To Bob
Chr
Merry 201...

MW00936890

Leo

Touched Up

Leo Dufresne

Leo Dufresne

Touched Up

Text Copyright © 2014 by Leo Dufresne

Cover art Copyright © 2014 by EDHGraphics

ISBN-13: 978-1501028809
ISBN-10: 1501028804

DEDICATION

To Cindy, who always believes in me, offers sound advice and celebrates my successes with heartfelt joy. "Thank you" and "I love you" don't seem to be words enough to begin to express my recognition for all that you have done for me.

To Dave Watson, may you never be afraid to ask someone if their "house is in order"

Chapter 1

No one should smile before the sun rises. On the happiness scale, content is about as good as you can get to in these dark hours. I wake early most every morning because content works for me. Since becoming the father of two, this tiny portion of the day is all the me-time I have left. If people were honest, which they mostly aren't, I think they would admit to wanting more time alone. It's 5:47 AM and I'm sitting quietly in the kitchen, where there are no responsibilities, no guilt, and no unmet expectations. Simply silence.

I'm using these precious morsels of time to pore over the latest edition of Popular Photography. A review of the top-of-the-line Hasselblad SLR catches my attention. The camera body alone retails for around $36,000 but it's just the piece of photographic equipment I deserve. Someday I'll own one. My plan is to reward myself after Alyssa and Jacob move out. I love my family; maybe I don't always show it, but kids suck the energy and money out of parents. When do we get to invest serious resources toward our own happiness?

This Hasselblad model is the supreme digital SLR camera on this planet. It has over 200 megapixels of resolution and captures colors in a way that is unlike any other man-made instrument. If a picture is worth a thousand words, photos from this apparatus would be the equivalent of an entire novel. I often imagine myself waking up each day to let the lens of my camera drag me about the world. No plans, spending my time capturing nature in its smallest, most intricate details. My wife, Stacey, had once suggested getting a video recorder. No way. Audio just mucks things up for me. People generally talk too much for my taste. Still shots, exquisitely taken, uncomplicated, unfettered – these are perfection.

"I hate you!"

My teenage daughter's voice destroys the silence as it thunders down the stairs. The recently adopted Pederson family theme song is starting again. I'm not sure when or how this drama crept into our house. Its departure will be none too soon.

On cue, my wife joins in the chorus, "There's a shocker, a daughter who hates her mother. Little Princess, I suggest you get your royal ass back in there and change your clothes. You won't be going to school dressed like that."

"Fine! I'll just change back into these when I get to school. You can't make me wear what I don't want to."

"Your dad and I will see about that."

There it is. My signal to enter the fray. I get up from the kitchen table and clomp along the hardwood floor, adding extra emphasis to each footstep as I move toward the base of the stairs. Sometimes just the bluster of my entering the battle causes it to end. I hope such bravado works this morning; I am not up for a verbal showdown. I continue noisily up the stairs when a door slam signals the battle is momentarily paused. My role in the family drama is complete and I turn to head back to the kitchen.

Arriving again at the breakfast table, I notice the cream cheese on my bagel. It's a color not nearly as appetizing as it had been. The once ultra-white spread is now streaked with shades of yellow. My photographer's eye is intrigued by the promise the bagel now holds. I could move the plate to the back patio. It might attract the Steller's Jay I have noticed in our yard the last few days. In my mind I see that long-bodied, blue bird hunched over the bagel, silently contemplating whether the mysterious yellowish object is safe to eat. These colors against the verdurous canvas that is our backyard would make for a compelling photograph.

"And a good morning to you too," Stacey says as she enters the kitchen.

Well-worn blue terry-cloth bathrobe, well-worn oversized fuzzy slippers, well-worn conversation to follow. "Morning."

"I swear there are moments when I dream of being born without a uterus."

I grunt. Stacey grabs a cup from the cupboard, fills it with coffee from the pot and takes her customary spot opposite mine at the breakfast table. I allow myself to sigh, softly, so as not to be too obvious. As I sit down, I slide the magazine back into my briefcase. Stacey drones on with the details of this latest clash with our oldest. I try to feign concern, but what exactly does a concerned face look like? I wasn't ready to leave the reverie of my photographic oasis. It annoys me that I'm expected to shift gears so quickly, effortlessly. A trick that I've never been able to pull off. Tonight I'll try to give them more of my undivided attention.

I steal a look at my smartphone, hoping not to draw Stacey's attention. It is still thirty-eight minutes from my normal departure time but the project review meeting was just moved up an hour. This is an event that will ripple through my Monday.

A non-work-related excuse to leave early is what I need. Stacey doesn't grasp the nuances of the corporate world. Her life is filled with black and white. Mine is one of grays. Maybe this is one of the things that draws me to photography. Colors that we can both appreciate.

An oil change. Yes. This time I look deliberately at my watch.

"Sorry. I've got an appointment at Jiffy Lube on my way in this morning. I really have to go. Call me at work and let me know what you want me to do or say to Alyssa when I get home tonight."

Stacey lets go with her own sigh, an audible one. Crap. She must have caught that the oil change was a diversion. I start to cross my arms, but fight the urge and place them back by my sides. I have to get out of this situation. My office is where I should be right now so I push forward with the lie.

Within three minutes I am easing my late-model BMW out of the San Diego subdivision we call home. My father would have hated this place. All of the houses look the same. No character. He probably hated a lot of things he never shared with us. Maybe even hated his family? Don't people who choose to off themselves hate everything in their life at some point?

Another twenty-eight minutes pass before I park my car in the spot marked Vice President of Engineering. Simply pulling up to the tan-colored office building gives my energy level a kick start. This is the place where so many of my life's greatest accomplishments have occurred.

I move quickly. Still have to get a status update from

one of my underling managers, Kwan Lee, before the meeting. Arriving at my office door, I unlock it and start to enter when I spot a large white company envelope just inside the doorway. It's common for other managers to leave semi-sensitive material shoved under my door like this. I stoop to pick it up as I continue moving toward my desk in the corner of the office.

Seated, I begin to scan the morning's email on my phone. It is the usual assortment of engineering updates and manufacturing issues. There's a note approving my request for a loan from my 401K and another warning from my broker that my margin account is running low yet again. Nothing here requiring any immediate action. I glance at the envelope. It's probably just an advance copy of an employee's review that I must approve before it goes to HR.

I should know the contents so I can assign it a priority. It's not yet eight and the day is already going to be screwed. As I use my right index finger to open the envelope, its flap buckles and cuts my finger.

"Shit."

It comes out louder than I wish. I drop the envelope. Wrapping my left hand around the wounded finger, I apply pressure to stem the bleeding. Although it is painful, it isn't that deep a cut and the bleeding soon stops. I could walk down the hall to the restrooms, but this would use more time than I have to spare just now.

I grab a letter opener from the top right desk drawer and finish the task. My phone buzzes before I can remove the contents; the meeting is only ten minutes away now. I toss the envelope back on my desk and rise to leave. A small portion of the envelope's matter slides out. As I examine the partially exposed page, I see that the paper is glossy, like that of a photograph. Why would someone use a photo in a performance review? I hesitate for a moment and decide to bring the envelope with me. I'll find time to look over its contents during a break in one of my meetings.

Kwan's office is to the left, but I detour to the right to grab some coffee. I'll need it for what follows. As I pour a cup, I glance at the pink, blue and yellow packets of chemical sweeteners. The man-made rainbow is pleasing to look at, but of no practical use for me. Coffee, black, straight caffeine, no additives.

Some hallway lingerers toss their morning pleasantries my way. I don't hear what they say. Well, I probably do hear but I don't give a shit. My energy level's still not up to dealing with people outside of the task at hand. I reply with the same rehearsed response I give every morning. My social responsibilities as a human complete, I execute a U-turn toward Kwan's office at the other end of the hallway.

I knock on the closed door. There are many Asian engineers in the high-tech world and quite a few have adopted American names. I guess they think it helps them fit in. Ironic the way their choice of a name often shows their lack of understanding about America. Kwan chose to use the name Jimmy and yet he maintains an air of formality about himself. He is the only CommGear employee who regularly keeps his door shut when he is in.

"You may enter," a voice responds from behind the door.

I step into the almost-dark office, shutting the door behind me. The walls are bare and there is no furniture in the room except Jimmy's desk and the chair he occupies. His title and tenure at the company landed him a window office. The vertical blinds, always closed, sway slowly with the air currents. With each oscillation they choke off the sunlight desperately trying to work its way into this pit.

My eyes slowly adjust to the lack of light. Jimmy clasps his hands together on the desk in front of him; a shock of black hair hangs over his right eye. He just stares at me. Neither of us offers a greeting. There is no reason to pursue small talk with Jimmy.

"I must provide an update on the Xanadu project in nineteen minutes. I need your team's status."

"I am managing everything properly. No one should have any concern." he says.

"Yes, I'm sure that you are."

Jimmy pulls his hands closer to his body, straightening in his seat. "Has someone suggested that I am not performing my project responsibilities well?"

Damn. I glance at my watch. I knew this wasn't going to be an easy conversation. Jimmy always gives his status to me by email at 11:30 each Tuesday. This request for an oral update, earlier than normal, is an unplanned change in Jimmy's routine. Jimmy doesn't do change well.

"This isn't about you."

Jimmy continues to stare at me. The glow from his computer monitor is not enough for me to make out his features clearly, but I can feel the contempt just the same. A movie starts in my head. I'm yanking him from his seat, pinning his arms to his side until he whines in submission.

"We're still 1.5 men short on our staffing needs?"

"If anything were deviating from previous guidance, I would have reported it to my management."

With this last answer, Jimmy refocuses his attention on his computer monitor. I have never learned to speak Korean but I am pretty sure that Kwan's name is derived from the Korean word for prick. As I leave the office I make a point of pouring the remainder of my coffee in the trash can by the door. Consider that a free lesson on how a *real*

American reacts to insubordination, you son of a bitch.

With a Band-Aid I snatched from a first-aid kit in the break center, I enter the company's main conference room. Strings of fluorescent lights cover the ceiling, forcefully illuminating every crevice of the room. A long walnut table sits like an island where thirty-five people may dock at one time. On one wall is a whiteboard and a pull-down screen to view presentations. This room is the center of activity at CommGear. Commotion, fuss, and sometimes progress occur here throughout the day and night. My usual seat next to the IT manager, Pete Talarian, is open and I take it.

"I thought this was going to be a productive meeting. Why do they keep inviting you?" I say.

Pete looks up from his notebook and watches as I fiddle with the wrapping around the bandage. "So you do bleed. I guess you aren't the superman everyone thinks you are."

"This may all be part of my scheme to fool mere mortals like you."

"Very clever. It's nice of you to humble yourself by living amongst us lower creatures."

To my right I place my time-management portfolio. It's open to the page set up for this date. A pen sits on top and at the ready. It's a silly habit since there will be nothing uttered at this meeting worthy of being recorded. I quickly slide the envelope under my portfolio. It's not quite hidden from view.

"I have been looking forward to this meeting."

"Anyone who looks forward to this crap must have had a bad morning."

"I did get a dose of Jimmy Lee when I got in."

"There's a pool running out on the manufacturing floor about him. The winner has to guess which CommGear employee will be the first to punch the little bastard. I think I'll go put another twenty on you," Pete says.

The meeting kicks off. Managers typically remain seated, trumpeting their team's progress and any known program risks. It is the same mind-congealing, bullshit routine each week. One of the newer marketing directors is running the show. They are all made from the same plastic and I have given up trying to remember their names. This one calls my name and I'm on.

I stand up and move toward the front of the room where all the useless ones sit. The head of marketing, O'Neill, looks at me quizzically. He was once an engineer on my team, but he jumped over to the dark side. It was just as well – he wasn't much of an engineer. I deliberately slow my pace. I'm on their turf and it gets the room's attention.

"This Xanadu project is our chance to move the company up to another level, but it is also an opportunity to ruin us. Failure here could start a downward spiral that may prove impossible to reverse."

I pause to give my words a chance to sink in. I know I should think better of these men, but it's become so difficult of late. The project is a drowning man going down for the third time and they're just watching. Some of these indifferent observers think they are actually my competition for the future CEO position. If they would just accept what I already know, that I have distanced myself from them, things would go more smoothly.

"For the last nine months we have been complaining that we don't have enough resources to bring this project home. And what do we have to show for it? A week from now I plan to go in front of the board of directors and demand they give us what we need. It's time for the company to open its wallet and let us bring in more help. I am wondering if there are any other leaders in this room who will back me at the board meeting."

I return to my seat not waiting for a response. O'Neill looks at me, silently. He couldn't make a decision when he worked for me either. I nod for him to move to the front. He looks at his team. They whisper amongst themselves. Seconds pass and he remains seated.

A software manager, feeling his oats, or more likely obtuse to the pecking order of this hen house, moves to the front of the room and agrees to back my proposal. In succession the heads of manufacturing, procurement, and quality stand up to voice their support. The parade of puppets has begun. I lean back in my chair. The eyes of the room are upon O'Neill as the false smile of a man who knows he's been beaten covers his face. He too rises and complies.

This Xanadu project is the biggest nut CommGear has ever tried to crack. Many in this room were naysayers when I proposed it. I've long since gone all in. If you're going to play with the big boys you can't be afraid to fail. I'm not and I won't.

Pete leans in my direction and whispers, "You may not actually be Superman, but you have this room of dumbasses convinced you are."

I fight back a smile of my own. What do you think of me now, Dad?

With back-to-back-to-back meetings, it is mid-afternoon before I can return to my office. Despite this drudgery, I am still on a high from the project review meeting. My plan is to tackle the action items that are sure to be piling up. I look at the still-unexamined envelope in my hands. What the hell.

I sit down at my desk and at last slide the contents fully out into view. The top item is an 8½-by-11 picture of –

my wife tending to the roses in front of our house. It's recent but not one that I took. Stacey is hunched over, pruning shears in her right hand.

Another look at the envelope reveals no clue as to the sender. Why would someone send me a picture of my wife?

The picture feels like it was taken from another yard; the subject has no idea she's being watched. Stacey's sandy brown hair hangs loose, tickling her face. Her lips are parted as if in mid-speech. She's does this when she's running through a mental checklist. She's beautiful when lost in one of her true passions, family or gardening.

Her yellow tank top and cut-off jeans offer no attempt to hide a figure still capable of capturing the longing glances of neighborhood teenage boys. My mind drifts back to a steamy summer night a few years ago. Stacey was in the backyard shed working on some lawn project. Lost to the time, it was well past ten and she hadn't made any motion to come inside. Her work wasn't done. The air that night was laden with the smell of gardenias in full blossom. Crickets chirped out a salsa-like rhythm. I caught her alone in the shed, kids were off somewhere, and I was able to turn her passion to better use.

My focus returns to the remaining item from the envelope, a single sheet of paper with a printed message:

```
Your future isn't as bright as it
once was. Why are you risking so much?
```

Chapter 2

My focus locks on the Japanese maple just outside my window. Over the years the tree has matured and taken on the traditional inverted bowl shape. A gentle ocean breeze jostles the leaves, never letting them come to a complete rest. I begin to picture the photo I'd take to capture the essence of this tree. Slow my shutter speed way down, probably below 1/20 second. The red leaves would blur against the still backdrop of the manicured lawn.

Most of the leaves arch downwards, but a select few stubbornly form tiny cups pointed to the heavens. An arborist would look to prune these. Not me. Tough problems don't have easy answers; the solutions are often made up from many simple steps. I like to imagine that each upwardly pointed leaf catches a small piece of the bigger answer. My job is simply to harvest the micro-solutions and piece them together.

Your future isn't as bright as it once was. Why are you risking so much?

The note is vague and inaccurate. My future couldn't be brighter. I'm going to be CEO; even a blind man could see this. Risk. You don't get somewhere important without risking something. And what does the picture of Stacey pruning roses in front of our house have to do with all of this?

I bound out of my chair and give the door a kick. It shuts with a slam that rattles the many framed awards hanging on my office walls. I return to my seat, looking for something else to kick along the way. Nothing is available. I settle for slamming my fist on the desk top. From outside footsteps approach followed by a soft knock.

"Busy!"

I pick up the photo with my left hand, the note with my right. Read the note, examine the photo and read the note again. The sound of blood pumping through my brain echoes louder in my ears than the door slam moments ago. My hand begins to tremble. Struggling not to harm the image of my wife, I put the photo down as carefully as clenched muscles allow. Losing my temper now would serve no purpose.

Why would someone send me such a note? Is it a threat? Has to be, or why the secrecy? Clearly they want me to back off on some perceived risk. Take my eye off the goal. What will they do if I don't change directions?

Shit. The important question, and the only one that matters, is what I should do. I don't have enough micro-solutions to make a decision. I need more facts. A real leader refuses to let time force him to make a decision. There is always an optimum moment to arrive at a conclusion and this is not it.

I decide to read some emails to give myself some distance. The first one that catches my eye is related to my retirement account. My request for a 401K loan has been approved and the money will be deposited in my checking account in three business days. That ought to get the broker off my ass for a while.

The desk phone rings. A quick glance at the caller ID reveals my home number. I gather the envelope's contents together and slide them into one of the desk's top drawers. Allowing one hand to linger on the front of the closed drawer, I use the index finger of the other to hit the speaker button.

"Hi dear," I say.

"The school called and *your* daughter is at it again."

Chapter 3

I bugged out of my office thirty-seven minutes early today. Not my preference. Traffic patterns heading east are altered from the norm. Congestion pops its head up in unexpected places. My commute is the mechanism I rely on to shift my focus from work to home. It's not working so well tonight.

I would like to give some more thought to the note and the photo, but I know I need to leave that alone for the evening. Last anniversary I asked Stacey what trinket she wanted me to get her. She surprised me with her answer: marriage-counseling sessions. Weekly meetings and hours of utterly pointless communication homework. The Xanadu project was at a critical stage and the counselor was narrowing in on minor items that could be dealt with at a less intrusive time. I stuck it out for almost four weeks. Stacey cried when I finally broke it off. We're still solid though, hanging in there. I guess we're better for having gone through it.

If I brought up the envelope Stacey would just ask me a bunch of questions that I couldn't answer. It would just leave me more frustrated. I did learn from that counselor they need me to be home, all of me. Despite what Stacey told the marriage-whisperer, this again will prove that I can leave work things at work. I deserve more credit than they both realize.

As I hit the button to close the garage door, I examine my watch. There is a different pace at home, slower, not so clearly defined. I've tried to impose my own timing here in the past and it has never ended well.

Twenty-some minutes later, the four of us are sitting at the kitchen table where dinner is turning out to be as unbearable as expected. Only my ten-year-old son Jacob seems clueless as to the heaviness in the air. Stacey calls tonight's main course tuna surprise, but it should be tuna tragedy. It is almost criminal that a poor fish had to give his life for this. I will force down enough to show gratitude to Stacey for cooking under these conditions. Mercifully, Jacob finishes his meal quickly and asks to go play video games. He knows he isn't allowed to play with his Xbox on school nights. Maybe he isn't as oblivious as I supposed.

Behind me a large yellow clock shaped like a sunflower ticks. It is almost three feet across and can probably be seen from outer space, during a lunar eclipse. It wouldn't be in my house except that it makes Stacey happy. The sound of its loud, slow ticking is extra annoying right now. I look to my left at my daughter, leaning her chair precariously backwards, inches from the china cabinet, defiance in over-drive. Stacey had been so pleased when we saved enough to buy the cabinet. It's a dark oak piece, stretching almost the entire wall. She has filled it with dishes given to her by her long-passed grandmother. I don't understand why we need it when we have plenty of cupboards in the kitchen. Having it in this room gives me a sense that her ancestors are always there, eating alongside us. During happy occasions it is comforting. Now it is just another object in the midst of a war zone. I can't imagine Stacey ever passing these family artifacts on to the person sitting next to me.

I stare at Alyssa, trying once again to understand her. She is petite and attractive, despite the piercings of her nose and the extravagant hair colorings she changes weekly. I was against these alterations to my little girl's physical appearance, but have eventually caved in. I wish I had been stronger. Did I let her down? Will she be disappointed with me in her twenties when she looks back at what I have let her do to herself? I have no clue what she is thinking most of the time.

From the living room an assault is launched on our ears. The sounds of a massive battle generated through electronics. I played the game with Jacob once. The graphics were amazing. Explosions and combat dialogue a bit too authentic. I think of having him turn it down, or better yet, off. Napoleon and Hitler both lost by trying to fight on multiple fronts. One battle at a time. Let the one before me begin.

"The school called today and said you weren't eligible to play in this weekend's tournament. Your grades weren't good enough."

Alyssa waves her left hand in my direction. Dismissing my comments while her right hand moves a fork load of cheese-draped tuna toward her mouth. In mid-bite she utters, "So."

My grip on my own fork tightens. I won't let this teenager see that she has that much control over me.

"You mentioned you had a chance at making varsity next year. This can't help your cause."

The rat-a-tat-tat of machine gun fire causes the glass on the china cabinet to rattle.

"It's just a stupid volleyball game," said Alyssa.

"I thought you loved volleyball?"

"You loved volleyball because you could brag about how good your daughter was doing at it. Now you can't."

"If you wanted to quit there are other ways besides trashing your academic record."

A soldier from the front room yells "Incoming!" For a

brief second all is still and then an explosion rumbles slowly through the house.

"You wouldn't let me quit. You said that I had to finish the season because the team was counting on me. I didn't ask them to count on me and now they'll just have to figure out how to lose on their own."

"Private. Get your ass over to that building and give us some cover fire!"

I look at Stacey. It's time to hand over the baton.

Stacey picks up my signal. "All we really want is for you to be happy. If you truly want to quit the team, I am sure we can work something out."

"I said that's what I wanted."

She doesn't know what she wants. She is an excellent high school volleyball player who has an above-average chance of getting a college scholarship. I know she doesn't really hate the sport. She is throwing away a good opportunity in something she loves for reasons that make no sense to me. We can't talk rationally about this now. It's the academics that I want to focus on anyways.

Thump, thump, thump. The low-pitched sounds of helicopter blades slicing through the air signal that a counterattack has begun. "Get 'em boys!"

It's my turn again, "Okay, I will agree to consider your leaving the volleyball team. Later. What I won't compromise on is your grades."

"What do you care? They're my grades."

"No, they are your future."

My stomach groans audibly. Another battle has started between the tuna dish and my digestive system.

"Yes, they are *my* future, so why can't you let *me* take care of them?"

"Because it's our job to protect your future, even

from you."

"I didn't ask you to protect me. I can handle things myself."

Stacey rises and begins to clear the dishes. I try to smile a silent thank you, but only end up belching. I mouth the word "sorry" and turn my attention back to Alyssa.

"I see an angry young girl making stupid decisions out of spite. What I can't understand is why you can't seem to grasp that this is hurting you more than us. Are you really that blind?"

"Obviously you need to make all my choices since I am so blind. So go ahead and decide this too. You were never going to let me make any choices anyways. Have at it, General Pederson."

"Okay. Since you can't play volleyball this weekend, you are going to stay home and study. In fact, you are grounded until you can get your grade in every class up to a B or better. You want your freedom; earn it like the rest of us."

"Permission to speak freely to the commanding officer?"

"You mean you have been holding back up till now? Wow, yes please do share more."

"You suck," Alyssa says shoving her chair back into the cabinet and stomping from the room.

Stacey continues about her task of cleaning up the dinner remnants. Family strife really gets to her. I've explained to her that this is just part of being a parent. She doesn't deserve this shit. Neither of us do.

I look at the congealed casserole on my plate and decide I have eaten enough. Sliding my plate toward her, I silently watch my wife soldier on. From the living room a trumpeted version of our National Anthem begins playing. Jacob must have beaten the game. That song, when played by a solo bugle, always brings me back to my senior year in high school. At 7:18 AM the Star Spangled Banner played over the school's loudspeakers.

Stacey and I would meet every morning in the library. She had been having a hard time in geometry. I was there to tutor her. That was her plan. I was a teenage boy with other ideas. Somehow she was successful in fighting off my testosterone-fueled advances long enough to memorize a few geometric theorems and pass that class. I still get excited every time I hear that song.

Our little girl got her act of defiance in, but I still achieved my goal. Everything will be dealt with in its appropriate order. All is well on this front.

Chapter 4

I'm in my office early. For almost two decades now I have arrived at my desk at 6:45 AM. A deviation in my start time by more than fifteen minutes can throw me off for the entire workday. Changes to my routine feel like a hose in my brain has broken free, allowing my mental fluids to spurt out on the floor. You can't get that stuff back in once it spills out.

Yesterday my role here was incomplete because of Alyssa. Some emails and action items were left unresolved. For work and home to coexist, such imbalances, no matter the magnitude, must be righted. This morning I cut short my personal time at home to come in and catch up. My door is open, but only a crack because it's better for all if I don't have to deal with anyone just yet.

After forty-three minutes my attention is diverted by a text message from the brokerage house I use. The price on the June Light Sweet Crude Oil futures contract I purchased has dropped a few ticks. If it doesn't right itself by the end of the trading day they will trade some of my Apple stock to cover my position. The price of the futures contract is swinging a bit more wildly than I anticipated. I need to place more money in my margin account.

Movement beyond my office door catches my attention. "Sheila, can you come here for a moment?"

"What can I do for you?"

"Monday when I got in there was a large white envelope shoved under my door. Did you see who put it there?"

Paper and pen appear in Sheila's hands. The woman's

desk is always covered in scribbled notes. There's nothing too minor for her to record. "No. Do you want me to ask around?"

"That's okay."

"Everything all right? You didn't seem yourself yesterday."

I give her a thumbs up and spin in my chair to face my computer monitor. It takes a few moments but she finally takes the hint and leaves.

CommGear policy forbids nepotism, and yet I find myself with a sister-in-law for an assistant. When my regular assistant left on maternity leave two months back, seniority landed Sheila this opportunity. HR decided to ignore this corporate taboo since Sheila doesn't officially report to me and this role is temporary. I tried to block the move on the down low, but I couldn't figure out how to do so without creating a family crisis. Now I live in fear that anything said in her presence could end up on Facebook. My work-family boundary has become too gray with her around.

Sheila does have some good attributes. I asked about the envelope because she is a bloodhound. Even though I told her it wasn't important, I know she will spend the next few hours trying to determine who put it under my door. I hope that I have deflected her curiosities regarding my well-being. She won't let that go either if she smells something.

I call Pete Talarian's extension. As usual he picks up on the second ring.

"Lunch plans?" I ask.

"Are you asking me out, big fella? Normally I play hard to get, but if you're buying, I'm in."

"Yeah I'm buying, you food whore. I'll come by your office at 11:30."

At 11:25 the alarm on my Blackberry goes off. I grab

my wallet, shut the door and head toward Pete's office on the other end of the building. The shape of CommGear's offices are a large letter U, with the lobby in the middle. It is quicker, despite the secured entry doors, for me to walk through the lobby.

As I cut through the reception area I notice a short, squat man signing in with the secretary. The man turns, gracefully for a person of his proportions.

"Hi Mr. Pederson."

I slow to look the individual over more thoroughly. His black hair is slicked back exposing a face that is too large for his body. He is the kind of person my mom would have warned me not to stare at when I was a child. Despite the climate-controlled office, there is sweat forming on the man's brow. He is wearing a dark tailored suit with an iridescent red silk tie. My eyes are drawn to the five large rings on his hands. Who needs five rings? I am sure this is the first time I have met this man.

The man seems to sense my lack of recognition. "Art Mancuso. I brought you Jason Blakely."

I nod. A head hunter, should have guessed. "Yes, Art, I remember you," I say as I step closer and shake the man's hand. The massive gold rings embed themselves in my flesh.

Art produces a business card which he must have been palming all the while. The card seems to magically burst forth from his olive-colored appendage. I am trying not to look as repulsed as I feel while I reach for the card. It's slightly moist from his sweat.

"Please keep me in mind if you need to find more talent or," the man pauses and steps closer, lowering his voice, "if, down the road, you might want to explore your own opportunities outside the walls of CommGear. I know many people in this industry."

I step back, restoring space between me and this being. Would prefer an extra six feet. "I'll do that Art. I have a meeting that I must run to. Please excuse me."

     ***

Pete and I arrive at the Cackling Cow, a hamburger dive I found on the internet. It's a safe distance from CommGear. Every table has a bucket of peanuts on it and patrons are encouraged to toss their processed shells on the floor. The hostess leads us to a booth in the back of the restaurant, peanut remnants crunching, crackling, and snapping under our feet.

Pete's attire consists of a Chargers football jersey, jeans, and tennis shoes. I would venture that I am the only one within 500 yards of this place who is wearing a tie. The booth we're taken to is small and it feels awkward sitting like this with another man.

After our order is taken, Pete begins, "So, what's going on?"

"With what?"

"With you. You wouldn't have picked this hole if you didn't have something you wanted to get off your chest."

"I received a strange communication yesterday I need your word that what I say stays here between us."

Pete stares at me, too long for my comfort. "You really don't get the idea of being friends."

I open a button on my shirt and tuck my tie inside. The silent pause allows the odor of truth in his remark to disperse. Composed again, I spend the next ten minutes outlining the previous day's events concerning the envelope and its contents. I am interrupted once by the waitress bringing our food. Pete just listens. When I finish with my narrative, I reach for my hamburger and take a large bite. Pete still hasn't touched his food and is leaning backwards, his arms crossed over his expansive chest as he seems to study me. What is it with this guy and staring at me today? Not the behavior I want when we are two guys sharing a booth. Finally he speaks.

"What do you want me to do?"

"Do? I want you to do the friend thing you're talking about."

Pete huffs. "Well it's not good."

"That's it? Some bastard sends me a picture of my wife in front of my house and it's not good."

Pete still has that strange look on his face, but now it seems to include anguish. He has been my friend for over seven years. I was originally drawn to him because of his intuitive nature about people. During my first stint at managing a small team, the group's progress had suddenly started going sideways. After a joint meeting between our two teams, Pete came to my office. He informed me that one of my key players was unhappy and was probably undermining me. Pete was right on the mark and he deduced this from one meeting. The mutiny had been in the works for six months and I never saw the signs.

Why is he being so dense now? I take another bite of my burger; looking away from him, trying to make some logic of his reaction to the story.

After swallowing I continue, "I need your help to figure out who's behind this."

"Why me?"

"Because you read people. You... you get them."

The waitress comes and refills our drinks. She asks if we want more fries. This place serves them family style, a big basket for the table. I've never been comfortable sharing my food. I didn't eat any from the first basket. Before I can refuse, Pete says yes and she scurries away.

"Maybe I'm not as good as you think," Pete says.

"What does that mean?"

"It means I have no clue why someone would send you something like this. I don't even know how to begin to help"

I grab my glass of iced tea. Too fast. Some of the tea sloshes over the rim, landing on the table. Ignoring the spillage, I take a big gulp. I put the glass back on the table with a slam and stare off toward the bar area. Silently I count to ten, fifteen, twenty.

"I didn't do anything wrong!"

"Maybe someone is just trying to get under your skin?"

The waitress returns with the fries. They're covered with garlic seasoning. Pete grabs a handful and shoves them in his mouth. I hope they cool quickly. When they're hot they're really tempting.

I continue, "I guess this could all be a joke."

Pete grabs another handful of fries, "I don't see the humor, but…"

I hold up my hand to stop him. "McGee's group down in shipping. They love this shit."

Pete is staring at me again. His mouth is open and I can see the partially chewed fries. I quickly turn my head away. Not soon enough to keep from storing this pre-digestive photo moment in my memory.

"Come on Pete. Remember when those guys let that porcupine loose in the women's bathroom? They're just yanking my chain like you said."

"But this is your house and your wife. That's a step too far even for those assholes."

A busboy with a handful of paper towels approaches our table. He starts to wipe up the spilled tea, but I grab the towels from his hand and wave him off. I hear him say something in Spanish under his breath as he walks away.

"Xanadu is at a make-or-break stage. Alyssa is being a pain-in-the-ass teenager. I got that board meeting coming up. There's no time for this shit. Help me find the son of a bitch behind this and I'll deal with him."

The manager stops at our table to ask how our meal was. I flip my credit card in his direction without taking my eyes off of Pete.

Pete looks from me to the manager and back to me. "Nice."

The manager silently retrieves my credit card and walks away.

"A lunch manager at a hole-in-the-wall restaurant. He'll get over it. You gonna help me?"

"I'll poke around in shipping, but nothing will come of it."

"You can't know that."

Pete finishes off the last of the fries while I check my email and transfer the 401K loan money from my bank to my brokerage margin account.

The ride back to the office is a silent one. More than once I feel Pete's eyes on me. Seems like he has another question to ask me, but he never does.

Chapter 5

Our son Jake is spending the night with a friend. Stacey and I are alone with Alyssa for dinner. The boy's the lucky one. I knew that someday there would be a time of alienation from my children; it's natural. Now that it's happening I'm surprised how painful it is. My beautiful little girl has become an emotional monster, attacking without provocation.

Alyssa's drama usually saps my energy. Lunch with Pete and the possibility, minute as it is, that the mysterious envelope problem may be solved has left me with a renewed sense of strength. I am determined to use it to good avail. I want a little peace in this home.

Placing my daughter under house arrest until her grades come up was punishment for all of us. The last two days have been rougher than normal. I wish the girl would learn to take her medicine the way we were expected to when I was little. When we acted up Dad would make us sleep in the garage. No mattress or pillow, just the cold concrete floor. We had special sleepwear for those times, garage pajamas. Made from scraps of clothing that Mom had stitched together. She didn't want us getting engine oil on our good pj's. I mentioned the idea to Stacey once and she just stared at me. It worked for my dad.

Stacey has made lasagna, Alyssa's favorite. Nice move on Stacey's part, feeding the dragon a good meal before the brave knight walks into the beast's lair. I glance across the table. Quickly, so as not to provoke my daughter prematurely.

Alyssa's hair is bleached almost white with streaks of

red and black. I am no longer shocked by this. Her eye shadow is a bright red that really contrasts with her blue eyes. Where can you buy make-up like that? Outside of rodeo and circus clowns, who would want that stuff? Somehow she is still a beautiful girl.

I put my fork down and address my opponent. "So how was your day, sweetie?"

"Fine."

"Anything interesting happen?" I ask.

"Nope."

"Half the day passed and nothing happened?"

Alyssa rolls her eyes upward. Will the caked-on make-up cause her eyelids to stick open? Will we have to make a run to the emergency room to get her lids freed? I should remember to take more pictures of her before this stage ends. This look will make a wonderful picture to embarrass her in ten years. I imagine myself asking her if she remembers how she looked in ninth grade. Then I'll whip out one of these shots. I shudder for a moment recalling my own freshman appearance.

Alyssa's teenage angst would normally be sufficient to stop a family conversation dead, but not tonight. This knight is carb-loaded on pasta and isn't ready to quit the battle so soon.

I point at her plate. "Food. That's enough to make most animals grateful. Share something with us?"

"Did you just call me an animal? What am I, a cow? Are you calling me fat?"

"No, but I did get you to give me more than a one-word response. I'll take that."

More eye-rolling from Alyssa, this time accompanied by a long sigh. She pushes her mostly-filled dinner plate away. She was probably looking for a reason to do that anyway. Stacey has told me that she's trying to diet. She doesn't need to, but somewhere, some asshole has convinced my little girl she needs to lose weight.

"Since I'm so fat, I'm done. I'll just go to my room."

"You aren't fat but you are stubborn. You want out of here? Tell us one thing that happened today."

Alyssa looks at her mom. I know this move. Before I can intercede, Stacey speaks. "You know Dad isn't going to give in until you share. Please, tell us something. We want to be part of your life."

Stacey's eyes appear moist. If I allow myself to keep looking at her I will really get mad. I've made this lady cry more times than I should have. All husbands do. It's honestly never been my goal, although there were times when I could have done more to stop the process. More often I'm at a loss to explain what brings on her waterworks. This may always remain a mystery to me. All I know for sure is God help anyone else who brings her to tears. Even family.

Stay focused on the dragon. Win this battle, brave knight. Alyssa crosses her arms and huffs. She sits there for a few minutes as if she hopes she can outlast us. Silly girl. Stacey and I resume eating. A smirk begins to ease onto Alyssa's face.

"Well, since you want to be in my life, let me ask you a question that has been bothering me all day. My boyfriend has been after me to put out and I have been thinking why not. Now, he's going to use a rubber because I took *that* biology class and I don't want no problems coming along in nine months. There are so many different condom textures to choose from. You guys got any recommendations?"

"Alyssa!" Stacey shrieks.

The corners of Alyssa's mouth turn upward. The fire-breather thinks she is winning this battle. You have no idea who you are messing with here.

"So you have a boyfriend. It's good to have friends. What's his name?" I ask.

Alyssa snaps her head toward her me. "That's it? Your daughter is thinking of losing her virginity and you only want to know his name. Yeah, you really care."

"I didn't say that's all I wanted to know, but it's a good place to start. Obviously the young man is in your good graces since you are thinking about sleeping with him. Winning your approval seems so hard to do lately. Maybe we can learn something from the boy. So what's this guy's name?"

"It's Dillon and you'll never meet him."

"Not sure I want to. Why don't you tell us more about him? Then we can decide if we want to spend time with him."

"He understands me and doesn't ask a bunch of stupid questions. So basically, he's nothing like you."

"Oh, I see. He's very smart. Must be if he understands you so well. So tell us something else about this smart young man?"

"He says he's going to need an extra large Trojan. I haven't seen it yet, but that sounds appealing." Alyssa winks at her mom while she adds this last part.

She is good. A better opponent than I supposed. I've sat across the table from some powerful men in the business world. Millionaires, power brokers. This little girl has got a knife pointed right at my heart. Sweat is forming on my brow. I won't allow myself to wipe it away. There's too much at stake here to show weakness. "So he's a tall man? Does he play any sports? Basketball?"

"He doesn't do any of that lame stuff. He makes movies."

"What kind? I hope it's not porn, although it would

be cool to brag that my daughter is an actress. I'm not sure I could recommend anyone see the movie. Have to think about that."

Alyssa snorts. I recognize this as the sound of someone trying to suppress a laugh. Stacey looks at me and laughs too. I have the dragon on the run now.

"No, he doesn't make *those* movies. He's into fantasy. He's going to be famous," Alyssa finally replies.

I lean forward in my chair, both elbows on the table, hands clasped under my chin. "I bet he is. You're a good judge of people. Has he shown his movies to any crowds yet?"

"He's waiting for the right time and place. But all his friends think he's great."

"Do you think he would consider a private showing for us?"

"Why? You aren't going to like it."

"You're probably right. But he's important to you and we want to stay in your life. Would you ask?"

Alyssa replies, softer. "Maybe."

This dragon is curling up in a ball. The good knight has won tonight. How do other less skilled knights fare with their dragons? I try to imagine Pete dealing with his child. He couldn't do what I've just done. Maybe the battles are somehow worse in the Pederson house? If I had a less stressful job would it be easier? Might there be a connection? Enough with this. I've won the battle and now the avenging knight needs to focus on the board meeting on Monday.

I will try to be gracious in victory with my daughter. It would not be so at work. "Thanks for sharing with us. You can get out of here now. And I know you were just trying to get a rise out of us with that condom thing."

"You better hope so, Daddy" Alyssa says, smiling as

she rises from the table.

Chapter 6

Deep in the bowels of a local hotel, the conference room lights are dimmed. The vertical blinds of two large windows remain partially opened. Natural light is much more soothing on elderly eyes.

Front and centered, eight men, sixty-plus, sit spread around a twelve-foot conference table. Eleven rows of chairs, haphazardly aligned, are located in the middle of the room. These lesser seats are for the audience. Only the revered performers may sit up front. For the moment I sit with the peasants. Someday they will ask me, implore me, to join them on stage. Today I will give them a glimpse of the greatness that lies within.

The CommGear board of directors would be intimidating to some. I succeeded in getting the request for more personnel added to their agenda at the last minute. Not unheard of but still a bit unusual. Some of my peers are concerned that this impudence will lead the board not to back us. No time for such trepidation. Real men make their surroundings important, not the other way around. Even a hotel conference room with unsightly trappings. I'm prepared to shine. Watch your eyes, old men!

I glance at my watch as the meeting progresses at a geriatric pace. My agenda item is near the end. There are no notes for me to go over. Such is not my style anyways. Men want to be led by true leaders, unlike the politicians of the last four or five decades, the kind who don't need to speak from prepared notes. I have slept, commuted, and lived with this project for two years now. In my stomach glow sparks ready to spawn a wildfire; I don't need any written scribblings to help me find the heat.

On both sides of the room food carts stand silently at the ready. Coffee, regular and decaf. Porcelain cups with their accompanying saucers. Stacked neatly in two mini-towers. Trays of sugar-laced pastries, brown muffins, yellow, orange, and red fruit slices. In the midst of all this is a large metal bowl filled with bottled water on ice. Beads of water condense on the outside of this bowl. Napkins, stacked too near the bowl, have become wet from these drippings. Life has natural pockets, things that should be kept at a distance, separated for safety and comfort. Even a waiter should know this. I resist the urge to grab my smartphone and snap off a handful of photos of the colorful food carts.

Instead I spend the time leading to my turn watching the interaction, audible and otherwise, between the board members. Frank Pinelli, my boss and CEO, sits in the second seat from the left. A curious choice. Many leaders would choose the head of the table or at least the center. He doesn't need a seat of honor to command their respect.

Two of the board members, one an investment banker, the other himself a former CEO of a long-standing CommGear customer, occasionally howl like old sheep dogs. Their barking echoes in the audience's collective souls like a dirge played on bagpipes, momentarily drawing us to their attention, but soon we learn to ignore it. The rest of the men range in temperament from Doberman to Chihuahua. I focus on the Doberman for several minutes and discover that he has no teeth. My daughter is a tougher audience than this collection.

At last Frank nods for me to begin. I rise to my feet and allow my gaze to pass among the men, pausing to lock on each one. Twenty, nineteen, eighteen... Silence can grab a room better than the loudest scream. The key is waiting just the right amount of time. Control them from the beginning and you have them throughout.

"Gentlemen. CommGear has been built on the backs of amazing men and women. Employees who thrive on challenge and back down from nothing. Some of my colleagues think I should thank you for allowing me to speak today. I don't feel the need to do so."

I pause to look at the investment banker. He momentarily meets my gaze and then lowers his eyes. Let's see you bark now.

"In the two decades I've been a part of the CommGear family, we've never missed on delivering against our promises. Along the way we've made some of you wealthy men."

Uneasy smiles cross the faces of two board members, a Beagle and a Chihuahua. I slow again, letting each one visualize the private golf club memberships, luxury cars, and high-end homes made possible by the success of the company.

"That's about to come to an end. We will not succeed with the Xanadu project."

Barking ensues, the volume increasing with every passing moment. Each breed struggles to be heard above the others. Several seem on the verge of barking themselves into apoplexy.

Sixteen eyes at the main table are focused on my every move. I force a phony cough and move slowly toward the bowl of chilled water. The big dogs have quieted but the Chihuahua and a Poodle continue to yip. Deliberately, I go about removing the plastic cap from one of the bottles and take a long gulp. Ice water clinging to the outside of the bottle drips on my shirt front. My instincts compel me to make some attempt to blot away this temporary stain. I resist. A distraught man wouldn't think to do this.

In semi-tortoise mode, I return to my original stance in front of my chair. I look the board members over again, using my gaze to silence the remaining yappers, and then continue, "Unless you open the coffers one more time."

The cocker spaniel to the right of my boss raises a paw, "We've already allocated more money toward this project than any other in the history of the company."

I like dogs, not this particular breed, but he reminds me of an uncle of mine, so I'll be kind and not punish him too badly. "True. The original contract, approved by this board, wasn't written tightly enough and now the customer is expecting more deliverables from us."

The kennel gate has swung wide open and another household pet dares to interject. "Can we ask for an extension or renegotiate?"

"That's a good idea. One that we examined months ago."

The two old sheep dogs are beginning to squirm. Chairs squeak as they adjust themselves to renew their howling. I hold up a hand to still them. "I realize that this added expense will cut into the profits we hoped to get from this project. Keep in mind that the real money will be made from follow-on contracts with Microsoft and other big fish whom we could never land before."

The Doberman snarls, "How many people are you asking for?"

"Four full-time and two contract."

The Cocker Spaniel yelps, "That's another half-million dollars in fully-loaded burden to the budget."

"Closer to six-hundred thousand," I correct.

The Doberman rises, locking his eyes on mine. His

stance is one of a once-mighty warrior. "If we approve this and it fails, you'll be coming back before us again. I can assure you that won't be fun. Have you given this any thought?"

The smell of testosterone overwhelms the room. I know that he's waiting for my tail to droop or a whimper to escape my throat. The corners of my mouth turn upward. This is not the right response, but I love this shit. So did my old man. I nod my head slightly, showing both my understanding and disdain for his threat. Someday you'll be my lap-dog big fella.

Frank shuffles the papers before him. My role here almost complete, I go on satisfying potential objections. Questions are asked and answered. All the canines are silenced. The battle was won from the moment I stood. If I believed in destiny, or some form of higher order, I might say that I was meant to lead. Statistically only a few men are wired to rule others and I happen to be one of them. It's just math, not some phony god's plan. Only the strong survive and I trust in nothing but myself.

Thirty-seven minutes later I leave the room with the go-ahead to hire more people.

Chapter 7

Frank Pinelli's office is not carpeted. Cool granite tiles reflect the light that dares to intrude. A small conference table with four chairs is the only furniture visible from outside. The walls are off-white, barren, antiseptic. This is the first of three levels in his work space. The unwashed only get to this point.

I stand at the gates of the palace having been summoned by the king. The reason for my presence has not been made clear. Sounds of a phone conversation coming to a close reach my ears. I recognize the tone of a father talking to his child. Frank has only a daughter. He loves her greatly but she tries his patience in equal measure. Chronologically she may be in her thirties, but Alyssa has periods where she acts more mature.

In a quiet moment in this very office, Frank shared with me his disappointment at never having had a son. It's one of the crimes of nature that a man like him will never see his line continue. Only the truly fortunate get fathers like this man.

Frank pops around the corner. "Come in."

He turns and I follow him. Fifteen feet in, the office angles sharply to the left. Level two. A massive oak bookcase lines the right-hand wall, leading to an oversized walnut desk. The desktop is bare other than a telephone and various framed community service awards.

Behind the desk are two floor-to-ceiling windows. Each window has white vertical blinds which are controlled by a hidden switch. Outside the windows is a private patio reachable only by a door located further to the left. No one has used this patio since Frank quit smoking seven years earlier.

This level is for mid-level managers and the occasional customer. Franks slows to look at the screen on the desk phone. I don't break my pace. I've long ago earned access to the highest level, executive informality. Expecting to hear Frank's renewed footfalls join mine, I stop when they don't. I turn to see him still at the desk, looking me over foot to head. We're going to level three, but I should wait to be escorted, invited. Slow down Mitch.

The office turns left again. A black leather couch and matching mahogany coffee table sit on a Persian rug. Autographed pictures of Frank with Schwarzenegger, Gates, Jobs, Ali, and even Sinatra adorn the walls. Frank chooses the far end of the couch, reclining with his arms crossed, his body angled slightly away from me. I pick the nearest end, sitting forward and studying his shoes. A bit of reverence is in order here after my earlier misstep. Level three should not be taken lightly.

"So you got the board to give you what you wanted. Where do you go from here?" Frank asks.

My shoulders are tense. I force myself to lean back. I look at Frank's face trying to pick up any clues. I don't know where he is going. Frank continues.

"We knew the project would be a success when we assigned it to you. You didn't need a board meeting to get approval for new hires. I have that power and you know it."

If I were a politician I would give him one of those noncommittal plastic smiles. I don't have one of those so I just keep looking at him, hoping his face will give me some idea what he's after.

"A little face-time with your future bosses, perhaps?"

My belt is starting to dig into my right side. I adjust

my posture slightly, hoping to relieve the pressure. It doesn't work. "Not sure what you want me to say."

I look up again at the photos on the walls. In my mind I picture my own photographs in their places. There won't be shots of me with celebrities. Family pictures and a few serene nature shots. This will be my inner sanctum someday. I don't know that I would ever bring someone back here.

Frank makes a soft clicking sound followed by what looks like a grin. "Your eyes are locked on this office. I think you have an interior decorator on speed dial already. You've got to learn to let things come to you. You always seem to be on the attack."

"I wasn't trying…"

"Yes you were. I've invested too much of my life building this place to pass it along to someone so focused on himself."

"I can lead this company."

"When you learn to care about the people here more than yourself."

The phone on the desk rings and Frank rises. "I know my time here is closer to the end than the beginning. I'm prepared to hand over the reigns, not have them jerked from me. I can see myself handing these over to a calmer, steadier version of Mitch than what I see in front of me now."

I stay seated in case the call is a short one. My thoughts drift back to the first time I was invited to this third level. It was five years ago and my team and I had just returned from a field trial at a large automotive supplier. An exec at the customer scheduled a call with Frank to let him know how the trial had gone. I was nervous and excited to be asked to be present for the call. I was sitting in this very spot as the man on the other end of the phone gushed about how good the results were. Frank put the speaker phone on mute as he hopped around the office celebrating. He ended his happy dance in front of me and gave me a high-five. Two months later I was promoted to senior director.

This call shows no sign of ending quickly. I round the corner back to level two and when I catch Frank's gaze, any hopes I have of righting this meeting are lost. The king gives me a half-smile and a half-wave. Dismissed.

As I walk back to my office, I am trying to picture a more patient Mitch. Of course no one has ever seen such a thing. If there is a vein of patience running through this body of mine, I don't even know where to start digging to tap into it.

It's almost 11:26 and I am hungry. No brown-bagging it in my office today. Some time away from this place. This future CEO of CommGear needs it. If I leave now I won't have to wait in line at a restaurant. Sorry Frank, lines suck. I'll work on patience when my stomach is full. As I exit the building, my sight comes to rest on something under the windshield wiper of my car.

Chapter 8

It's a small blue envelope, the kind you'd include with a bouquet of flowers. I look around to confirm that my car is the only one tagged. Signs are posted throughout the parking lot forbidding solicitation. Coming closer, I notice that my first name has been typed on the outside of the envelope. I remove the little card from inside.

Oil and Water. Home and Business. Some things just aren't made to mix. Maybe you should consider again the contract you agreed to? Your time is running out. Do something soon or your wife will know you really don't care about her.

I spin around quickly and scan the parking lot again. This time I take in the nearby surface streets. Looking for anything out of place. Two gardeners, Mexicans, at work on the landscape surrounding the parking lot, a mechanical engineer, can't remember his name, been here a couple of years, is getting out of a blue Volvo sedan on my right, a young man and a woman having an animated conversation on the sidewalk across the street. A crow starts cawing loudly somewhere to my left.

This is a business district. What is a couple doing on the sidewalk? I struggle to keep my pace beneath a run as I move in the straightest path toward them. My hands form into fists and I crumple the note. The hell with being coy. I start to run, keeping my eyes locked on them.

They're facing each other, hands on their hips, bent

forward at the waist. Two roosters squaring off for a showdown. I'm still too far away to make out what they're saying, but their mouths are moving rapidly. When the distance between us nears fifty feet the woman turns her head in my direction. The man follows her lead and twists his upper body toward me, hands remaining on his hips. I recognize him as one of our marketing types.

As I approach to within twenty feet, he speaks, "Can I help you?"

"How long you been here?"

The man's face contorts, "Almost two years."

"Not with CommGear you dumb ass." I come to a stop with just under five feet between us and point violently at the sidewalk he is standing on, "Here! How long you been here!"

The woman, blonde with a blue dress cut too short for this neighborhood, moves closer to the man. Sweat has caused her make-up to smear into an odd-looking mask. Her entire body is taut. The roosters are both facing me fully now as we each wait for the first act of aggression.

Wrong bogey. Before they can answer, I reverse course and sprint back across the street. The gardeners have stopped their work and now huddle together. I veer in their direction, not reducing my speed. As I near them they stare at me and take a couple of steps back. One of them mutters a word in Spanish I don't recognize.

The younger of the pair, bigger than his partner by over a foot, is holding a rake. He turns it over in his hand so the business end is up and facing me. The other man grabs his arm and steps forward. He begins to speak rapidly in Spanish. With every other word he seems to pick up his pace. It's been over two decades since my last conversational Spanish class. If he asked me where to buy a blue plate or when the library closes, I might be able to understand him. I turn again toward my building. As I head off I hear the voice of the other man. Many of his words I do know and they weren't learned in a classroom.

I race to the front door. No remaining suspects are outside the building. I picture someone peeking at me through an office window, laughing at how he's toying with me. All right asshole, you wanted to get my attention, you just did. You'd better be wearing some good body armor buddy, because I'm coming for your ass now.

Still breathing heavy from my parking lot dash, I arrive at Sheila's desk and motion her into my office. Both of us are standing near the door which I have just shut.

"The envelope I mentioned last week. What'd you find out?"

"Not much. What was in it?" Sheila asks.

I slip past her and sit down with a thump in my chair. "Nothing important. I just want to thank the sender personally."

"If you give it to me, I can show it around to some other people."

"Keep digging."

My desk phone rings and I can see that it's Pete. "I need to get this."

Sheila remains frozen, staring at me. I meet her stare with what I hope is a colder version. At last she leaves, closing the door behind her a bit too loudly. I hit the speaker button on the phone. "What do you have for me?"

"Fine, fine. And how's your…"

Still breathing heavy, I have no interest in conversational foreplay. "The SOB just left me another note."

"Sounds like I'm on speaker. Your door closed?"

I reply with a "yup" and grab a black pen and small notepad from the top drawer of my desk. I like to doodle when I speak on the phone. The distraction keeps my other senses in check. Allows my brain to focus more on what I am hearing.

"It wasn't a joke. I poked around down in shipping. McGee's got 'em all scared they'll lose their job if they pull any more shit."

"Then what the hell is it?" I hiss into the mike.

"Slow down. Tell me what this last note said."

"Some crap about oil and water not mixing and a contract I agreed to. It said my time is running out."

I rip the top page from the pad. The next page has indentations from the previous doodling. Rip that page off too. A new twist in the discussion requires a new piece of art. I grab a red pen from my desk. A second color will add depth to the drawing. I like to combine straight lines and arcs.

Pete goes on, "Contract? Have you signed anything lately? Could he mean Xanadu?"

I am drawing larger sweeping arcs with the black pen. Where the arcs intersect to form closed shapes, I color the interiors red. I decide to alternate the interior colors, black, red, and black again. I like the pattern.

"The note said something about home and business not mixing either. It's gotta be more personal."

Pete is mumbling now, "Oil and water, home and business, and a contract that's expiring."

I put down the pen and remove the first note from my desk drawer. It was focused on future and risk. The second one talks about things not mixing well and a contract running out.

I pick up the black pen to continue my drawing. Focused on smaller details now. Sometimes after I finish doodles I will hold on to them for a few weeks. They can act as a trigger to help me return to what I was thinking during a particular moment. This could be one of those drawings.

My phone chimes, signaling an incoming message. As I lurch to turn off the sound I read that my oil futures contract price has dipped again.

My attention restored, I stand and walk toward the window. Looking for help from the tree of knowledge. There seems to be no breeze blowing today. The red leaves remain idle, lifeless, silent. I'd like to go outside and shake the trunk, forcing answers to fall from them. That's not how it works, solutions come when they're ready. The tree has no clock. It's not synchronized to my life.

Twenty or thirty seconds pass until at last a zephyr gently rustles the leaves.

"Shit!" I yell at the speaker.

"What is it?" Pete asks.

I walk back to my desk and put my lips inches from the speakerphone. "Shit, shit, shit. I'm being blackmailed and if I'm right, I've got less than ten days to catch the bastard!"

Chapter 9

Glancing at the emails in my inbox, I can see no emergencies pending. Despite this, I quickly hang up on a confused Pete. I want to think this through and my friend will only slow me down. As a young engineer, wild with ambition and short on experience, I often sought out the advice of a simple, quiet man. His role at the company is not lofty but for me he always seemed to have just that right piece of wisdom I was missing. We don't run into each other much these days. The thought of re-connecting brings a sudden unexpected smile to my face.

The engineering development lab has eight gray work benches located in clusters around electrical power drops. Each of the benches has shelving that hold oscilloscopes, variable power supplies, digital volt meters, and logic analyzers. There are rolling carts with additional test equipment throughout the room. One of the benches is vacant and neatly kept, but this is a rarity in an engineering lab. The other benches are covered with circuit boards, test leads, laptops, schematics, notebooks, and half-empty soda cans.

As I walk in, heads turn my way. This is one of the last places in the high-tech world where a man can be real. Everyone here must act like a man, even if genetically they aren't. Conversations in this environment may be loud or soft, among just two people or involving more than five, but they are not bound by political correctness. Bonds and barriers are formed through all-nighters. Teams come together as they try to get critical designs to work before career-changing deadlines. The pressure to solve a problem at 3:00 AM doesn't leave much energy for worrying about whether a thought is worded so it doesn't offend someone.

I nod at Jackson as his glance catches mine. One of my lead designers. We were peers once. Ten years ago when we were pulling an all-nighter, he told me I was a failure as a father and a husband because I didn't have any guns in my house. Life-long NRA member, the world is so very black and white to his kind. His politics are shit, but he's a good engineer. Glad he's on my team.

I look at the bench in the far left corner, closest to the windows. Robbie Robinson, the senior technician at CommGear, works at this bench; it's the best one. Robbie has been here longer than I and although not a manager, he runs this place. He is alone and looks to be making some modifications to a circuit card. I head in his direction. As I get to within five feet, I announce myself.

"Not looking to bother you. Just wanted to get away."

He doesn't look up from his work. I don't expect him to.

"Figured that. If you'd planned this you'd a changed out of the monkey suit," Robbie says, still not appearing to look at me.

He's right. I am not dressed like someone who belongs here. Vice Presidents don't come in this room except for customer dog and pony shows.

"Can I sit?" I ask.

Although I'm now several rungs above this man in the corporate food chain and could have him terminated with a text message, this is his empire. Outside of this room I am Mr. Pederson. In here, I am somebody who needs to ask before I touch anything.

"Help yourself," Robbie answers.

"Still heading up to Montana to fish this summer?"

Robbie doesn't answer right away. He never responds quickly and slows down even more when he is troubleshooting a design. I don't mind this. I know what Robbie's response will be, when it eventually comes. The world could stop abruptly and he would still make this trip. I just want to keep the conversation moving forward while I consider how to get to what I really want to talk about.

I look out the window at the back parking lot. A car full of engineers is unloading. Probably just returning from a run to a nearby convenience store. The corporate bean counters might be upset by this, but I'm not. These guys will still be working here tonight long after those finance prima donnas are resting their heads on their 400-thread count pillow cases.

"Yup," Robbie finally replies.

"Ever had a guy try to steal something from you?"

"Mmmm."

"Something big, really big?"

It will be several minutes before Robbie replies and I look around for something else to occupy my thoughts. In the upper-left corner of the window, on the outside, is a large spider web. Sunlight is passing through its strands like a prism. The window further refracts the light, producing a miniature rainbow on the far corner of the bench. In the silence I find myself trying to identify the specific colors generated. Not an easy task. Stare at the rainbow too long and the colors start to run together. The trick is to keep looking away before it begins to blur. I'm just discovering the best timing for the intermittent glances when a movement in the direction of the main lab door interrupts me.

"Why are you looking over my design?"

I recognize Jimmy Lee's voice and then look quickly toward Robbie. His eyes meet mine and in a nanosecond I realize my day is about to get a whole lot worse.

"I stopped by to ask Robbie about mods to the lab."

"He has much to get done for me," Jimmy Lee says.

"We're also under a tight schedule. We need to make some decisions on the new lab," I suggest, trying to keep my voice even and low.

"Why you not call him to your office? Strange. Last week you ask for my status in person. Why you concerned about my work?"

Jimmy steps between Robbie and me. The space is quite small. He has his arms crossed. I notice a bubble of spit forming in the right corner of his mouth. A shock of black hair has come free, hanging in his face. There are many things in my life that I find difficult, disliking this guy isn't one of them.

"My work is good," Jimmy replies as some of his spittle flies toward me, landing on my left shoe.

I sense many eyes watching us now. He better stop pushing me.

"We'll talk about this later," I say as I spin around and head for the lab door.

"This is not right, what you do."

Okay, you want to play that way. The gloves are coming off. I stop and turn back toward him. The distance between us has widened to almost fifteen feet now.

"Do you like your job?"

Our eyes are locked on each other. I let a few seconds pass without a reply. It's as if the room is buried in syrup, everything is moving slow now. "I asked if you like your job. If your answer is no, I can help you lose it."

"This is not…"

"I'll tell you what this is. This is where you turn around and get back to work or hand me your badge."

Jimmy continues to stare at me. He makes no attempt to speak or move. I know he is angry but I think he is also confused. His culture doesn't do throwdowns like ours. This has always puzzled me. I thought it universal that little dogs put their tails between their legs when big dogs put them in their place. Maybe their men should spend more time watching dogs instead of eating them.

"I've got a lunch meeting. Why don't you spend yours thinking about your career?"

I head for the door once more, knowing that he is still staring in my direction. I quicken my pace so I don't get drawn back in.

Chapter 10

For the second time in under a week I find myself at the five-star diner that is the Cackling Cow. Sharing a table with Arturo Mancuso only adds to the enjoyment. I insisted on a table this time. My life is already overburdened and I don't want to spend a spare hour I don't have crammed in a tight spot with the likes of this Mancuso fellow. I chose this peanut-shell-encrusted hamburger dive to reduce the chances of being seen by anyone in the industry. Even though I have an easy excuse for meeting with a recruiter – we're always on the lookout for more engineering talent – people might talk.

I'm in my usual attire: white monogrammed shirt, open collar. Art has me beat in the race to see who is the most overdressed for the Cackling Cow. He has removed his tan suit jacket, placing two unfolded napkins on the seat next to him before laying the jacket down. To call his shirt bright blue is like calling the noonday sun yellow. It must be a sin to wear a shirt as loud as this without calling ahead to warn the other patrons.

His tie is a pastel green. No shit. In what universe do those two articles of clothing go together? His mismatched attire leaves me dangerously close to a seizure, and yet I am grateful he has chosen to wear a tie. The uppermost button on his shirt, the one beneath the knot of his tie, must be on the verge of bursting free under the pressure of his massive neck. His tie is the only thing saving patrons in a three-table area from this potential missile.

"Thanks for inviting me to lunch. This restaurant is a…surprise," Art says.

"My friend owns a piece of this. I'm helping him out."
It's a lie, but he seems to accept it.

"Good friend," Art says, as a waitress approaches to take our order. The process goes quickly because the place doesn't offer many choices for its patrons.

I start the conversation again as soon as she leaves. "How long have you been in the head hunting...recruiting business?"

"It's okay. I call it that too. About two years," he answers.

Engineers are always bemoaning the fact that they aren't treated with the reverence of other professions. Doctors usually come to the forefront of these comparisons. Some argue that these differences are due to the stakes of the decisions made; ours aren't a matter of life and death. All I know for sure is I can't imagine even the lowest quack having to work with this guy for his next million-dollar-a-year position.

"Well you're pretty good at this. Jason Blakely was a good find," I say.

"Thanks," he replies, with the smallest hint of a smile.

"What did you do before this?"

The waitress returns with our drinks. Water for me and something called passion iced tea for him. She approaches from the side closest to Art's suit jacket. He quickly puts his massive arm over the jacket. Probably trying to prevent spillage on a piece of clothing he spent too much money on.

I notice that his attention is on a TV. It's a large plasma model mounted on the wall just above head level. Not sure it was here last week. It is tuned to SportsCenter. This segment is covering some big horse race back east. At least something in this restaurant will be entertaining.

He focuses on me again and replies, "Sorry. I've got a thing for the ponies. Done a bit of this and that in my life."

Visions of a green 1979 Mercury Cougar being towed from our driveway pop into my memory. The neighbors watched as our family car was repossessed, a casualty of yet another of my dad's sure-fire businesses. Gambling on something is not bad as long as you have a good system. It's a bit like a marriage; once you pick the girl you have to stay committed to the end.

"I guess you've heard we got a couple of new positions to fill. What are our chances of landing some good people?"

"This bad economy will help. It's a buyer's market."

I nod my head, wishing that the waitress hadn't taken the menu. It would have given me something to look at while we talk. His bringing up the economy is good. I can use this.

"We're holding our own at CommGear. How about you?"

"I can't complain. There's always room to make money if you know what you're doing," he replies.

On the TV, SportsCenter is over and the next show has begun. It is all about horse racing and that big race coming up. Art nods his head in the direction of the TV. "I'm hoping to buy me a horse like that."

Wow, an over-dressed, bling-laden Italian is looking to get into horse racing. No stereotype there. "Those are pretty pricey. Head-hunting must be better than I thought."

"It's not that good," he says.

"We all have our hobbies I guess. Just need to have the right income to let us play at the level we desire."

The waitress at last arrives with our hamburgers. She tops off our drinks and asks if we need anything else. I don't bother answering. Maybe the food here grows on you or I'm hungrier than I thought. I take a big bite of my burger.

Left alone again, he returns his focus to me, "If you want something bad enough you find a way."

"More financial freedom would make it much easier to...breathe."

"That would be nice," he says.

Nineteen months ago I graduated from simple stock trades to dealing in options and finally futures contracts. It's the big time. No safety net. Along the way I've won some and lost a bit too. It's the price of perfecting your trading system. To really score, and have your name on the marquee, you have to be willing to take serious risks. I have and I am.

My current position in oil futures is the most risk to which I've ever exposed my family's finances. All of our available assets are being used to cover my margin account. We're at our limit. A serious turn of the market to the south could take away all of our savings and jeopardize our lifestyle. The contract expires in just over a week. My trading system is solid though. I won't allow myself to lose any sleep over this. Stacey doesn't know the situation because she's not built like me. She couldn't handle the pressure of trading on this level.

A CEO's salary, or at least a VP position at a bigger firm, would better cover my position in the market. Providing insurance that Stacey never has to worry. I've invested a lot in becoming the next CEO of CommGear, but after my last meeting with Frank it would be good to have a fallback.

Art stares at me. I notice that sweat is starting to form at his hairline. The waitress reappears to ask about dessert. I consider waving her off, but then welcome the delay. More time to move this conversation toward the goal I have in mind.

We both pass on more food and Art at last moves the

dialogue in a way that helps me out. "So what about you Mitch? Any specific needs I can help you address?"

I nod at the television, "Someday I'd like to be in a position to buy a horse of my own. Can't do that on a CommGear VP salary."

Art pauses to take a long sip of his fruity drink. "Rumor has it that you're the lead horse for the next CEO."

"The front-runner doesn't always win, does he?"

The waitress arrives with our bill and Art grabs it before I can offer to pay. He mentions something about it being a business lunch as he produces his wallet.

"I suppose that's why the smart horse people never bet it all on one race," Art says.

I take a drink of my water as I plan my next step.

"So, if I wanted to look at entering other races, maybe bigger-stakes races, would you be the man to help?

Art starts to rise. I remain seated, hoping he'll take notice that we haven't finished going where I need this meeting to end. The non-verbal cue doesn't seem to work as he continues to make himself ready to leave.

My face must give away my puzzlement because he slows the departure process enough to look fully at me and speak. "There are other races out there I could get you in. You're a rising star I've been watching for several years. While I would love the chance to help you out, your best bet is to win the race you're already in. Do that and after a few years I could get you in some really big races."

Mr. Mancuso extends a hand to bid me goodbye. I rise amidst the sounds of crunching peanut shells. Grasping his hand firmly, I give it a solid pump.

A meeting reminder chirps at me from my cell phone. I can't help but notice that my oil futures price has gone up two ticks since the morning bell.

Chapter 11

I turn on to my street. Something is off. Still several houses away and I feel like I need to speed up. Nope. It's getting dark. Don't want to run over a neighbor's pet again. Pulling into the driveway I notice movement near the rose bushes that run under the front windows. As I turn off the car's engine, I hear the snapping. It's rhythmic and savage.

In the semi-brightness of the exterior lights I can make out a figure. It's Stacey. She is on her knees, her back to me. The light reflects off the garden blade in her hand. With each loud snap her body lurches. Behind her is a pile of branches. Rose petals are strewn everywhere.

I have known this woman twenty-four years and I would be lying if I said I really understood her. I am sure of only one thing; she's pissed. I could put the car in reverse and go back to the office, but I know this isn't an option. I'm going to have to deal with this. I grab my briefcase and ease myself out of the car. Choose your words carefully here. Hello seems safe. I use it as I walk slowly in her direction.

Stacey doesn't turn around. The violent hacking maintains its pace. In my younger, naïve days, I would have pushed her to tell me what's wrong. She's not ready to talk yet and I know I'm not ready to hear what she would say if I forced her. Turning around, I head inside.

At the back of the house is my photo-developing studio. It's a small room that we added a few years ago. One half of the room has a desk with a computer and high-end printer for digital photography. The other side of the room is set up for 35mm processing. For this reason the room has special lighting and temperature controls.

I remove the bottles containing the developer and stop bath solutions from a locking cabinet. The cabinet isn't actually locked anymore since the kids are older. The stop bath I use is a type of citric acid, which can be dangerous to contact in this concentrated form. I pour the solutions into their respective basins. There's a particular roll of film I have been waiting to develop.

In ninety minutes the recently decapitated rose bushes have been resurrected. There are several very good shots in the final step of processing. They need to dry for another seventeen minutes. A knock comes from the other side of the door. I was hoping to finish before she came back in the house. I'd like to dispose of the chemicals in the basins, but it's best not to keep her waiting. I answer the knock with an "I'm coming out."

No one is present when I open the door. The sound of water running is coming from the kitchen, so I head in that direction. Stacey is at the sink washing away the evidence of the carnage. Numerous cuts crisscross her arms. The water dripping from her is a pale red.

"Hello," I say as I lean back against the refrigerator.

She doesn't look at me and continues to clean her wounds. "You've said that already."

"Yes I did. I wasn't sure you noticed."

"I notice a lot more than you think," Stacey says.

That doesn't feel like a good place to go. The level of her anger borders on the uncharted. What has cast her emotional ship in these waters is not clear, but I'm sure to be part of the reason. Time apart seems to have done little to calm the storm.

I mumble, "That looks painful."

Stacey turns off the water and spins to face me. She's

wearing one of my old T-shirts. It looks better on her than it ever did on me. Her damp arms are crossed in front of her. I start to offer her a towel but think better of it. In her defiance there is something beautiful I don't want to disturb. I'm left to stare at her like a helpless boy.

She breaks the silence. "Let me share some pain with you. Our daughter is using drugs."

"What the–"

Stacey interrupts, "It gets better. She never came home from school."

"Is she all right? Is she answering her phone?"

Stacey smacks her palm to her forehead. Her hand is still wet and the sound echoes through our kitchen. She opens her mouth to speak, but then shuts it.

Damn. I hate when she treats me like an idiot. "She's okay then?"

"No, I'm here pruning roses while our daughter is missing."

Stacey looks at me, unblinking. I wish she'd just tell me what's eating at her so I can deal with it. I'm making a 1,000-piece puzzle and she's presenting me one piece at a time. Can't she just dump the whole box over and let me put it together? Our arguments always have to be at her glacial pace.

I take a deep breath. "Would you please tell me where Alyssa is?"

"My sister's."

That's piece one in place. Move on to the next one. "What's this about drugs?"

"School security found marijuana in her locker," Stacey said.

Good. I guess. Marijuana is not as bad as it could be. "How much did they find?"

Stacey's eyes widen as her volume increases. "Who cares?"

Keep your voice low. Don't match her. I breathe again, deeper. "Did she have enough to sell?"

"You want to be a detective? How 'bout you play the role of father first?"

"That's what I'm trying to do."

"You're just trying to get back to your photography."

I can feel my face getting flushed. Why can't she stay on track? She's got no logic. "What the hell do you want from me?" I yell.

Instantly I regret this. Stacey looks at me but doesn't raise her voice. Her anger is a blue flame now. She doesn't need an increase in volume to make her point.

"More than the scraps you're giving us."

"I'm giving you all I've got. This...you make no sense to me!"

In three quick steps she is across the room and heading toward the stairs. Without looking back she tosses, "Maybe you should try as hard as you do at work?"

I consider following her but realize the futility. We'd just rehash old stale arguments. I'd be none the closer to understanding what the hell she is really mad about. Better to secure myself to the mast and hope for calmer seas tomorrow.

I head back to the asylum of my photo lab. The pictures of the rose bushes are dry and I spend the next forty-five minutes mounting them on some matting I have left over from a previous project. Stacey's face always glows when someone mentions her rose bushes. I leave the pictures near the coffee pot, hoping they will have the same effect tomorrow morning.

Chapter 12

For as long as anyone can remember, we have oscillated the naming of projects between engineering and marketing. My guys usually opt for a sci-fi or pop culture reference. The marketing types go for high-culture themes. It was marketing's turn and one of the directors in their camp is a big Broadway musical fan. Says he chose Xanadu because he saw a performance the last time he was in New York. A success among critics and viewers, after a year it went national and did well, or so he says. Wonder if he knows that the 1980 movie it came from is considered a monumental flop. It was the first movie Stacey and I walked out of.

The twinge of guilt I feel for being at my desk on a Saturday morning is almost completely overwhelmed by a corresponding peace. I can truly focus on what I wish with no possibility of interruption. At home, the kids are off doing their own thing and Stacey, with her attitude of late, wouldn't call me to let me know the house was on fire. I hope the photos I left by the coffee pot accomplish their goal, a truce fire at the Pedersons'.

Almost a year ago we signed a contract with Microsoft. They want a device to demonstrate a new social media software they hope to roll out soon. The handheld units will have dual 20MP cameras, 3-D video projection, VoIP teleconferencing, and a virtual keyboard that can be enabled on any flat surface. We haven't been privy to all that they plan on doing with their software, but rumors found on the internet have the tech media world buzzing.

Just the material costs for our deliverable units will exceed what they've agreed to pay per device. We'll be wrapping hundred dollar bills around each Xanadu as it goes out the door. Turning a profit on this project was never the motive. Being the demo device for any new Microsoft program is priceless. It's the kind of exposure CommGear can't purchase. We need Xanadu to be on time and flawless.

That's what has me here today. Slipping a couple of minor milestones on the Xanadu project has me...concerned. Blackmail notes have been stealing my attention of late. The boat that is my present life is barely afloat. Children, marriage, investments, and now work. I'm bailing as fast as I can but the waterline is rising. This kind of thing shouldn't happen to Mitch Pederson.

The company has enough in the bank to withstand a major loss on this project. Money would not be the issue. I'd make sure none of my team was let go. The real price would be paid in what CommGear would become. It would be years before the board could be convinced to take a chance like this again. The mere whisper of the word Xanadu would be enough to crater all but the most secure future projects.

Fear of another failure. Life on the sidelines, not being allowed to play with the big boys because we might get hurt. I will be CEO of this place, but I don't want to be running that kind of company. That's not a man's job.

Two hours of reading through status reports, emails and various data dumps have produced no discernable pattern. We aren't falling off the pace because people are getting lazy. The weekly timecards and email traffic show this is not so. My team is a very good one; results should be coming through. It seems as if we are moving backwards. I feel like I am the coyote chasing the roadrunner. The audience can see why I am losing ground, but it's a mystery to me.

I need the real story and that doesn't come through electronic media. Verity in this world comes from one place. The lab. It isn't always pretty, but it's solid. Not this modern PowerPoint crap. Honest engineering. Selfless trench workers putting their time in on the weekend. There's no extra pay for this and they would keep their jobs if they stayed home to deal with "honey-dos" and kids' soccer practices. These guys get it. It's about commitment. Loyalty. They are my brothers. I head to the lab where the light of truth shines brightest.

There are a handful of engineers huddled around various benches. They're the B team, none of them working on Xanadu. Strange that none of the A team is here. Robbie is in his familiar place and I head in his direction. No need for pleasantries. I can just jump into it.

"Is that Jimmy Lee's stuff you're working on?"

Robbie smirks. "Yeah, but you're safe. He was in, then left for a few hours. He does this every Saturday."

"Where's the rest of the team?"

Seconds pass as Robbie uses a large magnifying glass to inspect some solder points on a circuit board. He sips some coffee from the only mug he has used at work this century.

"They're not coming in today."

"That's odd, isn't it?"

"No reason for them to be here."

"Like hell. All of the peripheral designs are behind. They know they should be in here."

Robbie puts down the circuit board he's been examining and slowly turns his swivel chair in my direction. This is an uncommon act for him. He only stops when he has something very important to pass along.

"Their designs are on hold until the re-design of the main board is complete."

"Re-design?"

"Jimmy Lee is changing the architecture. He said the old approach was not good enough for Microsoft."

"Son of a...We don't have time for that shit."

Robbie turns back to his bench while I get up and

start wandering through the lab. Each time I approach a bench, the occupants grow silent. A wave of over-activity seems to be advancing before me. Knobs and switches are being adjusted at too fast a pace. Notebook pages flipped through at almost violent speeds. Those who didn't witness my last encounter here with Jimmy Lee have surely heard of it.

The public confrontation with one of my managers wasn't my best moment. A little fear of your boss is good medicine. It's the dosage that isn't always so easy to measure. I walk to the center of the room and turn toward the doors, my back on the group. A signal that I don't wish to interrupt their Saturday morning progress. They'll never know how much I miss the times when I could just be one of them. There are costs, often unmeasured, to being the big dog.

I search for an explanation. Jimmy Lee is a veteran of several projects. He knows we don't have time to change the system architecture this late in the game. This kind of step shouldn't have been taken without consulting management. This he also knows.

Is this a reaction to our run-in the last time I was in here? He didn't have the guts to stand up to me directly, so he's thumbing his nose like this? Nah. He wouldn't muck up the project just to get back at me. He knows he would suffer more than I would.

Maybe he really thinks this change in the architecture will make a huge difference for the program? He's trying to hit a home run and steal all the glory? He does have the ego for that, but it would be a big risk. If the approach fails, I would walk him out the door. He's not Americanized enough to go all in like that.

Unless the payoff is more than just this project. Maybe there's a bigger game going on here, one that's worth the risk?

Leaving the lab, I send Pete a text asking him to see me tomorrow morning. He asks me if it has to do with the blackmail. I don't bother responding.

I will right this boat, even if it means throwing a certain body overboard.

Chapter 13

Yesterday was a silent but unholy Sunday at our house. Not a scrap of harmony to be found. Something is eating at Stacey more than usual. Work problems to tackle first, and then I'll jump right into those home issues. Pete's on the top of my list this morning. I think I have the answer to my blackmail problem and I want to hit him with it right away.

No need to rush in this morning; Pete never does. I'm leaning on a wall near his locked office door. His perpetual lateness gives me more time with a photography magazine. I've read all the tech reviews and how-to articles. This month's feature story is the type I usually skip: build your own professional photography studio. Because I have extra time I run through the checklist included with the article. Seems I have most everything needed to make a go of it as a professional. Still shots, video, I could do it all. The thing I'm missing has no dollar value. To make a living in the photographic world would require a boldness I do not posses.

Walking away from the security of my present life is not fathomable. My father's attempts at being a proprietor scarred us all. His last venture failed less than a week before his life ended. I close the magazine and shake my head, trying to dispel these thoughts. Exotic and haunting for some, the land of self-employment is a country this family man shall never visit.

Although not yet in view, I know it's Pete that approaches. The jiggling of the keys in his hand, the scraping of the soles of his shoes on the tile floors, just the pace of his walk gives him away. The big man has a presence. I don't wait for him to round the corner. Things have been strained between us lately. I decide to make the effort to treat him better.

"How was your weekend?"

Pete rounds the corner with a perplexed look on his face. "A strange Monday. You want to see me first thing and you're acting civil."

"Don't push it. I don't have that much humility in me."

Pete unlocks his office door and moves quickly toward his chair. He flops the backpack he was carrying in a pile beside the desk. There was no laptop in it. He's not one to take his work home with him. Looking around his office, it's a wonder he gets much done here either.

Wild stacks of paper and magazines seem to grow everywhere, on his desk, covering a small conference table, smothering two chairs and even lurking behind the door. A large bookshelf in the corner doesn't contain a single row of books facing the same direction. The books do all have a uniform layer of dust on them. The lighting in here is bright and I wish deeply that it weren't.

An unspecified odor wafts in my direction. It doesn't smell like food, at least not from something prepared this month. I know I won't be able to sit here for any length of time with that aroma. I move toward the window to open it.

Pete must have ascertained my thoughts. "Had a little food accident in here. Facilities sprayed some kind of disinfectant last week. Let me turn on the fan."

One of those funny horns begins to make itself heard from the parking lot. It's the roach coach. I see Pete's eyes drift toward the window. My friend won't be able to resist the temptation. "All right. We can take a break. My treat."

One breakfast burrito, an apple turnover and two coffees later we return to Pete's office. I wouldn't have walked across the hallway for the coffee, but a friend doesn't let a friend dine alone. The food looks like it must be awful. My arteries pray that I never verify this. Pete takes a big chomp off the end of the burrito and instantly appears to achieve a state of bliss. I should have his attention until his stomach takes control again.

This will be a conversation I want to be seated for. I look at the chairs, but moving the stacks of written material is not appealing. Against the far wall I notice a couple of boxes for equipment racks. I pick them up and stack them in the middle of the room. My impromptu throne complete, I look to Pete for approval.

"Make yourself at home."

A smart-ass comment comes to my lips but I quench it. Instead I wipe a layer of dust from the top box and sit on it facing Pete. He has a silly grin on his face.

"Thanks for slumming it with me," Pete says.

"I got it figured out. The blackmailer. I should've seen this from the beginning."

Pete swallows the last bite of his turnover. The aroma of roach coach fare is dissipating, a blessing that is negated by the return of the original food odor. How can he work in here?

"Yeah. How do you know it's blackmail and what's with the deadline?"

I suspected he'd ask me this. He's been itching to know since I hung up on him last week. I saw a couple of his emails that I left unanswered. Maybe I'll share more with him another time.

"There's one guy I never considered. Our interactions have become increasingly *confrontational* and this weekend I learned that he has completely changed the architecture for the Xanadu project. He never consulted anyone in leadership about this."

Pete blows out a big breath. No doubt he's frustrated with my avoidance of his question. Sorry friend, not yet. He starts again with a new line of questions.

"Jimmy Lee? Butting heads with you is not unique. Why would he do something so stupid as this?"

These are inquiries I will respond to.

"I thought he was just a good engineer who happened to be a pain in the ass. Then I started thinking about our past interactions. He's always been a little too aggressive."

Pete winks at me. "Being aggressive doesn't single him out either."

"It's more than that. At his last review, I was trying to coach him on how to climb the ladder. The usual crap. He told me that where he ends up, how high he goes, is not up to me."

I grow tired of sitting on the boxes, so I move to the windows and lean on a wall nearby. Pete's office view includes the employee parking lot and a storage rental facility. Though not artistically pleasing, there's a good deal of random activity to keep your mind occupied if the conversation lags. It's almost enough mental stimulation to keep me from again noticing that strange smell. Pete is looking at me as if I owe him more.

"The guy's not one of us. Won't work on Sundays. Doesn't even try to fit."

"Maybe he should take lessons from you on fitting in?"

I give Pete a quick look meant to tell him to tread lighter with the truth.

"A few years ago we were alone in the lab one night. He starts asking me strange questions. Where do I get my life's priorities? What's my destiny? I had to get up and leave before he got all Confucius on me."

"Confucius was Chinese," Pete says.

"Okay, some Asian bullshit mysticism. The point is, he's not American. He'll never understand how we think."

"And vice versa."

I shrug my shoulders and reply, "I need your help to catch him."

"Not sure what I can offer."

"I need to make use of your real talents, aside from eating. You're IT. That's where you come in."

Pete rolls his eyes at me. Don't I get enough of that at home? The eating comment was probably a bit too far. What the hell; it was true. And he's been hitting me pretty regularly with "truth bullets" the last few minutes. I thought best friends got a free pass when speaking the truth. I think about mumbling an apology, but he'll get over it. Everything in this office is neglected. Maybe he will actually take my comment to heart.

"I got to catch this guy. Proof. Hard data. Somewhere he slipped up electronically."

Leaning back in his chair, Pete cocks his head to the side. The chair squeaks. His eyes never leave mine. Too much time elapses. He's doing that staring thing again. Does he have any idea how uncomfortable it makes me?

"I still don't get why Jimmy Lee would do this and now you want me to dig through his emails and such?"

"It's legal. He consents every time he logs on to a company computer."

"Technically. But morally, ethically. I could get in a lot of trouble here."

I stand and close the distance between us. Stopping within inches of his desk, I stare back at him.

"The bastard said he's going to tell Stacey. It would hurt her. He's going to make his move by Friday."

Pete holds his hands in front of him, palms upright. I take this as a signal that he won't help until he gets more details.

"Jimmy Lee referred to a contract in his last note. I don't want to get into it. I know what he's pointing to now. Friday's the day. I did nothing wrong and I won't let my wife get hurt. Neither will a true friend of mine."

Pete exhales and breaks his vision from mine. It's his turn to look out the window at nothing. After another minute he rises and comes around the desk to stand in front of me.

"Okay. But there are limits to how far I will go. I'll let you know when it's too much. I won't go beyond that. A real friend will respect this."

"When I'm CEO in a few years, Jimmy Lee will just be an ex-employee that people will have forgotten."

Chapter 14

It's 5:57 before I can get away from my desk. The Xanadu hardware design actually hit a couple of key milestones today. It's still behind schedule, but for the moment, no longer losing ground.

On my drive home I think about stopping for flowers for Stacey, but decide against it. It would be throwing a thimble of water on a forest fire. Whatever I've done is going to cost me more than pretty flora. There are problems to fix at home. With Pete's help at least the blackmail won't be a complication to this process.

As I walk in the house the silence unsettles me. It's strange how much more soothing it was when the house was filled with the chaotic noises of children underfoot. To think that I once wished for such noises to go away. The issues of those clamorous days were so much simpler and I was so much smarter. This silence permits my ignorance to ring loudly through the house.

The kitchen and living room are empty. I walk to my bedroom door but it is locked. This is not unusual. Stacey is no doubt secluded in the tub, trying to cope. She'll be in there for a few hours and finally, hopefully, come out human. We've all learned that this is a good thing. I move to Alyssa's bedroom door. I intend to knock but I'm slowed for a moment.

The door is a masterpiece crafted by Stacey years ago. Its background is a light blue that matches nothing in the house. I suppose an interior decorator would find fault with this. Stacey always says family trumps style. In the middle, standing almost three-and-a-half feet tall, is Tinkerbell. Her blond hair and green leafy dress seem to jump from the door. Coming from her wand are twinkling stars that randomly cover the rest of the door. At the top of this portal, in various alternating colors, handcrafted letters spell out that a princess resides herein. The artwork has been modified.

Tinker Bell is now sporting gothic-style eye shadow and rouge that would make Walt roll over in his grave. This fascination with death has always escaped me. It almost seems sacrilegious to do this to a pixie dust-spreading fairy. I have always dreamed of saving this door to give to Alyssa when she is finally a mother. Like the inhabitant, I hope these recent additions don't spoil the beauty underneath.

My knock is answered by a drowsy-sounding, "Yeah."

"Can I come in?"

"Hold on."

As I stand in the hallway, I replay in my mind how I would like this conversation to go. I want two things to come from it. An understanding of what drove her to use drugs and affirmation that she knows this is a terrible path to go down.

As I open the door a wave of strange smells hits my forty-one year old nose. I recognize oriental noodle soup, some type of fruity perfume, and nail polish remover. I don't smell anything that resembles what I think to be drugs. That gives me some relief as I hesitate in the doorway. I need time to assimilate the room before I enter.

The window blinds are open, the street lights providing the only illumination in the room. Alyssa is reclining on her half-made bed. She is wearing cut-off jean shorts and what look like three layers of tank tops. I move toward the chair sitting in front of her desk at the end of the bed. I am sure it was covered with clothes just a few moments earlier.

"Mind if I turn on a light?" I say as I reach for the switch on her desk lamp.

"It's your house, you pay the bills."

I take a deep breath and let it out slowly. "You scared us. Can we skip the confrontation this time?"

"We'll see."

"Why drugs?"

"You believe the school and not your daughter."

The chair I'm in is small and my back has to remain too erect to keep my rear in place on the seat. I won't be able to sit here long. I'm sure I've already overstayed Alyssa's wishes. I twist my torso hoping this will make things more comfortable. It doesn't.

"The school found marijuana in your locker. Are you denying that?"

"No."

"What do I have wrong then?"

Alyssa places two pillows between her back and the headboard of her bed. This allows her to sit more upright. She looks at me fully now. This is not something she has done for quite some time now. It makes me uneasy and I want to look away. I force myself not to.

Alyssa speaks slowly, "They were not mine."

"They were found in your locker. You have a lock on it?"

"Yes."

"So who did you give the combination to?"

"The school office."

This is the time when all parents get the proverbial kick in the stomach. You have cared for them since they were an innocent mass of needy flesh; putting them before your own well-being. Despite all that you have sacrificed, the time comes when they will lie directly to your face. Not the infant version where they're trying to escape a spanking. The full-on, screw-you-and-the-horse-you-rode-in-on, kiss-my-ass kind. I don't think you can ever prepare for this.

"Drugs were found in a locker that only you have access to and you say that they aren't yours."

Alyssa crosses her arms and continues to stare at me. Is this really the time when she wants to be defiant? Doesn't she know that her parents are all she has going for her now? The rest of the world couldn't care less. I rotate in the chair again. I know it won't help. Looking again at my daughter, I throw open my hands, beseeching her for more details.

"Well?"

"They weren't mine"

"You're not giving me enough to work with here. Can you see what I see?"

"You were always going to take their side anyways."

"I was hoping to find a way to support you. The amount of drugs they found was less than 28.5 grams. The police aren't looking at you as a distributor. The fine can be up to $100. Was it yours or your boyfriend's? I can stomach paying the fine for you, but I won't do it for him."

"They weren't Dillon's either."

"I'm going to take the money for the fine out of your bank account. If you want it back you can find the mystery owner of the drugs and get them to repay you."

"That sucks!"

"So does finding out that your daughter uses drugs."

Alyssa buries herself under the covers while she screams in frustration. I wanted to do the same thing five minutes ago. And she thinks we are so different.

My back is no longer willing to be ignored. The small chair has won. I stand and push it back in place. I stop to look at the desk, white pine, light but sturdy. I made it large enough for two chairs to sit beneath it. Alyssa and I painted it together. The whole project took two months of weekends and late nights. I remember sitting in a larger chair next to her as we read or solved homework problems. I don't recall when the bigger chair was banished from this room or where it was exiled to.

The noises from under the covers have diminished, but Alyssa won't be coming out. I don't know that I've accomplished anything here except insuring that everyone is equally upset. I suppose that's something.

I've got a lying, drug-using daughter who applies make-up like a circus clown, a wife who is so mad at me she won't come out of hiding except to throw verbal hand grenades my way, and the most pivotal project of my career is behind schedule. My life is the poster-child for legalized marijuana.

Chapter 15

My office phone rings. It's Stacey's mobile number. Another day has passed and things are still icy. I'm closer to righting things at work. I have to believe this. Soon enough I will start addressing the problems at home. Maybe I can book a weekend at a bed and breakfast? Stacey likes this kind of thing. She'll want one where there's no wireless access. It'll suck, but hey, if it helps thaw things out.

"How far away are you?"

Oh shit. It's 2:45 PM and I'm supposed to be somewhere. She's gonna kick my ass for this. I've got no idea where I should be heading.

"You forgot, didn't you?"

It feels like she calls me sometimes just to catch me screwing up. Whatever it is, my missing it will surely cause the world to end. I didn't mean to disappoint her, but that will amount to nothing. This will be just another example of why I don't care about them. I know how the rest of the conversation will go. Though I have no patience for it, it's going to happen.

"I guess."

"I know you don't care about me, but this *is* your daughter."

Alyssa. School. Shit. It's the appointment with the guidance counselor to get her back in. I forgot to put the damn thing in my calendar.

"I do care, about *both* of you. I just forgot. Sorry."

"You're using that word a lot lately."

"If I leave now I can make the last fifteen minutes of the meeting."

"Why bother?"

"When are you going to cut me some slack?"

"Do you think you deserve some?"

"This was an honest mistake."

I look at the four framed pictures on my desk. Three of them are of my own doing. Shots of the kids and Stacey. Two were taken before I had a digital camera. I went through many rolls of film looking for photos worthy of being on my desk. As adults we learn that to survive we must draw a curtain between the world and our fragile inner core.

Alyssa at seven, wearing a one-piece purple swimsuit. That was the summer she only wore purple. Hair tied back in a simple ponytail, running through the sprinkler on the front lawn, screaming in delight. There was not a cloud in the sky that day.

Jacob in his pajamas, skipping down the hallway, game controller held above his head, celebrating the first time he beat Halo. Immediately after the shot was taken he jumped into my arms almost causing me to drop the camera.

A summertime shot of the three of them squeezed together in a teacup carnival ride. Stacey in the middle, pulling her beloved offspring tightly to her. The kids raising their hands to feel the full effect of the centrifugal force. The faces of all three a mixture of emotions: fear, excitement, love.

The most important people in my life are before me every day, alive, joy on-demand, for my pleasure only.

The last picture, taken by an anonymous hotel staff member, is from our honeymoon. I was working here just over a year when we got married. Had to save up the money and vacation time. We're on a cliff in Hawaii, sun setting over the ocean to our backs. It was a great time. I remember being so totally relaxed, like I've never been before or since. Stacey sometimes asks if we could return again as a family. One of those things our schedules haven't permitted.

"Things have been pretty rough here at work. I'd like to think after seventeen years you'd understand this."

"There are a few things I thought you would've understood by now."

"If I'm doing something wrong, it would help if you told me. I can't fix what I don't know."

"I have been. You're not listening. If you cared you could figure it out on your own."

Here we go again. Another trip on the marital merry-go-round. There's no brass ring on this ride. Just the same monotonous circular path with the same old shitty music. You don't have to pay money for this ride. It only costs you a piece of your sanity; one slice per ride.

"Do you want me to meet you there?"

"No. Stay at work. Eat there, sleep there. It's your real home."

"People do treat me better here and they make a lot more sense."

"There you have it then."

The line goes silent. The ride has stopped. I shouldn't have said what I did. It was stupid to push her button like that. I'm risking my marriage by putting it on hold while I take care of Jimmy Lee. She didn't mean what she said about living here at work. Probably. I can fix it. I always have.

A quick glance at my trading account site shows the futures contract price edging the wrong way. There are still a few days for it to right itself. I've seen it before. A lot can happen in just one day.

I wish she would understand how difficult it is for me.

Chapter 16

Driving the streets of our suburb, I call my daughter's cell phone for the thirty-seventh time. It goes right to voice mail, just as it has for the last three hours. The logical part of me knows this is the sign of a dead phone battery.

Alyssa didn't come home from school again. The second time in two weeks. Night has long since fallen. There were no planned after-school activities. She's just acting out, got a good head and wouldn't do anything stupid. As I drive around, I keep telling myself this. It helps, but only a bit.

Stacey called me earlier to let me know of Alyssa's disappearance. Not the kind of phone call I wanted, but at least it was civil. Neither of us can figure out if drugs are to blame. It seems Stacey has an idea what's behind this, but she's not opening up. No surprise there.

Stacey gave me a list of places to look for Alyssa. A good parent should probably know where his daughter hangs out. We really only know what our kids choose to let on to us. At some point you have to trust the work you put in when they were young. Alyssa knows right from wrong. Next on my list is the bowling alley.

This oughta be fun. It's a Tuesday night. The place will be filled with league bowlers and teenagers looking to score illegal alcohol. I'm not sure which I'd rather avoid more. As I open an oversized blue wooden door with a bowling pin for a handle, the smell hits me. Eau de bowling alley. I don't know all the ingredients in this recipe. Sweaty shoes, plastic balls, alley oil, cigarette smoke, and other substances less appealing. I think if these places were around in prehistoric times, a few dinosaurs might have made it.

Nothing dies in here. Everything feels supernaturally suspended.

The café and bar are to the left. An amusement room is to the right. I make an unnecessary scan of the lanes. It would be too uncool, unhip, unfly, to be seen bowling in here. When was the last time bowling was popular with the in-crowd? I decide to start with the amusement room. Not because I think I'll find her here. I would just prefer it to the bar.

Electronically generated sounds drown out pins crashing and balls returning to their owners. Pre-teen boys swarm around the machines, focusing their attention on killing aliens and driving fast. The opposite gender are surrounding some kind of dance game. A computer is teaching them to dance. Isn't that the boys' role? The only kids in here that are close to Alyssa's age are social misfits. She would never hang with them. A bunch of nerds who'll end up as engineers and scientists.

I trudge to the other end of the alley. I close my mouth tightly as I pass through a curtain of cigarette smoke. Like all other buildings in the state, this is supposed to be smoke-free. Try imposing those laws on league bowlers. They're not the type to be worried about their health. There's probably not a one of them with a cholesterol level below 200. They're not convinced that smoking or bad eating habits will kill you. I think they make bowling pins black and white because that's how bowlers see the world.

I move quickly through the bar area. There's no sign of Alyssa or anyone else this side of fifty. I do see a couple of lizard-skinned women that may have been around with the dinosaurs. Their knowing glances assure me that they have taken off their custom-made bowling shirts for money at least once in their lives. If I believed in prayer, I'd request now that

I never have to come back here again.

The occupants of the café are the right age group. I stop before I fully enter. If she sees me first she may bolt. My dilemma is compounded because I may not recognize my daughter at first glance. What color was her hair the last time I saw her? I focus on height and body, ignoring hair and clothes. No one stands out. I'm going to have to go in.

There are only two rows of booths. I walk between them slowly, looking at each inhabitant. I was spotted long before I entered their dominion. The contempt is thick and genuine. I want to yell at all of them to kiss my ass. I know better than to ask any of them for help locating my daughter. Alyssa's not here.

Next on my list is the town's alcohol-free dance club. It's closed. It was started by a group of concerned parents a couple of years ago. I guess they're not concerned any more. Nothing is going on at the high school. I check Denny's and the 7-Eleven. My list is complete. I consider stopping by the police station, but their passivity when I called them earlier tonight eliminates that inclination. I was reminded that although this is my first teenage runaway, it isn't theirs. These things almost always turn out all right, despite what the media leads us to believe. The logic didn't work for me then and it is fairing worse as the night wears on. With no other moves left, I call my daughter's cell phone again. Same message.

I head home. Memories of bringing Alyssa home from the hospital for the first time try to creep into my thoughts. I stop them. There will be no crying. That will serve no good purpose at this time. I imagine seeing Alyssa sitting on the couch in full combative mode as I arrive. This thought sustains me for a few blocks. Then I realize that Stacey would call me immediately if Alyssa walked in. I will hold my feelings in check because that's what dads do.

As I walk in the door I see my wife and my heart finishes caving in on itself. My throat is so tight, I can't speak. I mouth the words "I'm sorry." Stacey tries to run off. I intercept her with a hug. She tries to pull away but I hold on tighter. Her body begins to shudder and then quake as sobbing takes control.

I hold her like this for several minutes. We don't speak, but I know her thoughts. She feels that she has failed, let her daughter down. There's no truth to this but nothing I say will change her disappointment. The only thing I can do is continue to embrace her as I feel inadequate myself. A good husband should know what to do here.

The executive ranks are filled with workaholics who have willingly sacrificed marriages and families. Superstar dads, the kind who make every one of their kids' school events and somehow truly participate in their families' lives, never get anywhere in the corporate world. Nice guys may not finish last in baseball but in the corporate world they do. I struggle to stay away from either extreme. I don't know any man who remains unscarred in this endeavor.

I'm holding the only person on this planet that I've ever made a public commitment to. The only person I ever will. Holding her so close, it feels as if the emotional barrier between us these past two weeks is dissipating. I consider sharing the troubles that Jimmy Lee is creating for me at work. She would like me to be more open with her; I know this, but to do so now would be selfish. The only loving choice is to hold her in silence.

Long ago, I learned that balancing the worlds of family and business is a zero-sum game. Anything that benefits one only hurts the other. Both sides can't win.

Chapter 17

My clothes for the day are stacked neatly on the end of the bathroom counter. I told Stacey this was in case we got news about Alyssa. Preparation for a quick exit. Truth is, I must go to the office today, but not for work purposes. A tiny piece of me feels uneasy, maybe guilty, about leaving Stacey alone. Work is the drug that helps me cope with family crisis. It's been that way for as long as I can remember. Today I desperately need a fix.

As I silently dress in the bathroom, my eyes begin to gather their focus in the light from the dawning day which is sneaking through the opaque windows. There is something amiss on the mirror above my sink. Letters are scrawled in a pastel color. Stacey writes me messages in lipstick if something occurs after I have fallen asleep. Willing my eyes to adjust faster to the paucity of light, I'm finally able to make out the three words.

Alyssa is safe.

I begin to raise my hands in the air as if celebrating a touchdown when a thought occurs. This small sentence is not concrete, definite. Is this a proclamation or a prayer? Could this just be the effort of a distraught mother willing herself to believe her offspring is well? Her notes always seem to leave room for misinterpretation.

There are times when you just have to believe that all will turn out right even when there is no evidence to support the conclusion. That's the way of a true leader, a father and a husband. Some might see this as whistling in the dark or false bravado. I prefer to look at it as steadfastness, willing the correct outcome. Throughout the rest of my readying for work, I fight the urge to wake Stacey and demand clarification. Whatever I'm doing must be working because the guilt I felt before seems to be diminishing.

There's an ebb and flow to my job. Like ocean tides there is much that is predictable. Pulling in to the CommGear parking lot, the waters have the feel of glasslike serenity. I won't be any use to my family if I'm less than my best. Time at work will be a much-needed pocket of peace in my life. I breathe in deeply as the first wave of this coping narcotic hits my body.

On my list is speaking with Pete about Jimmy Lee. I should be able to finish everything here in about an hour. Feeling more relaxed, I walk slowly into the building and pause for the receptionist to buzz me through the security doors. Seconds elapse and I don't hear the loud clicking of magnetic locks being released. I stop and look at the receptionist. She has her back turned to me. She doesn't look busy, but she also doesn't look like she's about to open the door either. Whatever. I use my badge and pass through the doors on my own.

Caffeine calls and I move to the coffee station to the right. Two marketing types are flirting with one of the executive admins when I walk up. I nod my head as a greeting but their conversation goes still. One of them mumbles about the amount of work they have to get to and they all scurry away. I grab some coffee and head to my office. Sheila told me yesterday there have been rumors of a layoff going around. Like internet hoaxes, no one knows who starts these things. Employment is secure here but people will continue to act strangely until the rumors peter out.

Up ahead there is a traffic jam of bodies in the main hallway. Office gossip I don't want to be drawn into. I decide to cut to my left through a mass of cubicles. Midway through the maze I notice several of the people from the hallway pile-up have turned to look at me. I fix my stare on them and they scurry like mice. The ability to create a little fear is a good thing sometimes.

As I near my end of the building I notice Sheila is at her desk. I check my watch because it seems odd that she is in before I am. Probably putting in some overtime to cover the next toy her husband has his eye on. I slow my gait to greet her but when she turns my way she has an expression that brings me to a full stop. No words pass between us but I know she wants to talk. It dawns on me that she must have heard about Alyssa. I nod my head toward my office and she follows me in.

I quickly shut the door behind her. "I'm only going to be here for a few minutes. You know what's up at home I take it."

"I'm surprised you came in at all."

"I've done everything I can do there. I want to tie up loose ends here and get back. We'd both be sitting there looking at each other waiting for the phone to ring. At least when it does, I won't have to worry about any fires here."

Sheila frowns and looks perplexed. "You seem calm."

How can I explain the feeling I get from being here? I pause for a moment and then go on. "There's no sense getting worked up about this until we know more. She's just acting like a teenager."

Sheila backs up two paces and looks me up and down. "I don't think I'll ever understand you."

Now my face must look puzzled. Sheila has worked for me for months now and seen how I manage a crisis. Did she expect me to go off the handle because my teenage daughter decided to stay overnight with one of her friends without telling us? If I can't run my home life how can I run this place?

"My family needs me to hold it together now."

Without any form of invitation from me, Sheila pulls out a chair from my conference table and sits down. She crosses her arms and her legs. It's a move her sister would make and it stops me for a moment. "This oughta be good. Explain how your family needs *you* to hold it together. It seems *you* might be the one tearing it apart."

Now I need to sit down. I sense I'm going to need all my energy to work through this. What is it with these two sisters and their convoluted sense of logic? I probably should have married an engineer, but they don't come as nice-looking as Stacey. Seated in my chair, I turn toward Sheila, take a deep breath and place my hands in my lap.

"Stacey's a wreck but we'll get through this. It's what happens to all families."

"Not every family."

I can feel the blood rushing to my face. I tell myself that Sheila doesn't have kids and doesn't understand this type of behavior. I'm feeling the need to defend myself and I don't appreciate it.

"All families go through this stage. Some just take it further."

Sheila shakes her head as if trying to free herself from where the conversation is going. "I've never seen someone as arrogant as you. Your life is going down the tubes and you're acting like all is normal."

My hands go to the arms of my chair and I feel them gripping tight. "You're crossing a line. I cannot allow this."

Sheila stares at me with a defiant look. "How many warnings do you need?"

I start to repeat the word warnings, but no sounds can come from my body. My mind is spinning at its highest speed but my mouth has come to a complete stop. The conversation needs a reset while I figure out where Sheila is going.

"Alyssa didn't come home last night. Something in her personal life, probably school-related. She'll show up today. I don't know what you're talking about."

"Alyssa spent the night at my place. Got there around 3:30 AM."

"Why didn't you call us?"

"Stacey knows."

And so would I had I understood the mirror scrawlings. I allow myself to take a deep, cleansing breath and it feels good. The need to go home quickly has been removed. I begin to mentally add to the list of things to be accomplished while I'm here. Sheila's frown brings me back to the moment.

"What warning are you talking about?"

Chapter 18

As I scurry out of my office, Sheila holds out a manila folder. I grab it without saying a word and quicken my stride toward Pete's office. I've got less than thirty minutes to check in with Pete, figure out how to deal with an upset CEO, and get back to my house before Stacey gets too worked up about the fact that I left her alone to deal with the crisis. At least Alyssa is okay. That's one thing going in the right direction. These may be scarce today.

Pete's not in yet. I duck into a vacant office nearby, shutting the door and turning on the lights. The last two people who occupied this space were let go. One for bad performance, and the other was thought to be stealing from the company. Pete manages the team over here and he's reluctant to put anyone new in this office. I don't blame him. I open the folder and remove its contents.

It's a folded piece of yellow construction paper. The type kids would use for an art project. I unfold the paper to its full size. Twenty-four by thirty-six inches. Around the perimeter of the paper are black diamonds. Each one appears to be hand drawn because they are not perfectly symmetrical and there's no pattern to their irregularity. Inside the border is a message written in bold red ink.

2 more days and then the whole world will know how badly. Mitch Pederson has managed his life!

I slam my fist down on the desk so hard the windows in the vacant office rattle slightly. Damn! Could Jimmy Lee have picked a worse time to do something like this? He couldn't know about how shaky things are at home just now? I picture myself sitting on the bastard's chest with a pair of scissors, cutting off his annoying long black hair in coarse lumps. I'm shoving a handful of hair in his open mouth. He's choking but I keep pushing more in. His eyes are wild. He doesn't seem to understand what's happening. I don't care.

From the hallway I hear keys jingling. Pete has finally arrived. I get up and open the office door. "You're not going to believe what the son of a bitch did now."

Pete looks startled to see someone come from this vacant office. He finishes opening his own door and tosses his backpack just inside the door. He turns and follows me into the cursed office. "Why here? This room is bad juju."

"No shit."

I point at the yellow paper on the desk. "Look at what the ass-wipe posted to the employee entrance for everyone to see this morning."

Pete rotates the paper so that he can read what's on it. I check the time on my phone and see that I only have eleven minutes left before my meeting with Frank.

Pete looks up at me. "How many people know about this?"

"Frank wants to see me this morning. The old man must have moved three other meetings to squeeze me in to his schedule."

Pete raises his eyebrows. "Shit."

"Yeah. You dig up anything on our friend yet? I need some proof and quickly."

"No, but I don't have to be subtle any more. I'll find something we can use."

"Do it," I say as I walk out the office door. I think about telling him to put the sign back in the folder and hide it. Who gives a rat's ass now? It's out. I'll smooth things over with Frank and then it's game on.

Frank's admin waives me directly into his office. As I turn the corner I see him sitting at the large desk. This isn't informal; he's wearing the captain's hat. I wish we could sit on the couch like the last time I was here. "Yes sir."

He doesn't get up. He leans forward in his chair and tosses his reading glasses on the desk.

"You know how I feel about family."

"I love this company too."

Frank waves me to take a seat as he comes out from around the desk. When he reaches the front he half-sits on it. His arms are crossed in a posture I can't recall seeing.

"Life outside this building is more important than what goes on here."

"This is not what it seems," I reply.

"If I called Stacey, she would say things are great at home?"

I begin to formulate what I hope will be a convincing answer when memories of my recent relationship with Stacey come to the forefront of my thoughts. "Marriage is a bit of a rollercoaster. We're not at our highest point just now."

"Maybe you should spend some time addressing that situation."

A creaking sound comes from the chair I'm sitting in. I look down and notice my hands are gripping the arms of the chair. "Things aren't going right on Xanadu. Besides I think this...this issue is all about work."

Outside a large cloud must have moved from in front of the sun, because a burst of sunlight suddenly enters the room. The polished top of Frank's desk acts like a mirror, spewing rays in every direction. I instantly squint and turn my head away.

Frank must sense my discomfort because he rises and

moves between me and the angry light.

"Tell you what, for the moment, why don't you go home? Take a few days off and work on things there. It couldn't hurt to spend more time with your family. I've already got HR looking into this business with the sign. We'll talk next week. Monday morning."

I open my mouth to offer another approach, but Frank's hands wave me to stop. The conversation is over. I can't read any emotion in his face. It's just as well since I feel enough disappointment without his help. I hate that I have let this man down.

Chapter 19

The weak-minded tend toward signs or superstitions. And yet, as I drive to work the fog rolling in from the ocean feels more dense than usual. The gray cloud cover seems to be stubbornly squatting over the La Jolla communities. Pulling into my parking spot, I hope the rest of the day doesn't shit on me too.

It's all I can do to sit in my chair. Pete's not in yet. He doesn't usually arrive before 9:00. Ninety-seven minutes of fiddling around. I took the better part of two days off as my boss suggested, but my home life is none the better. Now I'm struggling to stay focused on the simple tasks in front of me. I continue to return to thoughts of what might occur today.

It feels as if Jimmy Lee has been stalking me, hovering, waiting for me to slip. How the hell did he get his information? I've tried to prevent him from enjoying any real intrusion in my business life. There is no longer any choice. The deadline is today.

I grab a clean sheet of paper and the calculator from my bottom desk drawer. It's considered a relic now from my university days. I could do what follows faster on my computer, but there is something more settling about doing it the more old-fashioned way. Maybe I just want to slow down the arrival at an answer that I know will be painful.

I begin to write. Four months ago I purchased a futures contract to buy five units of Light Sweet Crude Oil at $98.00 a barrel. A unit is 1,000 barrels. This translated into an obligation to purchase 5,000 barrels of oil at the closing market price today. When I entered into this contract oil was going for $92.53 a barrel but my analysis showed that it would rise to $105.48 by settling time. If everything had gone as planned, I would have an extra $37,400 in my account today. I could have bought a nice gift for Stacey with some of that money.

The futures market is highly leveraged. That's the beauty of it. The ante to get into this game, my initial margin as it's called, was just $98,000. A damn sight easier to swallow than the full price of $490,000. The math was sound. It was the bastards running OPEC that were off. Who could have predicted that a prince from some sand-encrusted country no one gives two shits about would trigger a downward price movement that the market couldn't abate? Oil prices for Light Sweet Crude today are running at $76.52 a barrel.

Unlike typical stock trading, margin accounts in the futures market are settled daily. This is why as the price of oil plummeted I had to continue to pour more money into my margin account. Leveraged markets are an ugly bitch. Hitting a few keys on my calculator reveals that if the price falls to $72.93 today I will have lost everything. I use my phone to send an email to my broker instructing him to exit my position if the price hits $73.

The office phone rings. Caller ID shows that it's Pete and it's only 8:58. I move quickly to shut my office door, hitting the speaker button on the way back to the desk. "So you decided to work some overtime today?"

"Can you afford to alienate me?"

Point taken. Not a lot of people signing up to help me just now. I stare at the phone waiting for him to rescue me.

"Breathe, big man. Today's a rough day for you."

"Yes. I'd like to nail the bastard."

I look in my top drawer for the doodling I created during my last call with Pete, but decide against it. Before I shut the drawer, I grab the photo and blackmail note. I place them on the desk in front of me.

I stare at the picture. The quality still sucks, but even a photographic novice can't make my wife less than attractive. "It seems like a serious blackmailer would've done a better job with the photo."

There are several moments of unhurried breathing coming through the line. Pete exhales deeply and at last breaks the silence. "There's always been only one correct move."

Stacey's body is taut in the photo, leg and arm muscles straining against the work she is putting them through. Despite this, her face is at peace. She's content. A woman who knows what she wants.

Pete continues on, "Jimmy Lee's whole plan is nothing if you just talk to her. You married the woman, why don't you trust her?"

"It's not about trust. It's about protecting her."

"Bullshit."

"It's too late to bring her in now."

"Chicken-shit."

I pick up the receiver intending to loudly run through my own list of shit-types, but instead just slam it back in the cradle, ending the call.

***

It's 11:28. Jacob should be in school and Alyssa locked away in her room. Stacey would have called me by now if Alyssa wasn't home. It should be a good time to call. Stacey answers on the second ring.

"Hello."

Her tone is bright, coming through the line with a promise of a pleasurable conversation. Our children, lifelong friends, casual acquaintances, even telephone solicitors receive this greeting. She must have picked it up in the kitchen. We don't have caller ID on that extension. Maybe I can keep things warm with the right words. "How has your day been going?"

"Fine."

The word trails away along with any remnants of cheerfulness. One monosyllabic utterance and I know this isn't going to be a good call. It will take a lot from me to keep this civil. This is why I don't call home during the day. I need to make sure that Jimmy Lee hasn't followed through. I just want a chance to make things right before he makes things untenable.

"I was thinking of taking off early today. Maybe go out for dinner, just the two of us?"

"Suit yourself."

Strike one. So much for romance. Maybe something as simple as sincere interest in her day. "What do you have planned for today?"

"Picking up after your kids. Cleaning your house. Having everything ship-shape for when you finally come home. The usual."

Strike two and that one was ugly. I can take one more chance or silently head back to the bench. I should probably put my bat back in the rack, take a seat in the dugout and preserve what dignity I have left, but I'm not in the mood to quit. I decide to play the family card.

"No more troubles with Alyssa?"

"Now that you mention it, the FBI called and asked if we had any recent photos of her for their ten most-wanted list. I told 'em you're the photographer in the family."

There is no joy in Mudville today. Three strikes and I'm not sure I even got the bat off my shoulder. Screw it.

"Look I don't want to do this. I don't know what I've

done wrong, but I'd like to fix it. What are you looking for from me?"

I hear her exhale loudly. "I'm not giving that one to you Mitch. You're going to have to figure it out on your own."

The line goes dead.

An uneasiness rises in my stomach. I recognize the taste it leaves. It happens at work when I've failed to deliver my best effort.

Chapter 20

Sitting at my desk, I stare vacantly at the banner running across the screen of my laptop. The price of my futures contract is updated real-time from the floor of the Chicago Mercantile Exchange, the Merc, as real traders call it. The price has risen to $78.01. It would be smart to sell my contract now and limit my losses, but I'm determined to ride this out to the end. There's still reason for hope.

I lean back in my chair as a pre-children Saturday afternoon twirls to the forefront of my memories. Stacey and I were lying beneath a long-since-disposed-of quilt on a hand-me-down couch in the front room of our first apartment. The smell of impending rain drifted through partially open windows.

She was on her back, naked, her head resting on a tan throw pillow. I was on my side, equally naked, head propped on my elbow so I could see her face. Love-making completed, the two of us lay there enjoying a day free from commitments. I pulled the first photo from behind me. I had spent two weeks generating a portfolio for just this occasion. Some were my shots, others were magazine clippings.

Her eyes were closed. On her lips, the hint of a smile was forming in anticipation. I whispered, "Now."

From her throat and slowly deeper within her body came both words and non-words. Her face transformed into a window, making visible cravings, yearnings, and trepidations. The raw emotions she had tapped into were running unchecked. I laid there in awe, both at her courage in being so open with another human being and my ability to reach her soul.

We examined over fifty photos that day, each portraying some portion of a house. Front porches, kitchens, master bathrooms, backyards. Desires and dislikes were proffered freely. No notes were taken. The photos were merely stimuli for honest, unplugged communication.

For another four hours we shared our dreams. Exposing ourselves in the way young couples do. She spoke and I listened. Really listened. When it was my turn to jump in, she focused on me. No tuning me out as she browsed a magazine. I mattered. I was important. We were both convinced that we would always feel this way with each other.

Our conversations have long since become rigid, predictable, and lonely.

I continue to run our last *pleasant* exchange through my mind. Three meetings and four hours have passed since then. I know that I must call her again. There will be a remnant of anger from earlier today. It's an increase in her ire that interests me. The blackmail will cause a nuclear explosion. There's no way she can contain that. I must know what she knows.

Frustration with Jimmy Lee rises in me again. When is my deadline up? Did the clock run out with the closing of the Merc or do I get the whole day? Can I put this off further? Stacey's anger is something I've always handled before. If she doesn't bring up anything about the oil contracts I'm probably in the clear. Then I can spend the weekend fixing the family vessel. That's a ship I have repaired a time or two.

At 4:45 I make the call. It's been a decade at least since I called the house twice in the same business day. The warning flags will be up for Stacey, sailors beware, but there's no way around this. She picks up just before the answering machine kicks in. I can hear her labored breathing; she must have run for the phone. Good, that'll make her even more fun to talk to.

A flat "Yes" comes over the line.

"I feel bad about how our earlier conversation ended."

"You should."

I remember the woman on that couch so long ago. It was easy to love that woman. I want to love this version of Stacey too, but sometimes it's damned hard. As I allow her sarcasm to vaporize, I punch some keys on my laptop. Looking to see if there's a chick flick playing at the movie theater near our house. Success.

"That new Brad Pitt movie is playing. Want to go see it after dinner?"

"You hate his movies."

"You love them."

"Don't do me any favors."

Shit. I'm not in the mood to do anything for her just now. She treats insect predators on her rose bushes better than this. My vision lands on the oil contracts price, but I quickly drop the lid on my laptop. I need all my focus on Stacey.

"How's Alyssa?"

"Come home and find out for yourself."

"I'm planning on it. I'd like to know if I'm battling one or two opponents tonight."

"Are you afraid?"

"I don't think we can help Alyssa if we're at each other's throats."

The phone goes silent. Concern for our child's welfare trumps all. She'll regroup for another attack. I need to know if Jimmy Lee has followed through. I've done nothing wrong but this won't relieve me from needing to defend myself against some trumped-up charges. I'm going to have to push the envelope here.

"I'd like us to work together and solve the Alyssa thing and then work on our problem."

"What does that mean?"

"Our disagreements don't usually last this long. I'd like to really talk about whatever this is. That's probably not going to happen if I'm doing something to make it worse."

"So you finally want to talk to me about our *problems*. What brought this on?"

I mumble, "I guess I wanted you to know I still love you," and gently put the receiver back in its cradle. Replaying her final words in my head, it feels like normal marital anguish. Perhaps shielding her from this scheme of Jimmy Lee was the correct route all along. While my mind grasps at this hope, my stomach remains unsettled.

Chapter 21

As I walk to my car, I use my phone's app to check again on the crude oil futures contract. The market price sank to my $73.00 limit. My account balance, which was at one time $98,000, is now $350.

My mind is taken back to a sunny day four years ago. I was in a staff meeting when I got a text message to call my sister. Our mom had been found in her apartment, the victim of a major stroke. The second parent taken from me without a chance to say goodbye. It had seemed surreal to me that day that everyone around me could simply go about his or her business when my life was left with a gaping hole. Passersby were carrying on in animated voices, some laughing jovially. Pleasure and grief walking within inches of each other.

On my drive home today I pass joggers, teams of mothers pushing carriages, a noisy ice cream truck selling its wares. Photography has helped me through every major crisis in my life and it must be my savior again. I have some shots that need editing. Photoshop will let me transform the photos and my life into what they were meant to be. Iced tea, Van Halen, and two hours of solitude in the studio will begin to ease the pain in my heart.

Nearing my house, I see bundles of rose bush prunings left at the curb. Tossed aside, the colors are still vital, alive. Before I head to the studio, I'll grab my Nikon and record this image. There is still value here, worthy of reclamation. I punch the remote to open the garage door and simultaneously grab my phone to start up some music.

The peace blossoming in my soul rapidly fades when I see Stacey's car in the garage. I know I won't be able to slip past her into my studio. Any hopes I had of soothing myself in a photographic nirvana dissipate. Shit. I'm not ready to deal with anything emotional.

Walking through the living room, I hear the sound of a chair being moved across a tile floor. It's coming from the dining room. Like a condemned man, I trudge forward joylessly. As I near the doorway, I hear the ticking of the oversized sunflower clock. The familiarity of this sound is often comforting. Today it's just another thing that annoys me. Stacey is sitting quietly at the table. She's in Jacob's spot, middle of the table far side. A pitcher is sitting on the table to her left. In her right hand is a glass filled with some iced drink.

The blinds are drawn to a half-mast position, limiting my visibility. I reach for the light switch.

"Don't."

I pause for the briefest of moments, considering my options and then flip the switch. Turning my attention back to Stacey, I notice the redness around her eyes. She tops off her glass from the pitcher. An alcoholic odor reaches my nose.

"What's up?" I venture.

"Just chillin' with a pitcher of margaritas."

We don't typically have alcohol in our home. It's not that we're teetotalers. We came to an agreement a few years back that having alcohol in the house with teenagers was a bad combination. Holidays being the normal exception to this rule. It's May, a month not typically associated with drinking. I look at my wife, trying to decipher what would urge her to make a special trip to the store for margaritas. I must stare at her too long, because she adds to her last comment.

"Get over it, tight-ass. Jacob's spending the night with a friend and it's the weekend."

Her rebuff temporarily inhibits my movements. Freed again I turn toward the china cabinet. A drinking glass of my own in hand I reach for the pitcher, but I'm stopped by a new directive.

"There's not enough here for two."

Stacey pulls the pitcher closer to her glass. It's done too fast and some of its contents slosh over the pitcher's rim. Despite the spillage, there's enough for four more glasses. I focus again on my wife.

"So I'm just supposed to watch you get drunk?"

"I don't care what you do."

The spilled margarita is slowly making its way, in a serpentine path, toward the edge of the table. I have time to make it to the kitchen to grab a towel. Before I take a step, I realize that it's not necessary. The alcohol in the drink will evaporate soon enough and minimize any mess. The fallout of this argument will last longer.

"Why are you so angry?" I ask.

Stacey takes another long swig before responding, "Look closer. This ain't anger you're seeing."

"So what is it? Don't make me guess."

"You're no longer my concern."

I slam my open hand down on the table between us. The sudden meeting of flesh and oak makes a loud clap that rattles the glass in the china cabinet. My hand throbs, but I don't allow myself to examine it. Stacey doesn't even flinch.

"I've had my own shitty day at work. In fact, it's been a bad month. I don't have the energy to play these damn games with you."

"From where I'm sitting only one of us has been playing this *game* for quite some time now."

A good husband is supposed to give his wife a happy home where she can nurture her family, not burden her with his troubles. This is my lot and I accept it. And yet, as my partner, she deserves to know that I have put the family's future at risk with my investment fiasco. I'm at a loss to share this without really scaring her. I want her to trust my abilities to guide us through this storm, but I'm not sure I know these answers myself.

"There is something that maybe I should have shared with you sooner..."

Stacey's voice rises to another level. "Oh no, no, no! You don't get to do that now. It's too late."

Her increased anger crushes my attempted mea culpa. It's clear that she already knows something. I stumble to lock on new words that might resolve this issue. I use the silence to observe my wife closer. There has to be a clue that I'm missing. Maybe Jimmy Lee did follow through on his threat?

"Too late for what?" I ask.

"I'm not going to let you own up to what you should have done weeks ago."

Stacey begins to gently rock her half-empty glass from side to side. The ice cubes clink against the sides of the glass in a melodic rhythm. We both watch for a few seconds, mesmerized.

"I can't think of anything that I need to *own*."

"There you have it then," she responds.

I let out a big sigh while throwing my hands in the air. "Just for once I wish you would stop speaking in riddles."

"Okay. You want it to be clear, Mr. Engineer. Here it is. I want you out. I'm not willing to live with anyone who doesn't put this family first."

"I don't believe this. I'm not convinced you know what you want. This seems to be a problem for all the women in this house."

Damn. That sounded better in my mind than when it came out. She's been smoldering the last few days and now I've just given her reason to fully ignite. My back is to the china cabinet. I retreat toward the hallway. I want open space behind me. Stacey rises quickly and closes the gap between us.

I open my mouth to apologize, but it's no use. A thimble of water on a forest fire.

Stacey halts her movement toward me and raises her right hand. It's shaking. She points one finger at my face and speaks in a low monotone. Her lips part ever so little.

"Leave."

Chapter 22

The sound of the refrigerator door slamming shut interrupts our battle. We both look toward the kitchen. Stacey turns on one foot like a gymnast in the midst of a floor routine. The hand that was angrily pointing at me now shoves open the swinging kitchen door. Over Stacey's shoulder I can make out hair with streaks of various colors.

I follow Stacey into the kitchen. Alyssa turns. She must have heard our steps and maybe the conversation from the other room? In one hand she's holding a small plate full of cheese and vegetables. A bottle of ranch dressing is in the other.

Stacey moves in quickly, her arms spread wide like a great bird. The list of items more comforting than a mother's hug is quite short. Evidently Alyssa is not in need of such comfort as she sidesteps her mother's advances. All human activity stops for a moment.

The sound of a single water drop falling from the faucet echoes like a cannon shot. Still no one moves. Another drop falls and Alyssa flings the plate toward the sink. Vegetables and cheese slices tumble at different speeds to the floor. The plate hits the porcelain surface of the sink and shatters. She tosses the bottle of dressing to her mother.

Stacey fumbles in her first two attempts to catch the bottle, eventually clutching it to her chest. She takes two steps toward the sink and flips the bottle, end-over-end in a large arc. Moments later it ends its shelf-life with a loud crash. Slowly she turns and looks at Alyssa.

Returning her mother's gaze, Alyssa nods her head in my direction. "What has he done?"

How did this house get filled with such anger? It seems to have happened so suddenly. I despise this drama. It makes no sense for them to use their energy in this way. I look to Stacey hoping to see parental solidarity kick in. Our problems are secondary to our children's well-being. Nothing like this emerges.

Stacey replies in an even tone. "It's nothing I can't handle."

It's every man for himself. In what will surely be a futile move, I ask, "Can we not do this now?"

The refrigerator motor makes a thump as the fan kicks into a higher gear. The house around us continues to function, while the family coughs and sputters.

Alyssa crosses her arms, a perfect replica of her mother.

"Who did the bastard sleep with?"

In my firmest voice I yell, "Stop!"

Sometimes it's good to be a man. They both turn toward me, silent for a moment. I look first at Alyssa and then at Stacey. And then I realize what I've done. The battle lines are firmly drawn now and I'm officially outnumbered.

The refrigerator motor returns to its idle state. I try to soften my voice. "Tell her I didn't cheat on you."

Stacey puts her hands on her hips. She could not have chosen a more demeaning stance if she'd had a month to think about it. Is this a skill women are born with or do they take secret classes behind our backs?

"You don't live here."

Alyssa stares at me. I am surprised that Stacey has laid this before one of our children. I'm not prepared. My eyes focus on the faucet. It seems to be dripping slower and louder. I didn't cheat on my wife. How did I get here? I know better now than look to Stacey for help. There's nothing I can say that won't sound like an excuse. And yet, if I say nothing isn't that a confession?

Screw it. If this is the ground upon which I'll die, it won't be like a dog with his tail between his legs. As I begin to speak, I cross my own arms in front of me. "Unlike your dad, I don't have my eyes on every skirt that walks my way."

Stacey's eyes open wider and her nostrils flare as she sucks in a deep breath. And then she spews, "At least he was capable of loving someone other than himself!"

"So you'll be looking to keep up the family tradition and push me into another woman's arms?"

"You son of a bitch."

"I'm here now dealing with your irrational shit. What's that worth?"

"Not much." Stacey says.

"I have not cheated on you. Tell your daughter."

Stacey returns my gaze, unblinking. "It feels like it."

Alyssa pushes past me, accelerating toward the doorway. She's almost running now. She punctuates her leaving us with a resounding, "I hate this family!"

I hesitate to follow, unsure of the correct parental move. Stacey seems to have no such confusion as she sprints from the room. The three of us race down the hallway. We need to cut her off before she gets to her room. She'll lock us out and I don't know what she'll do if she's left alone. In the midst of accelerating, I realize that she's not going to her room. She turns sharply into my photo studio. Stacey follows her in, but my momentum carries me past the doorway.

I hear the destruction before I see it. Above the screaming is the sound of items crashing into the walls. She's tearing my studio apart! I retrace my steps and enter the room. I'm wrong. It's two vandals. Stacey is on the left destroying my digital processing set up. Alyssa is doing the same to my

35mm process on the right. Stacey is wrestling with my HP 6015 color printer. She has managed to maneuver it to the edge of the counter top. It cost me over $3,000, on sale. The old-school stuff that Alyssa has targeted is harder to come by, but less expensive.

I turn toward Stacey and wrap my arms around her, pinning her to me. "Please stop."

Stacey tries to squirm free. She's no match for me. I hold her firm but I'm careful not to hurt her. In a few seconds her struggling diminishes.

Softly I whisper in her ear, "I'm sorry."

Stacey turns in my arms. Tears are dripping from her eyes. Her face has a Halloween look from the wet mascara running down it. I pull my dress shirt free at my waist and unbutton the lowest two buttons. I begin to use the shirt bottom to gently wipe away the ghoulish make up.

From behind I hear a crash of metal against metal. I feel drops of liquid landing on my neck, ears and scalp. A scream explodes as agony saturates the room.

Stacey tears herself from my grip.

Alyssa is on her knees; her back toward us. She has her hands covering her face as she rocks forward and back violently. Her screams are replaced by a low, guttural moaning. Stacey is on her in a moment.

"What? Baby. What?"

My eyes survey the other half of the room. Torn pictures are strewn about. A pair of tongs and a lone plastic glove are on the floor to my right. To my left, on the edge of the work table is one of the metal basins. Muscles throughout my body begin to involuntarily tighten. The other basin is upside down on the floor next to our daughter. It's the one I use for the chemical stop bath. I left it full the night I developed the pictures of Stacey's roses!

I grab Alyssa under her arms and lift her upward, cradling her like an infant. Adrenaline is flowing in massive doses throughout my body. I whip her about like she's an infant in a car seat again.

Turning to Stacey I yell, "Grab your keys, we need to get her to the hospital now!"

Chapter 23

Stacey is driving my BMW in a way that would scare an Indy car driver. I would prefer to be at the wheel but Alyssa maintains a continuous whimper for her daddy. I am sitting in the back seat still cradling her. Neither of us has a seat belt on and my back is killing me from the odd angle I'm forced to assume. Alyssa hasn't removed her hands from her eyes and I don't make any effort to stop her. Her moaning is softer now. I try to remain calm and talk in a soothing voice. A good father wouldn't have let his daughter get hurt like this.

I brace my knees against the chair in front of me as Stacey cuts a corner too tight. The tires grumble as we come down off the curb. It's a ten-minute drive from our house to the hospital. My wife makes it in seven.

She pulls into the first open spot she sees in front of the emergency room. It's a handicap spot. Screw it, we'll pay the ticket. I jump out and half-run toward the automatic doors at the entrance. I can't make top speed with Alyssa in my arms. Behind me, I can hear the car doors being slammed and the horn tooting that the vehicle is locked. Stacey is at my side before I can make it through the door.

There are a handful of people in the waiting room. To our left is the desk where a nurse will check you in. We know the drill. We're parents; we've been here many times.

"Alyssa Pederson. She's been here before. She spilled citric acid in her eyes."

The nurse reaches her hand beneath the desk. I know she's hitting a button to get someone out here stat. She starts firing questions at us, taking notes on the computer in front of her. Stacey's answering her. Alyssa's moaning seems to get louder. It might be the acoustics of the room. I start singing the lullaby I sang to put her to sleep fifteen years ago. I don't know why I'm doing this. It seems to be helping. Both of us.

A male nurse comes out from a door to our right. He doesn't speak, just waves us to follow him. We obey. Stacey holds the door as I scurry past her, twisting awkwardly to keep Alyssa's head from hitting the door jamb.

This nurse is repeating many of the same questions that the attendant nurse asked. I always feel like I'm a criminal and they're the police trying to trip me up in a lie. Stacey tells him that Alyssa accidently spilled citric acid in her eyes. The nurse asks how this happened.

"It's the stop bath solution I use for developing photos."

We're directed into exam room number five. It's filled with instruments. The bright lights hurt my eyes. I put Alyssa on the table in the middle of the room. Stacey and I take up spots on either side of her head. Both of us run our fingers through her hair and alternate soothing sounds. The nurse is taking her vitals and recording them on a portable electronic device.

Without looking away from his work, the nurse asks again, "How did Alyssa get the acid in her eyes?"

I look straight at him with my best don't-mess-with-me stare. "It was an accident."

He looks up and appears ready to ask another question. He doesn't. Smart move asshole. Stacey grabs my forearm. She's right. I need to calm down. The guy's just doing his job. And if I had done mine properly we wouldn't be here.

A doctor pushes aside the curtain surrounding the exam table. Her name tag says Reynolds. She has long brown hair tied off in the back and looks to be in her mid-thirties. She tells the nurse to get her a large basin of distilled water, an eye flush kit, and extra towels. He almost runs out of the room. My stop-what-you're-doing look was good, but I've got nothing on her. There's no mistaking who's in charge now.

She reaches over to the light switch and extinguishes the overhead beacons. From her pocket she pulls a small flashlight and turns it on. She moves toward our end of the table and bends down close to Alyssa's head. Moving in close to our daughter's ear she softly says, "Alyssa, I'm Dr. Reynolds. I'm going to make the pain stop and see what we can do to fix those beautiful eyes of yours. To do that I'm going to need your help. I need you to take your hands down from your face. I know this will hurt a little but I can't fix things without taking a look. Can you do this for me?"

Alyssa nods her head slightly. The male nurse returns with the items he was sent for. Without saying a word the doctor waves him to take a position at the head of the table. Stacey and I move to where we can get a good look at our daughter's head.

A second nurse enters the room. She's carrying a syringe. The doctor signals her to wait a moment. She places her head near Alyssa's ear again.

"Alyssa dear, I'm going to have nurse Stevens here give you a little shot. It's a mild analgesic that will help take the edge off your pain. The needle is small and you won't feel more than a little stick."

The doctor holds her right hand up to the nurse holding the syringe. She squeezes her thumb and forefinger together three times. A signal of some sort that I don't understand. The nurse pulls an elastic cord from her pocket and ties it around Alyssa's right arm, just above the elbow.

The doctor's hands gently cradle Alyssa's face as she speaks softly to her. "I like your hair. My dad wouldn't let me have this much fun when I lived at home."

The female nurse swabs a portion of Alyssa's forearm with alcohol.

Dr. Reynolds goes on, "I bet your dad hates it too, but he's too afraid to try and stop you. What color streak do you think drives him the most crazy?"

Alyssa smirks and mumbles amidst obvious pain. "Blue."

I open my mouth to correct her; it's the white streak that bothers me the most. In the moment I decide to let this go unsaid.

The female nurse inserts the needle in a vein and starts to inject the drug.

"Now darling, while that starts to work I'm going to have to take a look at your eyes. I promise not to touch them yet. Can you take your hands down?"

Alyssa slowly moves her hands away from her face. Not down to her sides, just neck level. Stacey whimpers and I reach for her hand. Alyssa's cheeks are moist from crying. Her face is contorted as she keeps her eyes squeezed shut. There is a lot of redness surrounding her eyes. The left one appears to have been affected the most.

Doctor Reynolds motions both nurses to come closer to Alyssa's head. She stops them just short of touching her. "Alyssa let me walk you through what I'm going to do. First I'm going to rinse the area around your eyes with distilled water. It won't hurt. Then I'm going to have to rinse your eyes using the same fluid. It's going to bother you some to open your eyes. That will be the worst part. You won't even feel any pain from the rinsing. It might even feel good.

"The thing is your eyes have to remain wide open

while I rinse them. I know you are a brave young lady, but no one can hold their eyes open that long. So I've got this little metal contraption called an eye speculum. It just helps me keep your eyelids open. A surgeon used one on me when I had Lasik surgery. It doesn't hurt, but it can be … annoying. Like our fathers.

"When I've got your eyes open wide, it's important that you don't get your hands anywhere near. Your eyes can be very sensitive to infection. I know you're going to try really hard to keep your hands down, but just in case I have a couple of my assistants here to help you."

The doctor motions to the two nurses and they take hold of our daughter's arms, pinning them to the bed. Doctor Reynolds begins to rinse around Alyssa's eyes, working her way outward. She then grabs the eye speculum and nods to the nurses. Gently she uses the device to hold open Alyssa's right eyelid. Alyssa squirms and whimpers. The nurses tighten their grips on her arms. Stacey mirrors her daughter's facial expressions and movements. I'm probably doing the same thing.

Doctor Reynolds rinses each of Alyssa's eyes for ten minutes. The frown on our girl's face has lessened. Stacey and I scoot around the table trying to take in everything. I can't be sure if Alyssa's eyes are functioning. It may be the low light in the room. I try to glean information from the doctor's face but it's no use. Her expression is a rock of concentration.

The doctor at last removes the medical device from Alyssa's eye and motions to the male nurse to turn the lights back on. "Alyssa, you did well. Thank you. Now my friend, Nurse Jonathan, is going to place some protective pads over your eyes. We're doing this to reduce the risk of infection for the next few days."

As the larger nurse moves in, the doctor looks at us and nods toward the hallway. Stacey and I follow her outside the room and over to a nearby nurses' station. The doctor turns and faces us. She reaches out and takes Stacey's hands in her own.

"I have a little girl. I know you have a lot of questions. There's not much I can tell you right now. Her eyes are in a state of shock so we don't know what if *any* long-term vision impairment she will have. The good news is that citric acid is relatively weak. An alkaline could have been much more damaging."

Stacey is leaning against me. I slip my arm around her waist as I feel her begin to droop. She straightens up and focuses on the doctor. "What do we do?"

"Keep her eyes covered. I'll write a prescription for Tylenol 3. I paged the ophthalmologist on call. He should be here within the hour. Alyssa will need to be looked at in two days."

I pull my arm from around my wife and face the doctor squarely. "That's it? Our daughter may have permanent vision loss and you send us away with pain-killers and an invitation to see another doctor in two days? Don't they have someone around here who knows what they're doing?"

The smile that was on the doctor's face just a moment earlier fades. I expect her to get angry but there are no signs of this as she speaks.

"The role of the emergency staff is to remove any immediate threats to a patient's health and stabilize the situation. This I have done. Determining a protocol to repair any damage brought on prior to arrival here is in the hands of a specialist."

"So get the damn ophthalmologist down here."

"As I said earlier, your daughter's eyes are in shock. There's nothing *anyone* can do until the flaring settles."

"Well you've done your part, now haven't you? We're her parents and we'll do the figuring about what's best for her from here on."

Forty-six minutes later the ophthalmologist shuffles in. He examines Alyssa's eyes, makes indecipherable grunting sounds, and then echoes Dr. Reynolds. Thirty minutes pass before we are all back in the car heading home. This time I am behind the wheel. Alyssa is exhausted. She falls asleep in the back seat before we have gone more than two blocks.

I look over at my wife. She is slumped down in the passenger seat. I struggle for a comment to break the silence.

"Rough day."

Stacey nods her head.

"I believe her eyes will be okay," I say, hoping she'll buy my false optimism.

We don't speak as I pull the car into our garage and turn it off. Before Stacey can get out, I touch her arm. She looks at me with emotion-filled eyes. I can feel my own eyes getting wet.

"I want to work this out."

Stacey shakes her head. "It's not going to happen tonight."

"How– "

Stacey turns away from me, grasping the door handle. "Carry her to her room and leave."

Chapter 24

The effort to sleep last night was tiresome. It wasn't just because the hotel bed was uncomfortable. I lay awake hour after hour, going over the events of the past weeks: the arguments with Stacey, Alyssa's anger, the terrible accident, being dismissed from my home. Everything that's screwed up in my life points back to the blackmail. Something must be done. Something tangible.

I arrive at CommGear on Monday morning but I don't remember the drive. I make no effort to remove my employee badge from my shirt pocket. It takes only a curt nod in the direction of the doors to get the receptionist to let me in. I wonder if she knows that I would have broken the doors down if she had hesitated.

He's either in the lab or his office. I'm trying to keep my pace to a professional level as I hurry to his office. It's empty. The lab. Screw decorum. I break into a trot, stopping abruptly at the door.

My hand is trembling as I reach for the handle. I come up short. My balance is off. A buzzing sound is rising in my ears. The skin on my face and neck is getting warmer. A second attempt at the door succeeds and I'm quickly inside the lab. No need to scan the room. I know where he'll be. Robbie's bench. There are people in my direct path to him, but this doesn't matter.

I'm not going straight at him. I circle to my left. I want to keep my prey from reacting until I'm ready. Like a bird dog, I'm locked on my target. I sense a stirring. Others have noticed me. My hand rises as if on its own and waves them to be still. I keep my pace in check. Faster movement could create sounds and visual cues to alert him.

There is an opening of ten feet between the last group of people and the bench where he is standing. I'm exposed as I bridge this gap. My gait quickens to a trot again. The bastard will not get away from me. My daughter may live in a world of darkness because of him.

He is turned slightly, looking at an oscilloscope. He removes his glasses and puts one of the arms in his mouth. Appearing lost in thought, he chews on the plastic. His other hand moves through his thick black hair. Both hands are occupied.

Now.

I grab his shoulder and spin him around to face me. Off balance, he struggles to maintain his footing. The eyeglasses fly from his mouth and bounce off the nearby bench. Jimmy Lee catches himself on the window ledge, stopping his fall. His eyes are open wide. I have his attention now.

I close the gap that has opened between us. Jimmy puts his hands in front of his face, palms outward.

My voice sounds strange as it comes from me. It's low, almost a growl.

"It's time for me to darken your world."

Through his fingers I see tears form in Jimmy's eyes. He is working his way to his right. I move quickly to cut him off.

"I do not understand."

"You hurt my family. Now I'm gonna hurt you."

Jimmy squirms. A pathetic little bug that I've tolerated until now. I hear someone yell my name. Without turning from the cockroach, I tell them to shut up and stay out of this.

"I did not do these things."

"Don't they grow real men in your country? My

daughter spent the night in a hospital because of you. She may never see again."

I raise both my fists. Jimmy stares at them. His body starts to shudder but his feet remain planted. I lead with my left hand. It connects with his temple. Not as hard as I'd like, but it feels good. He moves now to protect himself from another left. I can see a clear path to his chin now and my right hand doesn't miss.

I step into the punch the way my college boxing instructor taught me. Jimmy's entire body spins and his temple bounces off the window with a loud thud. He goes down in a heap. He's not in my weight class but I would have gotten an A for that punch.

Jimmy pulls himself into the fetal position. A trickle of blood is flowing from his lip. I'm not done.

I pull back my foot and kick him in his ass. Straight on, point of my shoe right up the wazoo. I feel soft tissue in him collapsing before my foot meets bone. Jimmy lets loose a scream like a teenage girl. I heard plenty of those yesterday.

I kick him again and again. First my left foot and then the right. Jimmy Lee rolls and slides on the tile floor, trying to put distance between us. I circle him and find new spots to deliver my blows. The back, the knees, the stomach. Other bodies come near me now. I instinctively avoid them.

Jimmy Lee's body no longer responds to my kicks. I can't stop. The scales are not yet balanced.

I position myself for another kick, but multiple hands grab at me. I try to resist but there are too many. I'm forced to the floor and pinned on my back. A face appears only inches from mine.

It's Pete. He is on his knees with his hands on my chest.

"Mitch. Stop. This isn't you."

I can only shake my head. Jimmy Lee is still whining. I hear the voice of some hypocrite consoling him. No one here likes the man.

"Let me up."

Pete asks, "Are you done?"

"Maybe."

Pete repeats himself, his voice rising an octave. "Are you done?"

I take a deep breath and nod once.

Pete waves them to let me go and helps me to a nearby chair. I'm not quite steady and plop down in the seat harder than I expect. Adrenaline still courses through my body. I look around the lab. All work has ceased. Those not tending to the combatants are milling in groups. I consider telling the gossipers to get back to work. My breathing is slowly returning to normal.

A technician, can't recall his name, brings a first aid kit to the huddle around Jimmy Lee. Two of his would-be helpers try to raise him to his feet. He's not able to stand.

I know there will be repercussions for my actions, but justice must prevail. Frank has to see that I had no choice. Any real father would have done the same. The explanation I'll use is beginning to form in my mind when movement in my periphery catches my attention. That will be Frank. I'd like more time to compose myself. The lab goes quiet, too quiet.

I turn my head to see two uniformed police officers walking through the lab door.

Chapter 25

The two officers have just escorted me, handcuffed, out the front door and into a waiting police cruiser. I twist uncomfortably, my hands pinned behind me, to look out the rear window. The car is put in gear and we leave behind my hopes of being CEO.

Everything progresses in a haze. I recall being read my rights. I'm not saying anything, but it's not because of legal concerns. My cell phone rings. It's in the front pocket of my pants. I can't get to it. I look to the officer sitting in the passenger seat. He shows no concern for my dilemma. The ringing stops and vibration begins. An email has just arrived. How long before Pete has to turn off my email account? People outside the company walls will soon be finding out that I no longer work there.

The car pulls around the back of the police station. There are high whitewashed walls topped with razor wire surrounding the back lot. An automatic gate slams shut behind us with a loud clang. Although the front of the station has a polished granite exterior, no efforts have been made to enhance this side. No one really cares about the aesthetic appeal of the ass end of a police station.

We stop in a spot reserved for booking. The officer on the passenger side gets out and opens the car door to my right. A small rectangular badge on his shirt says Erickson. I think about addressing him, but his expression says don't bother. He unfastens the seat belt around my waist and helps me exit the car. The other officer is at the top of a small flight of stairs holding a door open.

It's difficult to walk up stairs with your hands cuffed

behind your back. I imagine you get better at this with practice. I hope not to. Once inside the building a wave of industrial cleaner assaults my nostrils. I want to stop and retch, but Officer Erickson pulls me along. At the end of a long, barren corridor we turn left. More nothingness. The only sounds I hear are the scraping of our shoes on the white, nondescript tile floor. A turn to the right and then quickly to the left. Another strange concoction of sounds and smells hit me. Sensory overload temporarily causes me to lose focus.

My eyes come to rest on a rotund man sitting behind a large wooden table in the middle of the room. He looks like he should have retired last century. If he'd stopped eating then he'd have enough body fat to still be alive. In front of me is a row of colored plastic chairs. I am placed in the green one. I don't like green. On my right are two hookers and what looks like a drug dealer. The specimen on my left appears to have just finished vomiting on himself.

The officer who drove me here is talking to his fat uniformed brother. I'm guessing the big fella is a desk sergeant. My knowledge of police proceedings is limited to the occasional movie or TV show Stacey has made me sit through. I wish she would have made me watch more. Officer Erickson turns and points at me while the gelatinous one takes notes. Amongst the hookers, felons, and homeless types he feels like he needs to point me out?

A fourth police official, this one female, enters from a room behind the sergeant. As she heads in my direction I am struck by her walk. Feet scraping with each step, never seeming to lift from the ground. Her toes are pointed outward like a penguin as she ambles closer. She doesn't make eye contact with me even as she beckons that I follow her. I look at the two officers who brought me in to see if it's okay for me to stand. They are deep into a conversation with yet another deputy and no longer seem to have any use for me.

The penguin directs me to the room from which she came. I am photographed and fingerprinted. She puts me back in the green chair. The hookers and the puker are gone. I'm left to enjoy his lingering aroma. A very large deputy appears next to me and grabs my right bicep. He's closer to seven feet tall than six. The grip he has on my arm causes me to wince. We move down yet another hallway, stopping at a table with a stack of large interoffice-style envelopes on it.

A deputy sitting at this table grabs an envelope and marks it with my last name and a number which must be my new identification. My possessions are inventoried into a computer. The robotic deputy slows his movement when he comes to my CommGear badge. He must have noticed the words "vice president" printed in small letters underneath my name. He looks up at me. I can't read his expression. Contempt, disgust, pity, envy? Confused about what's expected from me, I just nod my head.

The behemoth moves me forward into a room full of individual stalls. The handcuffs are removed and I'm told to undress. Inside a stall, I look for a curtain to pull shut, but privacy does not exist here.

The deputy who inventoried my possessions enters while I remove my clothes. There is a small stool in my stall where I guess they should be placed. I start to fold my shirt, but a grunt from the big guy seems to signal this is not right. I look up to see the smaller deputy noisily putting on plastic gloves. Blue. They look like the kind worn in hospitals, but I know the next steps won't be focused on my health.

The bigger one spins my now naked body about and places my hands back in the cuffs. I'm turned around again and seated roughly on the stool. My eyes are at chest level with the shorter deputy now. One gloved hand grabs a fistful of my hair. My head is held firmly in place, chin pointing upward.

The other hand violates my mouth. My jaws hurt as they are forced open wide. The process lasts almost a minute. My eyes begin to water from the pain.

The big deputy grabs me again and in one motion lifts and spins me so that my back is to the gloved one.

The giant speaks, "Bend over."

A small whimper escapes my clinched teeth as I bend forward. I put my hands on the stool for support.

A plastic-covered hand grabs my hip and I hear a snort from behind me.

"Never done this to a vice president before. Gonna check out some royal ass today."

Tears run down my face as the blue glove again enters my body. I try to remain still, but my body sways with every thrust of his hand. The exploring probably doesn't last more than twenty seconds. It will remain with me for a lifetime.

The examination is finished. They've checked every orifice they can see. They don't know about the hole left in me when my dream was ripped from my chest this morning.

Chapter 26

I've never understood the fascination with tattoos. Alyssa and Jacob both want one. I continue to veto that idea. Stacey has hinted she may also take the plunge someday. If I had my camera I think I could use this room as my argument against such body "art". Ranging from tear drops to full-length masterpieces, there is nothing appealing about the work being displayed in this holding cell.

I've lost track of the time. It may be a new day. Sunlight doesn't reach these bowels. The pace here is set by an unseen force. Sometime ago I was lead in front of a magistrate where I was formally charged with assault and battery. My bail was set at $2,000. I'd instinctively reached to my back pocket for my wallet. My wallet was of course not with me and I was told that this was not how it worked. I don't get to do things myself in here.

I think it was about an hour ago I was allowed to make a phone call. It was strongly suggested I call a lawyer or bail bondsman. I called Pete. Some decisions are still mine. He asked a few questions, took down some information and then said to hang tight. He's a better friend than I will ever be. Better than I deserve at this moment.

The door opens and my last name is bellowed. I obediently follow the deputy; we plod back to the inventory table. My possessions are poured out in front of me and I am instructed to sign a form indicating everything has been returned to me. Wallet, keys, watch, belt, wedding ring, CommGear badge. What about my dignity? Anyone looking to give that back to me?

I sign the form and pocket what they do offer me.

I'm led out front. This is the part of the station the obedient get to see. It's still loud but it smells better. The floor tiles and wall coverings give evidence that there are colors in the spectrum besides bright white, eggshell white, creamy white and off white. I look at the patrons. There aren't any happy faces here either.

A deputy at the front desk hits a switch and I'm buzzed through a small wooden gate, the final barrier, back into the real world. What's left for me in this realm remains to be seen. I recognize Pete's face. He looks tired, but manages a smile. The deputy slips behind me and removes my handcuffs. I extend my hand to thank Pete and he brushes it aside. Instead he envelops me in a big hug. This is foreign to me. I don't know if it's from the exhaustion of the last twenty-four hours, but it feels good and I go with it. I hold on longer than my norm because I need the time to compose myself.

Easing away, I'm finally able to say, "Thank you."

Pete waves me off. "Let's get out of here."

Since the fight with Jimmy Lee, my every movement has been ordered about. I feel myself wanting to sprint out the doors, down the stairs and back into a world that I control. I remember the bail.

"If we stop by my bank, I'll withdraw the money to pay you back."

"No rush. It wasn't as bad as you think."

I stop walking and look at my friend. His face is contorted. It's not pain though. He's holding back one of his booming laughs. I start to laugh too, although I still don't know why. This is too much for Pete and he lets go also.

"I told them you'd be the first one to hit him."

My laughing subsides. I look at him, confused.

"The pool in the shipping department. The first one to

hit Jimmy Lee. I won $975. They paid off quickly because no one wants Jimmy Lee or HR to find out we had this thing going."

A picture of Jimmy Lee lying on his side whimpering like a dog enters my thoughts. He's a son of a bitch, but I'm not comfortable knowing anyone earned money for what I've done. In the pit of my stomach I feel the presence of a churning uneasiness. It's not fully developed but the distaste begins to bubble with gusto as I recall my Catholic youth. Damn those sisters and their guilt trips.

We walk in silence the rest of the way to Pete's car. As he unlocks the doors he asks me, "What are you going to do?"

"Back to the office so I can get my car."

"I meant with your life."

Before I can tell Pete that I'm not sure I have a life anymore, his phone rings. He answers it and then hands it to me. "It's Stacey."

Chapter 27

As a junior engineer at CommGear I once received an unexpected bonus. It wasn't that much, but money was tight for our family then. I had been coveting a new camera lens for several months and the bonus would almost cover it. My officemate kept telling me to just order it. I rationalized that this extra money was mine, I had earned it. I bought the lens that day without talking to Stacey.

And then the guilt set in. I walked into the house and saw clearly all the things that could have been repaired or replaced with the bonus. Every room had something. I couldn't escape. I moped around that evening until the kids were put to bed. Stacey cornered me in the hallway and asked what was wrong.

It was the first time I felt afraid to talk to my wife. I had let her down. After a few moments of silence, I told her about the bonus. She was excited and then asked why I was down. I wasn't man enough to admit I'd already spent it. Told a half-lie. Said that I was depressed because it wasn't enough. She deserved a better house. The kids deserved more.

The agony I felt that night hit a new level when she began to insist I get myself the lens I had been wanting for so long. Three days later the lens came. I took it out of the box and showed it to her as she gushed for me. The next day I returned it and eventually put the money back in our bank account. From time to time, she'd ask about the lens and I'd tell her it wasn't the right choice for the photos I was going to take that day. A few years later, I bought the lens again. Our family budget was rosy by then.

A decade has passed and once again I find myself

afraid to talk to my wife. I can't believe I've let her down like this. Blown our whole future. Lost a big chunk of our savings and no one's going to touch me in the electronics business after this. I put the phone to my ear, not sure what to say. How do you tell someone that you may have destroyed all their plans for a happier ever after?

"Where have you been? I've been leaving messages all night. Alyssa's not doing well. We're scared."

"What's wrong with Alyssa?"

"The pain in her left eye is getting worse. She's having headaches and the medicine isn't helping."

I tap Pete on the arm and give him the signal to turn around. We are on the way to the office. I mouth the word hospital. "Get her in the car and meet me at the hospital. I'll be waiting for you."

"I'm afraid she may never ..." her voice trails off.

"Focus on getting her to the hospital."

"Sure thing!"

She's upset again. This time I counted on it. Her anger with me will allow her to concentrate on the immediate task. I'll take one for the team to get them both there in one piece. She's been pissed at me on and off for the last two weeks anyway. This time at least there's value in her emotions.

Fourteen minutes later I am standing in the emergency room parking lot when Stacey pulls in. She jumps out and grabs items from the back seat. I open the passenger door and scoop up my daughter. I try to offer soothing words as I move hurriedly to the doors. Alyssa moans. Her words are difficult to make out. I think she asked me to make the pain stop. Stacey's starting to cry. I look away. I won't allow myself to go there yet. I have a mission to accomplish and it's in my arms.

In less than five minutes we are in an exam room.

Doctor Reynolds walks in. Thank God she's on duty again. I was a bit rough on her last time, but that comes with the territory for ER docs. Right behind her is an orderly. As she turns to speak to us, he noisily releases the brakes on Alyssa's bed.

"We're going to run some tests and give her some more powerful analgesics. I've already called the ophthalmologist."

Dr. Reynolds turns to a nurse that has just walked in. She fires off a list of instructions of which only half make any sense. Stacey is leaning on me now. Her body is starting to shake noticeably as she sobs. I put my arm around her shoulders and kiss the top of her head.

The doctor is facing us again. "This is not a good development. The pain should have subsided."

I give Stacey a squeeze without taking my gaze from the doctor. "What are we looking at here?"

"I can't say. Citric acid should not have caused this much pain, even in concentrated form. It must have reacted with something else. Perhaps her makeup. I'm concerned there may be long-term effects on her vision."

Stacey lets out a wail and buries her face in my chest. I wrap both my arms around her. We stand like this for quite some time, swaying as if to some imaginary music. The doctor leaves without saying anything further.

For the next three hours we accompany Alyssa through a round of X-rays, MRIs and blood tests. The ophthalmologist, Dr. Buckwalter, motions for us to come out in the hallway. He has papers in his right hand, probably the summary of all the tests they have done.

"I'm very concerned for the health of your daughter's eyes."

Stacey and I just look at him. Any ability to react has

been drained from our bodies in these past few hours.

"The burns have begun to heal, but the scarring is our biggest problem. We will continue to ease the pain. Her vision will likely be severely impacted. I can't say yet how much sight she will have."

Alyssa is moved to a new room. The drugs have kicked in and she finally sleeps. Stacey and I slide two chairs next to her bed and take turns stroking her hair and muttering soothing words. At some point we drift off too.

It's 3:14 AM when a nurse nudges us awake. She suggests that we go home and grab some of the things that make our little girl happy. Maybe get a couple of hours' sleep ourselves in a real bed. We're going to need our energy.

Stacey shakes her head, but I begin to ease her from her chair. She doesn't resist.

Chapter 28

As we walk through the hospital lobby, I realize my car is still at CommGear. Unless Stacey invites me back home, I need a ride. Eventually she'll ask where my car is, if just out of curiosity. After the day we've shared, I have no energy or hope of keeping my work troubles from her.

We'll soon have no income and no company-provided health insurance. There's no telling what's going on with our daughter. If we liquidated everything, we could get by for six to seven months, nine if we really cut back. I could end up in prison with a hefty fine. I don't know what the penalty is for misdemeanor assault and battery. What if Jimmy Lee decides to go after us in civil court? Could we lose our house and what's left of our retirement? The kids' college funds? Even if we win, there are the legal fees.

Stacey has been through a lot today. Am I being selfish if I share this with her? Is it better to continue keeping it to myself? I wish there was a guidebook for good husbands. Shit, even if there were, I wouldn't have read it. I'm operating on instincts here and I'm exhausted.

"My car's not here."

"We came out a different door. The cars are outside the emergency entrance."

It's dark now and the temperature has dropped. A brisk wind whistles through the trees. Stacey zips her jacket all the way up and crosses her arms to hold in more body heat. I think about putting my arm around her. In a moment she may not want me touching her. We both walk faster than our normal pace.

"Mine's at CommGear."

"Someone gave you a ride here?"

We arrive at her Honda Odyssey. She hits the clicker button to unlock the doors. I use the act of getting into the car to put off what I know is coming. Stacey doesn't start the car immediately. My delayed response has probably kicked in her radar. I try to give her a comforting smile. She pulls the key from the ignition, unlatches her seatbelt and turns to face me.

This is going to hurt her. I hope it's not too much.

"I wasn't at work today," I finally reply.

Her voice wavers. "Where were you?"

The words I need to paint the picture right elude me. I'd pray now if I believed in such things.

"Jail."

She looks at me, eyes widened now, and non-verbally prods me to continue.

"I hit someone at work yesterday."

"You *hit* someone?"

"He hurt us."

"Who was it? Was he badly injured?"

"Can we get out of here? I'm sick of this place."

Stacey starts the car and drives toward the exit. We drive in silence. I want to wait until she turns from the parking lot before I speak. A left is to our house; a right is to CommGear. She gets in the left turn lane.

"I don't think he's as bad off as Alyssa. That's not the important thing, for us I mean."

Stacey's gaze is fixed on the road in front of her. She appears to be alert to the road but I know her better. She brakes too late at a red light and we're both pitched forward slightly as the car jerks to a stop. She mutters an apology.

"I'll tell you everything if you let me drive."

We pull over into a convenience store parking lot. Teens are clustered outside looking to find an adult to help them score alcohol. As Stacey and I switch places, one of them starts to approach. Before he can start his appeal I tell him to get the hell away from me or I will call the cops. I've seen enough of the men in blue the last twenty-four hours, but he doesn't know that. The boy retreats. Stacey doesn't react. This time she seems to understand my anger. Maybe she'll comprehend that I had no choice with Jimmy Lee.

Once I have the car back out on the main road, I begin again. "A man was trying to destroy our family and I hit him. Multiple times. I was arrested and spent the night in jail."

A green Lexus changes lanes in front of me with no turn signal. I swerve into the right lane and hit the horn in disgust.

After pausing for a few seconds I go on. "I'm pretty sure I'll be fired. Frank has no choice. I'm going to have a very hard time getting work. This stuff follows you around."

In my periphery I sense the Lexus slowing down. I refuse to look at him. Eventually he punches the gas and speeds off.

Stacey runs her fingers along my forearm. It is gentle. Her hands are so small, so beautiful. I remember how happy I felt the first time she let me hold her hand. During the last twenty-four hours I've been touched many times; this time it's with so much love.

"We'll get through this," she offers.

My voice breaks once, then a second time as I attempt to speak. "I hate that I brought this pain on our family."

She pulls on her shoulder harness, allowing herself the slack to turn in her seat. She puts her right hand on my forearm now and strokes my face with her other. I feel the urge to pull away. I don't deserve this kindness. She is my queen and I promised her a fairy-tale life. It was right in my grasp and I've crushed it.

I can feel tears slipping from my eyes again. In a moment of weakness, an emotional knee-jerk, I have destroyed so much.

"I've lost everything for us. Our dreams were built on my hope of being CEO. That's gone. I won't be able to get a position in management at another engineering firm and no one will let me start over as anything less. We've got some savings we can tap into, but that's just a Band-Aid on a bleeding gash. We may have to get rid of everything, the house, the cars, everything. Or we will end up losing it."

"It can't be that bad?"

During my first year as a manager at CommGear I would share some of the confounding personnel issues with my wife. Performance problems, office politics, nothing major. I knew she understood people and their complexities better than I did.

She would listen patiently, smiling all the while. Then she would offer up what she knew was a sure-fire solution. I tried to explain that the world I worked in wasn't like the one she lived in. She said that I just needed to get them to act like adults. I told her that she didn't know what she was asking me to do. After a few months I quit sharing my work problems with her.

My voice rises against my will. "I'm untouchable. Most managers will be afraid that I may go off again. They'll be too afraid of the risk. The ones who aren't scared of this will be worried that I'll eventually take their positions. I'm very good and they know it. I haven't made many friends. No one but Pete will stick his neck out for me."

I pull the car into our driveway and hit the opener for the garage door. I'm too tired to go to the hotel. I hope she'll let me sleep on the couch. It seems so distant, the argument that caused her to kick me out.

"Can I sleep here? On the couch is okay."

She shakes her head. I probably could convince her to let me stay, but I've got no more energy to fight this. She may be right. I walk to the kitchen phone to call a taxi.

Chapter 29

"You said this man was trying to destroy our family?" Stacey asks.

Like a puppy yearning for his mother, I turn around, hoping for one more chance to persuade her to let me stay.

"Tell me what happened," Stacey says.

Stacey walks down the hallway to the living room. She sits in her recliner. I follow, moving toward my chair, then stop. Pointing at the fireplace I say, "Cold?"

She nods. I take a few sheets of newspaper from a stack nearby. After rolling them in balls, I use small branches, twigs and shavings to construct a pyramid over the newspaper. The bigger logs are placed around these. This will create the base coals that will keep the fire going for hours. There's a system to this.

I've tried to teach this to Stacey. She'll spend hours on her rose bushes. When it comes to fires she wants the heat immediately. She fills the floor of the firebox with newspaper, covers them with logs and lights the pile. Quick heat can be generated this way, but it's not sustainable. You have to plan ahead.

"About three weeks ago an employee of mine, Kwan Lee, we call him Jimmy, sent me a blackmail note."

Stacey pulls her knees up to her chest and wraps her arms around them. I try to read her expression. Her eyes are wide. There's emotion but not anger. I turn back to the fireplace and remove a large wooden match from a box we keep nearby. Striking it on the side of the box I move it quickly to the base of my would-be fire. The flame almost jumps off the match to the newspaper.

From over my shoulder I hear, "How do you know it was him?"

"I didn't at first. I… investigated others. He was the only one with a motive and the means to do this. He probably wanted me out of the way so he could move up. Maybe I drove him to it. He got his wish."

The flames are licking the kindling and I see places where sparks are attempting to take hold.

"So you hit him?"

The newspaper is reduced to embers and there are several small flames coming from the kindling. It's time for me to act. I gently blow at the base of the embers. Blow and then pause. Fires have a natural rhythm. If you match the pace the fire explodes. Flames begin to leap toward the top of the firebox. In a few minutes the bigger logs will be engulfed.

"Last week he put a big sign on the employee's entrance telling everyone I was mismanaging my life. Who is he to judge me? That very morning Frank changed his whole schedule to get me in his office. He told me to take some time off and work on things here. He's a good man. A better boss than I deserve.

"Obviously I didn't make much progress in repairing the damage here. I wanted to explain to you what was happening. I didn't know how. Before I could figure out how to do this, Alyssa had her accident. Our daughter was blinded because some son of a bitch wanted to get promoted more than anything else. It was more than I could take. It's not fair. I cornered him in the lab and punched and kicked him in front of everyone. He cowered like the chicken shit he is."

Tears flow down Stacey's cheeks. I stand and grab a box of Kleenex off the coffee table. I offer her the box but she refuses. She pulls her knees up even tighter and hides her face.

I fall to my knees in front of her. I want to touch her and ask for her forgiveness. I can't.

Stacey begins to rock in her chair ever so slowly. The room is silent except for the creaks of her chair and the crackling pops of the growing fire. One of us must speak, but I don't know how to continue.

This natural music of the room continues unabated for several minutes until Stacey finally speaks.

"Why?"

Nothing in my life has hurt as much as this moment. Every breath I take causes fingers of pain to clutch my heart. I want to cry, but I don't deserve to.

"Why didn't you just talk to me?" Stacey asks.

"I don't know. I wish I would have."

A thud comes from the fireplace behind me. One of the bigger logs must have burned through and settled amongst the coals.

Stacey's next words are barely audible above the noise of the fire.

"It wasn't him."

I look up. Stacey's head is buried. I wait. I can't bring myself to ask the question that must come next. A nauseous feeling rises in my stomach. Pain is forming behind my right ear.

My voice returns and I ask, "What are you saying?"

She continues to rock. The sound of her sobbing joins the chorus of fire and chair.

I repeat my question, louder, sharper. "What do you mean, it wasn't him?"

Stacey raises her head and looks straight at me. Mascara is smeared. Her blush is streaked. Hair is beginning to matt to the right side of her face. I reach for the box of Kleenex and then stop.

"I just wanted you to spend more time with me."

On a January day three years back, I recall pulling on to our street. A complete stranger could have picked out our house from the corner. It was dressed in a fanfare normally reserved for soldiers returning from the front. Balloons were tied to the mailbox and the tree in our front yard. Congratulatory signs, hand-made, hung over the garage and the front door.

On the kitchen table sat a white sheet cake with the words "Vice President" written in red icing. A cardboard crown, hand-crafted by Stacey and the kids, was placed on my head. My face hurt from smiling so much that night. A casual observer might have seen the party for what it was, cheesy. But they would have missed the look on my wife's face.

Since the birth of Alyssa and Jacob, I had slipped lower and lower as the center of my wife's attention. That night, the clock was rolled back. Stacey knew she had done well in the husband department. She was proud of her choice.

As I looked into the faces of my happy children that night, I reflected on how they would react when I got to CEO. They were younger then. Excited because they got unexpected cake and because mom told them to be happy for their daddy. When I hit the next level, the last rung, big dog, they would be old enough to understand.

A moment now that will never be. Ripped from me by this woman, the one who has shared my bed for the last nineteen years. My legs waver as I rise. I put my hands in my pants' pockets to keep them from curling into fists.

"Well, you got your wish."

Stacey stands and moves toward me, arms outstretched. Her eyes are that of a child pleading for forgiveness. I step back, my head shaking.

Stacey whimpers. "This wasn't supposed to happen."

"No shit."

I walk to the kitchen; feeling my back getting colder as I leave the warmth of the fire. Stacey doesn't follow. I call for a taxi and head outside to wait. I would rather be in the cold than spend another minute with this woman.

Chapter 30

2:37. 3:14. 4:33. Sets of digits I was awake to see on the alarm clock in my hotel room. My mobile phone rang eight times throughout the night. Despite my insomnia, I didn't take my wife's calls. I don't know how to forgive this. Stacey didn't marry that big a man.

Since my teens, folks have hung labels on me. Zealous, fanatic, driven, myopic, anti-social, prick, Asperger's. Some might be true, but mostly it's jealousy on their part. People on the whole don't understand focused, successful men like me. Life ain't no popularity contest. It's about picking a target and taking out anything that gets in your way.

At the end of my college semesters there would invariably be a mad rush of activity leading up to finals week. Adrenaline would carry me long past what my mind and body felt possible. When the last test was complete emptiness would hit. I would walk around zombie-like for a few days. I had no goal in front of me, a human-shell with no reason for existence. I'm back there again and there's no new semester on the horizon.

In just over four weeks she has dismantled a lifetime's efforts. I can't act like this doesn't matter. This can't be glossed over. What the hell would her damn marriage therapist say about this shit?

A tone comes from my cell phone signaling a new text message has arrived. I start to ignore it too, but check it out of some sense of duty. It's from Frank. He's asking me to come by his house in two hours. I reply back with a yes even as I remember this is the same time that we are supposed to meet with Alyssa's doctor.

My little girl deserves to have her father at her side, despite what her mom may have done. I know I could push the meeting with Frank back. It will look bad if I skip out on the doctor's meeting. This I know. And yet, if I go I'll be checking my phone for texts and emails every few minutes. Isn't it better to just take care of business and come back to the hospital focused on my daughter?

Frank could have just let me go with a phone call. There may be one last chance to salvage a role at CommGear. I owe it to my family to take this shot, no matter the odds. If necessary, I'll find a way to convince my girl later that this was the best choice for all. Any hope of being the father she deserves requires my meeting with Frank.

Before I leave I send a text message to Stacey telling her to remind our daughter I love her. A response comes back seconds later. This one I do ignore. My wife will have to handle this herself. Seems only fair.

Frank lives in a gated community. The kind that until yesterday I expected to live in too. The man has done so much for me. I know I shouldn't but I'm hoping that he will give me one more chance. Maybe that's why he called me out here.

I'm held up by a security guard who must confirm with my host that I'm welcome. Frank gives the okay and I'm let in. Before I can finish parking my car in his driveway, Frank is outside and walking my way.

He shakes my hand and asks how I'm doing. It really depends on how things go here. He doesn't want to hear that. I give a noncommittal answer. He motions me to a gate on the side of the house. This is good. His home is terrific but the backyard is even better. He's proud of the landscaping. I would be. It cost more than the whole Pederson house. If he were going to simply dismiss me wouldn't he have done that from the front study?

It begins to sprinkle. We can't sit in the sun and enjoy the view of his swimming pool, tennis court, and putting green. Instead we take a spot under the covered portion of the patio, near a space heater. In spite of the drizzle, workers are giving the flora their weekly once over. Stacey's been here twice and has fallen in love with the flowers. I think that's why Frank first took a liking to my wife, this shared adoration for all things green.

A servant brings us each coffee. Franks waits until she leaves. "Am I right to think that the note on our back door and this altercation with Kwan Lee are connected?"

I take a drink. Only a fool would add cream and sugar to this nectar. It's so damn good. Frank would be insulted if I didn't drink it *au natural*. He's a bit of a java snob. I couldn't guess how much the beans cost to make this cup of Joe.

"They are. It's complicated."

"It generally is. Has he done something that warrants my terminating him?"

This is a test. Frank knows more than he's letting on. He always does. In the past I would have gone slowly here, feeling for the right answer. I decide to go with an honest response whether it's what he's looking for or not.

"I've never liked him, but he hasn't done anything wrong. He's also one of the best engineers you have. Ask him, he'll tell you."

Two birds swoop down and land on the expansive lawn beyond the swimming pool. They begin to poke fervently at something in the grass. I can't make out what has drawn their interest. Three more birds join them. Even in nature the insignificant are always lurking about to feed on those who have fallen.

"How's Alyssa?" Frank asks.

I place the china cup down too hard and it clinks loudly. I examine the bottom of the cup to make sure I've done no damage, then I look up at Frank to apologize. He smiles graciously and waves away my act of clumsiness.

"We don't know. The damage to her eyes may be permanent."

"I'm sorry. Sheila asked for our prayers."

My sister-in-law. Was she in on this? She had to be. She knows this world. A good sister would have talked Stacey out of this nonsense. I need to save thoughts of Sheila for another time. I stare out at the swimming pool where gentle waves are being formed by a light wind. This is calming. I could use another hour of this water therapy.

"Please keep me informed about Alyssa."

I nod slightly. Everyone at CommGear is his family. His concern for others is something he managed to hold on to despite his rise to the top. Some have suggested it played a part in his ascension. Until this moment, I've considered it a weakness that he managed to overcome.

All that's left to discuss is what's in the big box we have been dancing around for the last half hour. Do I still have a job? I'm a fish struggling on the end of a hook. The fisherman can either reach for a mallet to smash my head or a knife to cut me free. Not knowing my destiny is the worst. I can't bring myself to ask. I'm not sure how to do it without seeming terribly ungrateful.

The servant returns to top off our cups. I don't need more caffeine, but to refuse might look bad. Frank didn't say no either. Maybe he's planning on this being a lengthy talk. Another sign that it's not over for me?

"I don't want to make excuses, but there is a reason..."

Frank leans forward and interrupts. "The hospital bills may get high. If you need my help, don't be too proud to ask."

Chapter 31

Frank gave me six months severance.

With my poor prospects for re-employment I don't need to be spending my money on a hotel. But the room is paid through the weekend and I've got nowhere else to go. I call Pete.

It takes me nine minutes to explain what Stacey has done to me. Another three to outline Frank's generosity.

I conclude my narrative with "I'm lost."

"This is going to be a long trip. Just start walking."

"I don't know how." I slam my palm on the flimsy hotel TV cabinet. "She took my compass."

A long sigh comes through the phone line. "Linda just made pizza. Why don't you join us?"

Memories of a Datsun B210 that always reeked of pizza come back to me. It was my first car and my dad made me promise to cover the gas and insurance before he let me buy it. The pizza delivery gig was the answer to this teenage dilemma.

I found the job on my own and to my surprise, and I think my old man's, I excelled at it. Fast and efficient, I still took the time to speak with my customers. I remembered their names and something about them. At some point customers were actually ordering their pizzas and requesting that I be the one who brought them. Within a month I was bringing home more tips than any other delivery person. It was my first shot at being in control of my destiny and I loved it.

Two large, thin crust. One pepperoni, mushroom and onion, the other one half cheese and half supreme. Every Friday night the order would come in and it was soon my favorite stop. It also became the one I dreaded. The second time I delivered to 4784 Wilkerson Street, the door opened and my trouble began. Cut-off jean shorts and a faded blue Adidas sweatshirt. She was fifteen. I couldn't speak. I handed the pizzas over and almost left without collecting the money. I was less than a foot from the most beautiful girl I had ever seen.

When Friday nights came around after that I had to will myself to leave 4784 Wilkerson. I had responsibilities. A promise had been made to my dad. Stacey was almost worth reneging on the deal. Screw the job and the car. I might have chucked it all, but she wouldn't let me.

Eventually she started riding around with me on Friday nights. This was against company rules. My boss looked the other way. I was the best he had. What could he say? I don't think I've ever loved a job as much as that one when Stacey was sitting next to me.

I shake my head hard to stop myself from reminiscing. Thinking back to Pete's invitation, I realize that I haven't eaten since yesterday at the hospital. I'll deal with that later.

"Just ate. Thanks."

"Come over. Don't do this alone."

"You're a good man Pete."

I am pacing the hotel room. Movement through the window catches my attention. There's a small strip mall across the street. It's Saturday night and the place is abuzz with patrons. A motorcycle thunders to a stop near the entrance. The rider removes his helmet and sits watching the passersby.

A minivan pulls up two spots to his right. A father and mother exit the van and begin the laborious process of loading their two small children in an over-sized stroller. In under three minutes they've packed the stroller with enough sundries to make an attempt on Everest. The intrepid group at last begins its trek toward mall heaven. I ponder the mom's face. She doesn't look tired or frustrated. She's almost smiling. The dad looks like he's ready to hang it up. I feel like yelling at him to knock the motorcycle rider to the ground and make a run for it.

Pete interrupts my reverie. "How can I help you?"

"I don't think there's anything to be done. It's over."

"What does that mean?"

"My life."

"Lighten up. You're creeping me out."

My voice rises, "Stacey was the blackmailer. She cost me my job, my future. I'll never achieve anything with my life because of her selfishness."

"Have you stopped to ask why she did this?"

I called Pete to help and he's going off in the woods somewhere. I reach out and smack the drawstrings for the window curtain. They bounce off the windows and the weighted end hits me in the temple before I can move. It stings and I'm mad because I've brought myself more pain.

"Hold on for a minute," I growl into my mobile phone.

As I move the phone away from my face to rub my forehead, I glance at the screen and notice that I have six unread text messages. Five are from Stacey. The other is thirteen minutes old. It's from Alyssa and it says "call me please."

"Gotta go."

Chapter 32

I hit the speed dial for my daughter. She picks up immediately. No sound is forthcoming. At last there is a whisper. "Hello."

"Is everything all right?"

"They don't let you have cell phones in this place."

She must still be in the hospital. That's not a good thing. I picture her lying in a bed, her cell phone cupped in two hands in an attempt to keep it hidden. With no vision it would be tough to know if someone had entered the room. She would have to listen for silence, speak quickly and then listen again.

"Where's your mom?"

"Bathroom."

"How did you send me a text?"

"Dad? I'm a teenager. I can text with my eyes shut."

I smile at the humorous front my little girl is trying to portray.

"How are you feeling, sweetie?"

A ruffling sound fills my ear. She must have slid the phone down her leg under the sheet. I can hear the scuffling of shoes on a tile floor. A few garbled words are exchanged and then there's silence.

"It still hurts. Not as bad though."

My throat is tightening. She's trying to be brave for her dad. She's my little girl and it isn't fair that she's being forced to do this. I want to say something to break the tension, but I need more time to find my voice. Alyssa beats me to it.

"I need you here, Daddy."

Alyssa hasn't called me this since she was eight. My

heart aches. I would give my life for this one. Tears are escaping from my eyes. I know my voice will give me away but I don't give a damn now. "I love you more than you can know, little one."

There's a longer pause. I can't be sure if it's because of what I've said or her need to hide the phone. I think I can hear a muffled sob. I wish I could wrap my arms around her. She needs me to tell her it's going to be okay, even if it's not true.

"When are you coming?"

A question I can't answer. How do I explain all this to a teenager? I would like nothing more than to be there to hold this family together. The ability to right all this family's mishaps is slipping from my grip. Alyssa needs a father who can rescue her, save her. I hear the sound of the phone being moved again. There's another voice in the room and it's not muffled this time.

"The doctor stopped me in the hallway." An audible sigh follows. The emotion captured by the releasing of her breath tells me more than Stacey could say in another hour. A lifetime together in marriage has taught me that what follows will be agonizing for this lady.

"When can I take these off?" Alyssa asks.

She must be talking about the patches on her eyes. My daughter doesn't like to be restricted in any fashion. I have no doubt who she gets this trait from.

"Soon. There's a problem."

Stacey's voice is starting to falter. She must be curling her bottom lip inside her mouth so she can bite on it. It's what she does to get through such times. She had this look when we heard that her brother had finally succumbed to cancer. I want to scream at them to wait for me. Alone in this hotel room, tears run down my face. I make no move to stem the flow. No longer a man, I'm a fragment of the husband and father I'm called to be.

Stacey continues, "The chances of you getting all your vision back are not good."

The sound of sobbing pours out of my phone's speaker. There are two people crying. I can hear the bed springs. Stacey is probably climbing in with her to hug her close. If I were there, there would be three of us in that bed. When Alyssa was little we would lay her between us and fall asleep just watching her breathe. My heart hurt then, but it was a good hurt. The sobbing subsides.

"What does it mean?"

"No one knows. You will have some vision but not what you had before."

"Will I be blind?"

Stacey's eyes are green. They are glistening mirrors reflecting back all that is good in this world. I was captured by them the first day I handed her the pizzas. I have never been able to wriggle free. Alyssa's got my brown eyes. I was disappointed when we found this out. She's a beautiful girl. I would have been happy if she'd inherited nothing external from me.

"Maybe. Probably not."

"Can I drive?"

"Not right away… I don't know."

"Will I look … Will anyone be able to love me?"

I toss the phone on the hotel bed and slam my fist into the wall. The light fixtures rattle. A commotion begins next door. They'll probably call down stairs to complain. Screw them.

I pick up the phone and put it back to my ear. The dialogue has continued.

"… no medicines for this. Surgery might bring small

improvements."

"So there's no hope. I'll be a freak."

Alyssa's collapsing. Come on Stacey, hold our girl together.

"No, you're my daughter!"

"Who will ask the pathetic blind girl to sign their yearbook?"

I scream into the phone. "Stop it!"

No one seems to hear me as the drama goes on.

"There's no reason to live!"

"You don't mean that, baby."

The crying picks up again. I put the phone down gently on the desk and turn on my laptop. An idea begins to form in my head. Finally, I have what may pass for a plan that I can focus on.

       ***

Even though night has fallen, I park my car in the farthest reaches of the hospital parking lot. It's imperative that I limit my contact with people, especially family, at this point of the plan. Despite this concern, I will not move forward without one more moment with my daughter.

From just outside the emergency room doors I place a call to the hospital operator. The main entrance will be closed since it's past visiting hours. I request that the attending nurse for Alyssa let Stacey know she has a visitor in the lobby. The operator offers to put me through to the room, but I hang up before she can proceed.

I move inside the building and sprint up the back stairs to the fourth floor. I don't know why I'm hurrying; it will be several minutes before they follow through on my request. The pace of hospitals would unsettle me if I ever were forced to be a guest for any length of time.

From a sign on the wall and the room numbers nearby,

I deduce that Alyssa's room is at the other end of the hallway. The elevators lie between us. Perfect. I stand to the side and feign that I am engrossed in something on my phone. Minutes pass as I furtively glance to see if my ruse is in the works.

Distant footsteps catch my attention. I spot my wife advancing to the elevators. She looks frustrated. I'm sure she's not happy to leave her injured child for some unknown purpose. I quickly step back inside the stairwell and listen for sounds that she has boarded the elevator. A bell chimes. Doors open and then moments later they close. I wait ten seconds and then peek into the hallway. It's clear.

I walk quickly to Alyssa's room. I only have a window of five, maybe seven, minutes before Stacey returns. Arriving at the room, I see that a nurse is monitoring the medicine being fed into my little girl. Probably pain killers and something to let her sleep. I stand at the doorway and count the seconds until the nurse finishes. I'm down to maybe two minutes to complete my objective.

The room is empty now except for my daughter. I move to her bedside and gently kiss each of her eyelids. She stirs slightly, not fully breaking free of the drug-induced slumber. I put my mouth to her ear and whisper.

"Your daddy will not let you down."

Chapter 33

Outside my hotel room all is dark. The silence of nightfall is sporadically interrupted by cars traversing a nearby street. All that happens beyond this room is irrelevant as I continue my research.

Eye transplants are the oldest and most common transplants done in America. Actually they don't replace the whole eye, just the cornea. The success rate is quite good and has even improved with the advent of microscopic surgery. There are several reasons these procedures are normally done, one of which is in response to chemical burns. This I learned from a few hours spent on the internet.

The engineer in me wants to dig deeper into the procedure, but there's no time left for that. My plan must come together quickly. The average wait time for an eye donor is one to two weeks. The surgery can run over $10,000 and insurance doesn't usually cover it. At this point I'm looking at COBRA insurance to cover us and that's almost a guaranteed no. This doesn't include other incidental expenses such as therapy and post-op care. Even if Frank helps out as he suggested, all that would ensure is that Alyssa would have twenty-twenty vision of my inability to support our family.

The remaining equity in our house and what's left in my 401K would net us around $150K, give or take $10K. Enough to get us through a year. Then what? If I fail to land a job in that time, I'd have completely mortgaged our future and dug an even deeper financial hole.

There is only one foolproof way to solve everything. I have two good eyes and a large life insurance policy, $2.5 million.

Throughout the day I've tried to picture myself dead. Try as I might, this is a shot that won't come into focus. My heart beats faster and I feel sweat forming on my brow. Discipline has always been an area of strength for me. I'll tap into it when the final moment arrives.

God once cared about me. We were Catholic, the largest religion in the world, clearly His chosen people. Communion, check, confirmation, check. Keep up the good works and I was safe. A pain in the rear, but worth it. Or so my dad said. I actually believed it myself until the year I turned fifteen. It was then that two events set me straight.

Ted Murphy was my dad's best friend. Lived a couple of houses down. Of course he was Catholic too. Dad wouldn't think of befriending someone who wasn't one of God's people. Ted was married with seven kids. He really bought into the Catholic thing. Never missed a mass. Gave a lot to the church. His life made sense before the fire.

On a Thursday night, I think it was May because school was still going, my mom screams from the kitchen that the Murphys' house is on fire. Dad and I rush out to see three fire trucks, lights and sirens trumpeting as they pull around the corner onto our street. Thick black smoke was rising several hundred feet in the air.

We crossed the street to join the forming crowd. Flames were visible from several rooms inside the Murphy home. We later learned it was an electrical fire that spread through the walls, following the wiring. There was no way out; the fire cheated, cutting everyone off from any hope of escape.

A commotion broke out to our left. Ted was working the night shift at the power plant. Someone must have called him. He was fighting with two policemen to get to the house. His words were jumbled, but his face. His face. I'll never forget his expression. A man whose life was being destroyed before his very eyes. My dad went to him.

He held him as they both silently watched the rest of the tragedy play out. Fire eventually took the whole home. The firemen were brave. Two of them went in the inferno and came back with bodies. Three of the eight humans trapped in that house were brought out. From across the street I stared at the objects lying on the lawn. Two were bigger, one very small, just over two and a half feet. Their skin, at least I think it was skin, was black. Charcoal with a touch of licorice. Steam rose from the bodies as they continued to cook before us. Around me people cried and prayed. The man next to me vomited.

I ran home and hugged my mother.

The second incident occurred two months later. Dad's latest ill-conceived business venture actually seemed to be working. He even bought Mom a tennis bracelet. She cried when he gave it to her and then she showed it off to all her friends. Things were going so well that he arranged to buy back his prized car, that damn green Mercury Cougar. The very car that our neighbors had watched us lose earlier that year. At Mom's prompting, I asked him if I could go with him when he picked it up. We knew how important this was to him. That's why I was stunned when he turned down my request.

The Cougar was found on its roof at the bottom of a ravine. He didn't leave a note, but the insurance investigators were convinced it was a suicide. There were no signs of the brakes being applied and he wasn't wearing his seatbelt. It made no sense to me. Unlike his friend Ted, Dad had a family that was very much alive and needed him.

I remember thinking, why would God let this happen? An omnipotent creator could have easily stopped these things.

Ted didn't deserve to have his family ripped from his existence. How could a great God permit my father's selfish act? Did He not see what this would do to the Pedersons? Ted and my family, innocents forced to live on, expected to cope with their own personal truckload of steaming, unholy shit. Any God who would sit on His far away throne and passively allow this to happen to His people was not one I would follow.

A small part of me, a stubborn Catholic remnant, feels guilty about violating the sanctity of life. That portion of my being will just have to die with the rest of me. I won't stand by and watch my family suffer.

I have more immediate problems. I need to do what my father could not. My death cannot be considered a suicide. Some or all of the death benefits from my policy would be denied. With time I know I could craft an accident that would fool the investigators. It's a shame I don't have the time. It would be a worthy problem to solve.

I need someone to take my life. There are parts of town where I could go and make this happen. With the right coaxing I could end up an innocent victim. I'd have to rely on the would-be killer to get it right. If he merely wounded me that would just add to my problems. If he did kill me but in some way damaged my eyes, an important part of the solution would be lost. I need to control the output.

The person participating in my ruse doesn't actually have to know what they're doing. They just have to force me into a situation where I'm killed. I could be escaping from one danger and run into a worse one. There is one person who's got to be very angry with me about now. Could I get Jimmy Lee to strike back? Probably doesn't have it in him.

If I'm successful with the death, instructions must be left for Stacey to manage the funds that will come her way. A letter won't work because it could be discovered and prove that I anticipated my life ending soon. How can I get her the information she will require without leaving a trace? There must be someone I can trust to guide her but not reveal where he has gained the knowledge. A priest or psychiatrist might work. They're bound by the oaths of their professions. I don't have much use for those kind of people and it could take months to find one I could count on.

It needs to be someone I already know. Someone that Stacey would listen to without him letting her know I was behind all this. Can't allow Stacey to find out that I took my life. That would be an unfair burden to place on her, even with what she's done.

Who are my choices?

My doctor. He's got an oath of confidentiality. He's not hurting financially. I've talked to him about investments a couple of times. He relies on others' advice too much for my liking. I'm not sure his oath would apply to this. He's out.

My personal financial advisor. The guy would probably just try to get her to invest in more of his firm's products. I've never really trusted the guy myself. I can't do that to my family.

Frank. He would have the desire to help my family and the financial wherewithal to provide good advice. I can't be sure he would agree with my plan. Also the risk of him being exposed as a conspirator is too great. It would harm the company if it got out. He's a no.

Sheila. She'd do anything for her sister. Would Stacey trust her financially? She certainly leans on Sheila in other aspects of her life. I picture myself struggling to share my suicidal plans with my sister-in-law. The hurt I imagine in her eyes is a weak reflection of what this will do to my wife. I shake my head firmly. These thoughts won't help my plans.

Move on.

Pete. He'll want me to change my plans too. With him I can remain focused. He won't cry. There will be some anger, but I can turn him around to my way. I always do. He's a good man who would want to help my family. Stacey likes him too. She's said so in the past.

A strange peace envelops my heart. Some will see my actions as a quitter, but I know I can't win. I've given my all and this is where I'm at. I don't see any other way out. In this moment I feel my bitterness toward my father start to melt. We all must eventually check out of our earthly existence. At least my old man and I will have done it on our own terms.

I look up. The sun begins to peek through the blinds of my hotel room's window. I grab my car keys.

Chapter 34

Pete doesn't live in a master-planned community. He did at one time but the regular notices from the homeowners' association grew tiresome. It's not like he had an old car on blocks in his front yard. He's just not interested in appearances. Some people think he's lazy. I know that's not true. His life is built upon a different set of priorities.

The unpaved road leading to his house has potholes that could break the axle of a tank. It forms a barrier that would keep all but the hardiest of salesmen and missionaries at bay. It takes me almost two minutes to make it the quarter-mile stretch from the end of the pavement to his driveway. Three large, nondescript dogs escort my car with a fanfare of howls and yelps.

I changed into old jeans before I headed over. Exiting the car, I'm immediately set upon by the dogs. They're stubborn creatures, adamant in their efforts to leap upon any visitor. Pete says they're just happy to greet newcomers. The dirt road allows their victims to bring home paw print souvenirs of their happiness.

Surviving the canine gauntlet, I arrive at the front door. The doorbell doesn't work and the door itself doesn't appear it will survive a solid knocking. I rap loudly on the wall. This is probably unnecessary since the dogs have already signaled my arrival. I hear stirring from inside the house.

I called ahead the first time I wanted to visit Pete. He said they had nothing to hide so there was no need to warn them. This transparency is both strange and compelling. His is a quiet confidence that contrasts with the bravado of many of the leaders I work with.

Pete opens the door. "Hey."

This is a lower octave than his normal greeting. He's probably still hurt or confused from the way I ended our last conversation. "I'm sorry I had to run out on you last time. Alyssa needed me."

Pete turns and walks to a nearby recliner. Everything in the house is nearby. These are people who see no value in solitude. Pete grabs the remote and pauses the video playing on his sixty-inch plasma television. Mel Gibson's face is frozen in a contorted state.

Pete's wife, Linda, enters from a back part of the house. She's wearing a yellow blouse and a flowing white skirt. She appears to float into the room. That's quite a feat for someone pushing two hundred pounds. I've been in her company at least twenty times and have never seen her without a smile. There's an oversized purse dangling from her right shoulder.

She greets me warmly as she hovers in our presence. "I'm making lasagna tonight. Gotta run by the store. Stay and eat with us, Mitch."

A vision of eating alone again in my hotel room pops into my head. Dining with the Talarian family won't be lonely. Or quiet. I think about accepting the invitation, but realize it won't work after my talk with Pete.

"Thanks. I might just take you up on that."

Knickknacks throughout the house rattle as the front door slams behind Linda. I wait for the tremor to abate.

"Are we alone?"

"Jonathan is at a friend's."

The Talarians have only the one child. He's two years younger than Jacob and was the product of many fertilization efforts. Linda miscarried at least three times that I know of.

Stacey reached out to Linda the first time. There was no need. Linda refused to allow such extraordinary pain to change her disposition. My friend married a remarkable woman. I'm hoping that he will be the remarkable friend that I need now.

I move a hassock to within four feet of Pete, between his chair and the TV. I choose to sit here because I don't want to see Mel's face while I make my proposition. I also need to be able to read Pete's emotions clearly. Even now he's looking at me strangely.

"You're a better friend than I deserve."

Pete leans forward in his chair. Our faces are only two feet apart and he's staring into my eyes.

"Anything that we have, food, money, a place to sleep, is yours. You know this."

For once I don't look away. I will myself to face my friend for what may be the last time.

"Thank you. This is about my family. They need more from me now and I know how to do it."

Pete leans back in the chair. Its springs creak out their annoyance at the shifting of his weight. He pulls down the front of his UCSD sweatshirt which has ridden up his protruding stomach. Remnants of recently devoured potato chips are catapulted over the arm of the recliner.

"I've been driven for years to be the next CEO of CommGear. I've given up a lot to achieve this. My whole family sacrificed."

I rise and start to walk from one end of the living room to the other. My hands are in my jean pockets. Despite the need to observe my friends reactions, I know I won't be able to look at Pete for this next part.

"I married a beautiful woman and fathered two great kids. One's blind now and it's at least partially my fault. The kids are innocent and all three of them deserve better. I should never have let this happen."

Pete makes a sound. He's probably going to object but I cut him off. "Don't be kind. I don't need that. I see the truth and so do you. Some of this may not have been my fault, but there's still a way for me to be the man I should've been. I need your help."

Pete nods for me to continue.

"Alyssa's never going to see again without a corneal transplant. That's an expensive surgery and I no longer have health insurance."

Pete holds up his hands, palms outward, urging me to halt like a flagman at a road construction site.

"Linda's aunt has money-"

I mirror Pete's actions with my own hands.

"Thank you. Frank offered to help too. There's physical therapy and other expenses. The kids have another ten years at home before they go off to college. There'll be braces for Jacob, cars and insurance for both of them. Not to mention proms, iPads, and other things they must have to fit in with their friends.

"I'm not going to be able to land an executive position. I'll have to start over as an engineer, if I can convince someone to take a chance on me. The delay will cause us to eat through our savings and 401K. When I do get a job, the salary may not be enough to cover our mortgage. Stacey hasn't worked since Alyssa was born. The best we could hope for is that she lands a minimum wage position. The whole thing is a losing proposition."

Pete shakes his head. "Let the house go. Start over."

The frustration brought on by this last interruption gets the better of me. My next words come out louder than I mean them to.

"That's not an option."

I force myself to sit back down on the hassock and reach out to Pete, grabbing both of his forearms. I look him in the eyes. In a moment I begin again.

"My family is teetering on the brink and I'm still not sure how it all came to pass. There's enough blame to share between Stacey and me. I'm not willing to put my family through that kind of financial upheaval. I can't and I won't. I can still give them the future they deserve.

"If I get the money to get them through this, I'll need you to help Stacey manage it. It will be a lot of money and there will be no end of people telling her what to do. You're the only one I trust to guide her. She'll listen to you."

Pete gently frees his arms from my hands. He cocks his head slightly to one side and seems to be sizing me up. "You're not going to be around?"

Unable to speak, I lock my eyes on his and shake my head.

Pete is shaking his head more violently than mine. "I don't like this."

I get up and start pacing again. He's going to get angrier with me. I didn't think it was going to be this hard. I feel like I'm about to let him down too. I hate it but I won't allow myself to turn back.

"I need to know that you'll steer the ship in my absence."

"Any plan that doesn't have you at the wheel isn't a good one."

Scanning the room, I see the TV remote on the table next to Pete's chair. I reach for it and hit the power button. I may not be able to stem my friend's questions, but I can put an end to Mel's judgmental eyes.

"Pete. It might take years for me to get you to see the wisdom of my plan and I don't have that time."

"And yet you expect me to agree to something I don't even understand?"

"You probably think I'm dense when it comes to being a friend. Mostly, you're right. But I've learned a thing or two from watching you over the years."

I replace the TV remote, not taking my eyes from Pete.

"You will do this for me," I say.

Pete rises and approaches me like a bull after a matador. He thumps my chest with his forefinger in rhythm with his speech. "Don't be so sure of yourself!"

The thumping of my chest is too much. I use my left hand to smack away his finger.

Pete goes on. "I used to think you were a big man, larger than life. Whatever this plan of yours is, it reeks of cowardice."

I step forward until our foreheads are within inches of each other.

"Has your life ever been as screwed up as this? No. I didn't think so. Who the hell are you to tell me what's right?"

He raises both hands and shoves me backwards. It's not enough to knock me off my feet.

I keep my hands by my sides and force myself to take calming breaths. My family needs me to convince this man to be there for them.

"I didn't come here to ask for your approval of my plan, just your support."

"I have no doubt that in your convoluted sense of reality you see yourself in a hero's role. Trust me here my friend. You're full of shit on this one."

I picture my father in the moments before he jerked the wheel hard to the right, sending his life careening into oblivion. He left his family with no hope, nothing. I have this one chance to stop the train of destruction. My last chance to be in control. Tears start to leak from my eyes as I mouth a single word.

"Please."

Pete turns away from me to face the window. "Damn you. Have you stopped to think about my loss here?"

I walk toward him, hesitate and then place a hand on his shoulder. He's in pain and this is solely my fault. My actions in the next few hours will only make this worse.

Seconds pass before I speak. "You won't let my family down."

Pete drops his shoulder from my touch and steps away. He spins to look at me as he continues.

"You expect me to blindly accept your going away forever? That's bullshit!"

This next step is crucial and the part I have dreaded the most. I breathe deeply and work to put the correct look upon my face. My hands are raised in mock disgust.

"Whoa! What's with this forever shit? I won't be out of the picture for good, just temporarily removed."

Pete stares at me without speaking. I brace myself to bear the full weight of his inspection. In the space between us his silence batters against my lie. Slamming and crashing violently. A tsunami beating on a city's dike. Which one will break first?

Pete finally interrupts the still of the room. "If your goal today was to confuse me, you've done it."

"This pains me more than you can imagine. It will all become clear in due time. I need to leave here today knowing that you will be there for my family."

Pete flops himself into the recliner and grabs the TV remote. Just before he starts up Mel again, he speaks.

"It seems you have it all figured out. I'm friend

enough to support your family but not good enough to share your plans with."

I open my mouth to continue, but Mel's voice has taken over the room. The apology I should offer remains unsaid. I move to the door and let myself out.

Chapter 35

On the way back to the hotel I send Stacey a text asking her to meet me for dessert at a restaurant about forty-five minutes from home. She balks when I ask that she bring the children too. I mention that the kids love the place and we've had some good times there. She relents.

My window of opportunity will be small. I park my car on a side street two blocks from home. Looking out my car's back window, I have an unobstructed view of the road they will take when they leave. Forty-five minutes there, fifteen minutes of searching and phoning for me and then forty-five minutes back. I've got just short of two hours to do this.

The minivan passes. I wait three more minutes and start my car. All the lights are off in my house when I arrive. I pull into the garage and slam the car door when I exit. I need to be sure no one is here. A quick survey of the house confirms that I'm alone.

I must leave my family notice without leaving a note. They can't know that what I will do later today was planned. The burden of accepting that their father, husband took his own life can be crushing. This, above all else, I know. They will have to deal with police and insurance investigators. At some point they may discover the truth of my actions and I desperately need them to know that I loved them. This is not a selfish repeat of my father's last hours.

I head to the photo lab and retrieve my favorite digital camera, a Nikon D90. Jacob's room is two doors down. Superheroes and sports stars greet me as I enter. A Captain America mural commands one wall while a life-size Phillip

Rivers poster patrols another. I snap pictures of each of my son's idols.

The room is about a six out of ten on the Jacob cleanliness scale. There are no food wrappers or empty pop cans lying on the floor. I put my camera down and spend the next ten minutes tidying up and making the bed. He won't care about this, but Stacey will appreciate it.

Back in the lab, I download the pictures I just shot onto my photo computer. It takes about ten minutes with Photoshop to put my son's head on each of his heroes. Matching the skin tones is not a trivial task. I print each picture in 8 ½ x 11 format. They're not great, but he'll flip when he sees them. I should have told him that this is how I see him. He's just ten years old, but he's my little hero. I wish I were going to be there to witness his life's achievements. Tears fill my eyes as I return to his bedroom and place the modified pictures on his pillow.

Alyssa's room has a handful of her own pictures posted to a corkboard. She must have shot them on her mobile phone. They're of marginal quality but her natural talent shines through. She knows how to capture the spirit of her subjects. In a few days she will have my eyes. Will a piece of my photographic-soul be transferred?

Returning to the lab I grab my copy of The Art of Photography. This book taught me to speak a new language, one of self-expression. The author, a renowned photographer, holds an advanced degree in mathematics. Early in his life he walked in my world of engineering. With the gentle prodding of this tome I too embarked on the journey to understand the artistic half of my brain.

A good photograph should wrench an inescapable, emotional response from its viewer. A great one burns a hole in your soul. In Mitch Pederson lies the undeveloped, untapped, unappreciated skills to produce such artwork. Photographs capable of eliciting soulful tears. There's so much more I could have done with this life.

My own sixteenth birthday was only five weeks after my father's passing. Amidst the pain, my mom presented me a gift. She said it was from dad. Something he had wanted to give me for some time. It was a camera. A camera?

I had never expressed any interest in photography. Desperately wanting to maintain a connection with my father, I launched myself into this unknown world. Maybe Dad knew I would need this? Maybe he bought that stupid camera because he never really knew me? Wisdom or ignorance on his part, I'm grateful for the role of photography in my life.

I place the photography book and my camera on Alyssa's desk. She will see again. I want her to use her gifts and passion to shake the world one viewer at a time. Even though we have trouble speaking to each other now, someday we would have said so much to each other by just our photos. I love the woman she will become. I hope when she's older she can look at my work and understand the man I tried to be.

A glance at a wall clock shows I have sixty-two minutes left. Stacey's next. I take two steps toward our bedroom, but can't go further. There are dangerous things in there. Things that will bring me to my knees. In a frame above our bed is the tear-stained letter I wrote to her the night she gave birth to our first. The lingering scent of Stile Crème Bouquet, the fragrance that I've breathed in so many times as she allowed me to remove her clothes. Framed portraits of her deceased parents, adorned with flowers on their birthdays. I pray that the pain I will soon cause her will dissipate enough over time that she can decorate my picture in the same manner.

The hallway to our bedroom is a story not finished.

There are two rows of pictures beginning just outside our bedroom door. One row for each child. A pictorial map of their life's journey. Kindergarten graduation, first time riding a bike, gap-tooth smiles, favorite stuffed animals worn threadbare from love. I took these pictures. Stacey and I are the only two people qualified to interpret the story of these photos. The long hallway is only halfway filled. A chasm is about to be created. There will be more photographs added at some point, but I won't be there to interpret them. My part in the telling of the Pederson story is coming to an end.

I walk away from this part of the house. The kitchen will be less painful. I lean on the counter and look out the window at our backyard. A Steller's Jay is sitting on a tree limb just a few feet from me. I never found time to take pictures of him. My life has been a painting best viewed from a distance. There are great successes that look impressive from afar. A finer inspection reveals important details that are missing. Why did it take so damn long for me to see this?

A strange odor wakes me from my reverie. I look down. In the sink are dishes covered with food yet to be scraped into the disposal. They had a casserole for dinner. Probably leftovers. To some this room would be passable because the sink is where dirty dishes should be stored. Not to my wife. Her contractions were seven minutes apart with Jacob and we were scurrying about this room cleaning before she would go to the hospital. This room is a reflection of how she would like the world to see her. She left it like this to throw her children in the car and visit her husband. A man who she may soon feel has ultimately let her down.

I spend what will be my final thirty minutes in this house washing dishes, cleaning kitchen surfaces and crying.

Chapter 36

On my phone are six text messages from Stacey, each more frantic than the one before. From the last one I can infer they are on their way back home. It was sent twenty-one minutes earlier. I hustle to the garage and use a large screwdriver to remove the right front hubcap from my car. I put the screwdriver back and toss the hubcap into the passenger seat. With my headlights off, I back the car out of the garage and ease down our street. It won't help my plans to be seen exiting our home at this time.

I take a back way out of our neighborhood so as not to pass Stacey and the kids. Two blocks later I switch on my headlights and pick up speed. My heart is pumping faster as adrenaline courses through my body. Is it better for someone to remain calm before they take their life? Not sure I have much choice. I can't slow my nerves as I race westward over to the I-5 corridor.

I've been down this stretch of interstate hundreds of times. In several locations the road's shoulder becomes narrow. The third overpass I come to looks like it will do. I take the next exit and swing back south to retrace my steps. Five minutes later I am on the northbound side of the interstate again. My hands can barely hold the wheel as I slow down and pull over about fifty yards after the targeted overpass. I come to a stop just short of a sign for the next exit.

The beauty of southern California is that traffic is heavy no matter the time of day. I'm counting on this. I reach for the hubcap, fumbling it once, then finally securing it. I exit my car as a wave of automobiles whooshes past me; the tailwind pinning my shirt to my chest. The speed of these masses of steel is too close and too fast for my eyes to capture. Roaring engines bellow for my attention while the smell of diesel exhaust is almost overwhelming.

I work my way south along the shoulder, in the direction of the overpass. Dressed in dark clothing I'm difficult to see. I stick very close to the guard rail. This is not the way I want to be facing when I'm hit. I need to be clipped by a car from behind. It has to appear to be an accident. At about the midpoint of the overpass I stop and bend down like I'm retrieving the hubcap. A trivial act on my part, but it might be necessary to have a witness come forward that saw my *purpose* for walking along this freeway.

I turn to head back toward the car. Before I begin what will be my death march, I look west hoping to catch a glimpse of the ocean. As the day expires, the sun's final rays peek over the trees. I have been privileged to witness some beautiful sunsets over this ocean. Today a small hill obstructs my view. My last moments on this earth and there is nothing worthy of a photograph. Perhaps this is a fitting end to my life.

My thoughts return to my father's last moments. Did he struggle when it came time to veer his car into the chasm? Was it difficult to overcome his human need for self-preservation? Was I anywhere in his last thoughts?

I walk on the white line identifying the edge of the road. My personal balance beam. On one side is death; the other this pitiful existence. I fight to slow my gait, trying to give my would-be assassins more time to do me in. Despite my black shirt and slacks, drivers must be seeing me. I hear and see evidence of them moving out of the right lane. Eventually one of them won't make out my dark figure.

I think of praying for this to end quickly. Who would I pray to? If I believed in a higher power I would have asked for help long before this. If there is such a power He obviously doesn't give a shit about me. I'm not worthy of His concern. His face has long ago turned from mine.

I try to imagine my family happy once again. Will they still consider themselves my family after I'm gone? How long will it be before they recover? I know in this moment that Pete was right. I've ignored my wife's concerns and let her down time after time. Tears drip from my cheeks. My family's faces flash before me, one by one. I long to explain to them that this final act is one borne of a loving father. I have nothing else that I can give them. It would be selfish of me to go on living.

Maybe my father did it right. Things were looking up for him when he cashed in, but it was only temporary. He knew that soon enough the tide of his fortunes would have receded. Was it easier for him to go out on top?

The front of a semi passes within a foot of my left shoulder. At this speed it creates a sort of vacuum that pulls me into it. Somehow the trailer doesn't make contact. Once past me I hear its angry horn screaming at me to get off the road. I raise my free hand and flip him off. I wish he would see my gesture and turn around. Run me over.

God help me. Please!

My plan requires that I die here. Today. There must be a horrific collision between a technological mass and this weak body of flesh that I inhabit. I picture myself lying on this oil-soaked pavement, writhing in agony as the life ebbs from me. I shudder involuntarily.

My thoughts are firing in rapid succession now. I can't seem to focus. I'd like a drink or some chemical way to dampen my brain. Tears continue to stream down my face. I have never felt so cold.

So alone.

Looking over my shoulder, I consider leaping into the path of an oncoming vehicle. The muscles in my legs are rubbery now and I know I don't have that kind of bravery. I tilt my head backward and scream into the blackness.

"Hit me you sons of bitches!"

Once more I hear a horn. It's from a smaller vehicle behind me. Tires squeal and more horns sound. I tense.

The impact doesn't come.

Seconds pass and my body begins to settle. I walk the balance beam again, slower now, coming at last to a stop. There's a scant eight feet left before the shoulder widens.

I take three deep breaths, sucking in the carcinogenic-laden air. In the midst of the roaring traffic a strange calm settles over me. My tears stop. Maybe this is the moment I have been seeking.

The hubcap slips from my hand, spins on its edge like a top until it slowly, crazily settles in the path of an oncoming vehicle. I reach for it. My balance wavers for a moment. Just let go, Mitch. Do the right thing.

I feel myself falling, falling …

I pull back suddenly, inches before being struck by a green Honda Civic. I stand tall again and scream obscenities into the night.

There is no hope.

Why can't I do this? What is holding me back? I pick up my pace now, almost running, until I arrive at my car.

There's an open field to my right that looks to be in need of a late-model BMW hubcap. I fling the hubcap with all the strength I have. In this moment I realize that hubcaps don't fly true. It veers upward and to the left, heading straight for the exit sign I parked near. It's as if a magnetic force were acting upon it. The hubcap clangs against the sign and rebounds in my direction. The demon-possessed Frisbee smashes into the grill of my car. Instinctively I move to the front of my car to inspect the damage. Seconds ago I was prepared to leave this earth and now I give a shit about the paint job of a used car!

From the south I hear squealing tires again. The interior of my car is suddenly lit up like someone turned on stage lights in the back seat. The whole car lurches violently toward me.

My ears are filled with the sounds of metal groaning, crunching and finally relenting. In my periphery I see chaotic motion. Cars on the freeway are attempting to stop, too fast. They swerve like giant snakes. The odor of many cars simultaneously applying their brakes hits me like waves crashing on the beach.

Arms waving, my feet no longer touch the ground. I don't know which way to lean to right myself. I am being propelled along a path I cannot see.

My body is suspended above the ground. I'm floating. I don't feel any pain. My descent starts. Time begins to slow.

The landing will be abrupt.

I manage to bring my hands up to my head.

Chapter 37

Bedeep…bedeep…bedeep. Slow sound…a one-hertz rate. Electronics. Not digital data…millions of times too slow. An annoying sound. I can't place it.

Lying on my back. Roll my head in the direction of the sound. Sharp pain erupts from my neck. A low growl emits from deep inside me. Something's missing. Something necessary.

Ticking of a clock. Distant shoes scuffling on a tile floor. Muffled voices, the words unintelligible. Metal wheels squeaking, probably on a cart. Human activity. My eyes, they're locked shut. No pain there.

Where the hell am I? Is this hell?

I take a deep breath through my nose. Repeat this act again twice to collect more data. Body odor. I need a shower. Another smell, vaguely familiar. It masks everything… an overpowering aroma. Another breath. Alcohol, not liquor, antiseptic.

Numerous unrelated sounds, strange smells, still no visual input. The rate of the beeping sound picks up. Maybe two Hertz now. I need more information.

I carefully roll my head in the other direction. There's some pain, but it's manageable. More smells. Flowers, not sure what kind. Nothing else here.

I spread my fingers, focusing on their sensory inputs. A process that goes much slower than it should. A sheet is on me. It's stiff. The weight is too much for a simple sheet. A blanket too. I turn my focus to my toes. Nothing there. I arch my back and try to push my toes further outward. They refuse to offer any help.

Sweat is forming on my forehead. The beeping sound doubles again.

My eyelids remain heavy. No more waiting, it's time they help. I tighten the muscles in my face. I'm only able to generate a twitch. Two more sweat-inducing attempts. The beeping gets louder now and faster. My right eye partially opens. Light pours in. Pain, shut it, shut it!

Tears seep from behind the unresponsive lid. Don't you quit. Tough it out. Open it, you wimp.

The eye opens after a few additional moments of agony. Images begin to reach my brain. Something brown. A blanket. Looks itchy. It doesn't completely cover my body. Stops at mid-thigh. Beyond this is the explanation for why I couldn't feel anything with my toes: two large white objects. Casts. One for each leg.

My left eye decides on its own to fully open up. A tube is connected to my left forearm and a finger wrap is on my right hand index finger. How have I ended up in a hospital room? I'd like to shake my head to knock loose this brain dust and get my synapses firing again, but the potential for more pain leads me to dismiss the thought.

To my right is some sort of heart or breathing monitor. I can't make out the numbers on the display. The absence of alarm sounds is sufficient information at this point. An open door lies beyond this contraption. Bodies scurry past, their associated noises invading my enforced solitude. I groan and struggle to roll my upper body away from this activity. The bottom half of me is pinned in place. I achieve some success as my head is now facing the left side of the room.

Vases of flowers and large Mylar balloons overpower half of the room. Ubiquitous, trite requests to get well adorn the balloons and numerous obnoxious colored ribbons. Past these obligatory hospital room adornments, I can make out a narrow sliver of a window. Sunlight trickles through in a half-hearted attempt at lifting a patient's spirits.

My mind returns to my last memories before this hospital bed.

I was parked on the shoulder of the I-5. My plan to get a reckless motorist to end my existence failed. Beyond this a blurry haze foils my ability to recall. The casts on my legs indicate that at some point I met with harm. No other injuries are apparent. Strange.

The fog that hovers over my brain is slowly lifting. I still feel miles away from the shore where normalcy has chosen to dock its boat. My legs are impaired, but how much more of me is injured? How long have I been here? Where are the nurses? Doctors?

The incidents on the freeway were in the early evening. The presence of daylight sneaking into this prison cell proves that several hours have passed. You'd think I'd be joined by at least one of the people who were responsible for the flowers and balloons.

No, there are too many gifts for just one day. It would take time for the word of my ill fortune to get out and then for people to interrupt their normal schedules to fit in their condolences. It must have been at least two or three days, perhaps four. There are actually more items here than I'd expect.

My eyes begin to droop. I struggle to come up with a reason to fight sleep. It's then I spot movement from high up on the wall in front of me. I hadn't noticed a TV there. The sound is off, but I recognize the show. It's that quack from Oprah. The typical condescending, psycho-babbler type you see in the afternoon. Dr. Phil, that's it. If I were on his proverbial couch he'd spend fifteen minutes pretending to listen to my issues, all the while calculating the uptick in his investments, then hit me with a "How's that working for you?"

I search for the hand-held remote. It's on a bedside tray. My reach for it is interrupted by a cramp just below my ribcage. If I ever hit it big, I'll be a staunch supporter of realicide, the methodical and thorough killing of anyone in any way connected with reality TV.

I suck in a deep breath and ignoring the pain, manage to secure the TV remote. It has two buttons, one that controls the TV and another that calls the nurse. I push a button, not caring which one. Electronic or human assistance, I'm not concerned as long as the damned thing gets turned off.

Chapter 38

The sound of wheels half-rolling, half-skidding on tile floor stirs me. I fight the response to open my eyes. To do so would require my interaction with whatever annoyance has entered my space. I won't participate in a phony conversation in which a nurse on the last hours of her shift pretends to care about how I'm doing, while I pretend to be grateful for her concern, while we both pretend that we're enjoying the conversation. The only thing I'm interested in now is feigning sleep.

I sigh and twist my upper-body to my left, away from the sounds. Carefully I open only my left eye; it's the one closer to the bed now and shouldn't be visible to the mystery meddler. Daylight still slinks through the crack of window I've been granted. It feels like it's just past midday, but my body clock is not yet reliable. Time of day is irrelevant in hospitals, prisons, and nursing homes. It's a path to insanity to count the days until you get to leave. Your focus should be solely on gaining your freedom, either walking upright or in a box, the exact manner making no never mind.

I once more attempt to categorize the sounds coming from outside my cell. Various alarms being ignored at the nurses' station, carts getting pushed from room to room by Neanderthals masquerading as human life forms, the clang of a dinner tray being put back on a rack of similar trays, the "food" remnants to be disposed of in a location far from where anyone can be harmed by exposure to the lime Jell-O, and finally the higher-pitched dinging of the elevator bell signaling the arrival of yet another visitor to this palace of pleasure.

Shoes are making their way down the hall from the

elevator, shoes not of this place. These shoes have a quicker pace, an almost happy canter, not the scraping, sliding sound of a body trying to make it through one more day, toward a weekend, a vacation, a retirement and the ultimate exit from this hell. A cough first and then a partially stifled laugh reach my ears. These are familiar in some way. The rhythm of a muffled conversation finally gives them away. People I know are just outside my door.

I'm not sure I've enough in the tanks to deal with them just now. They'll want me to show them something I don't have, the will to be happy. I shut both my eyes and decide to maintain the sleeping ruse. Multiple bodies enter my room.

"Is he awake?" Stacey asks.

"He's conscious but napping now." It's a reply from what must be the nurse. "We don't usually allow more than two visitors for patients on this wing."

"He's been awake for almost two days now. The doctor said the effects of the drugs should be wearing off and seeing the whole family would be good for his recovery," Stacey replies.

"His crack is showing," Jacob says.

Sheets are being firmly tugged over my backside. I fight the urge to say thank you to Stacey. No kid should ever have to see his dad's hairy ass. I saw my old man's once and shudder as the picture flashes through my memory.

"Mom, can I have the eye patches back?" Alyssa giggles.

"Me first," Stacey says, and they all break out in snorts and squeals of laughter.

Despite my best efforts, I feel myself becoming energized. My family has always done this for me. They're all here and excited. I can fake it for a few moments. They deserve that much from me. I roll slowly onto my back trying to give the appearance of someone gradually awakening. Eyes fully open now, I begin to take them all in without speaking.

A look passes between Stacey and the nurse. Corporate rules are no match for a mother's love. The nurse shuts the door as she exits.

Jacob lurches forward, hugs me and kisses my cheek. It pushes me to my limits not to cry as he thanks me for the pictures of him and his heroes. As I fumble in my attempt to hug him back I notice that his hair is longer and appears to have gotten darker, almost black. I hope this isn't his sister's next project. He seems to also have grown since I last saw him. The smell of cologne lingers after he breaks away from me. When did this start? Somewhere there is a girl behind this.

Alyssa swaps positions with Jacob while I'm still trying to wrap my head around the changes in my son. Her hair is red, and it's not the clown-like variety. Okay, there's some highlighting, but it's within a stone's throw of normal. My focus drifts to her face, one that's not covered with excessive cosmetics. Rolling slightly to get a closer look, I notice that her eyes are tracking me.

My baby sees!

She smiles broadly, having picked up my recognition. I frame her face between my two hands and kiss her forehead gently.

I stare for several seconds into her now-functional eyes. This is a joy I never thought to experience again. She is whole. Tears well up in my eyes and I make no effort to hide them. My brain rummages for the right words to show my bliss, but her expression tells me anything I say is not necessary.

She returns my kiss with one of her own, planted

lightly on my cheek. Something's way off. Parents of teenage children don't get kisses, at least not voluntarily. Maybe I did succeed in killing myself and this is heaven?

As Alyssa gets up, Stacey grabs both of my hands. Sitting down on the edge of the bed, she brings my hands together and holds them tightly to her chest. Tears are dripping from her cheeks, falling onto my forearms. Her hair is tied back in a way reserved for her gardening time. She never leaves the house looking this way, not for anything. I lock my hands around hers and pull her down toward me. I kiss her face, slowly and methodically, letting my lips trace the paths of her tears. The salty taste lingers in my mouth.

Each of my kisses seems to extract a small portion of the loneliness that flows in her. Our foreheads touch and we remain still, connected, unspeaking. We linger like this for almost a minute and then she sits back up, freeing her hands to finish wiping her face. I notice her shirt. It's blue and has golden arches embroidered over its pocket. My quizzical look prompts her.

"It's from a job."

"Since when do you work at McDonald's?"

"It's just something I was doing while my husband was away."

What else has she been forced to endure while her husband was AWOL? In her eyes I catch a fleeting glimpse of the tip of her pain. It runs deep. I shake my head in self-disgust. Whatever she has suffered, she will not voice. She stood her post for the family, defiant and alone. How much of her agony did I create?

"You've spent the last sixteen weeks in a medically induced coma. The doctors were concerned about the swelling around your brain. They said it will take some time for you to re-adjust. We've missed you."

The kids chime in with their agreement. I work to create a happy look of my own. I owe them this much. It's difficult to push a counterfeit smile through the thickness of my disappointment. Taxed by the effort, I yawn and momentarily close my eyes.

Stacey rounds up her chicks and scoots them under her wings and toward the door. She instructs them that I need my sleep and they can come back tomorrow. I mumble my goodbyes when prompted.

Sixteen weeks. It's October. School has started again. Life for my family has continued without me. I'd hoped somehow they would find happiness after I left them. I just didn't expect to witness it.

I replay the snippets of the conversation we shared.

Stacey didn't ask for my advice. There were no desperate pleas for assistance. How long did she wait before taking her place at the family's helm? Forced to captain the ship, she weathered whatever storms beset her. Despite the need to take on a fast food job there are no signs of shipwreck or mutiny. Do I still have a position above deck on the Pederson boat?

Alyssa and Jacob seemed glad to see me. Were they filling the roles their mom asked them to play? Four months would be long enough for them to learn to cope without me. Many children find a way to succeed in single-parent homes.

I roll back over toward the window as I hear a chime indicate the arrival of the elevator. The sun is setting. Soon the temperature will drop outside. Inside I cling to the images of my family's smiles. The warmth of their love may be only embers, but it's enough to calm me as I drift into sleep.

Chapter 39

Three days have passed since I awoke. This place has gone from health care facility to prison cell and it's a short jump to insane asylum. Shuffling footsteps in the hallway signal the arrival of another guest. Yes. Free at last, free at last. I don't care who or what is out there, please stop and talk to me.

A short man with a massive comb-over knocks at my door. He's wearing a tan corduroy blazer over a white polo shirt, faded blue jeans and well-worn Nike Airs. Someone just walked straight out of the 1980s.

"Can I come in?"

I give a nod of approval to my visitor. The overhead light reflects from something dangling about his neck and instantly I realize my mistake. I'm about to be evangelized.

When my children were little we had a routine when these religious types came to the door. Upon hearing the doorbell and spotting them through the peephole, we'd immediately hit the ground, keeping silent, playing dead. We'd lay there trying to stifle giggles until the unwanted visitors left, no new recruits to add to their list. The ritual fell from grace one evening when we were welcoming a new family, the Richardsons, to our neighborhood. In an awkward moment of that initial conversation it came out that they were Mormons, the most common of the religious types who frequented our doorstep. As I struggled to look for another topic to keep the dead silence to a minimum, all eyes became locked on happenings behind me. There at my feet lay my children, reacting as they'd been trained.

It seemed that the frequency of evangelistic visits to

our home declined after this incident. The Richardsons probably sent a message through the spiritual network that we were to be avoided. This guy didn't get the memo. Too late to play dead. I settle on the least enthusiastic smile I own.

"Hi, I'm Paul Reynolds. And you are?"

"Not about to be converted."

My guest chortles, "Not to worry, I get paid whether you buy into what I'm selling or not."

"Good, then you can skip the hard sell."

"Not my style. Just work this beat to bring some peace to troubled souls. You were in a coma for a few weeks."

"A bit of a snoop, are you?"

"It's common for people to be edgy, frustrated when they first awake from a coma."

"Not me, people think I'm an ass most all the time."

The fanatic winks and offers a crooked smile, "Good, then you're recovering nicely."

This guy has the potential to be much more entertaining than most of his kind. Appears to have a functioning brain. Maybe I'll play along for a while.

"So, funny man, what religion are you hawking here?"

"You sure you want to go there? Tell me what fills your days."

No harm in opening up a little. Better than staring at the walls. If he goes too far, I'll kick him out. "I am...was a VP of engineering at a local firm."

Seeming to sense my guard dropping, my visitor removes his blazer and folds it over the arm of a nearby chair. He plops down in the same chair and continues, "Isn't it interesting that men always introduce themselves by what they do to make money?"

"You wear yours around your neck."

Another soft laugh escapes from him. "Less of an

anchor around my neck than money is around yours?"

No running from the bantering. If he wasn't wearing that religious symbol on his body, we might become friends. Not in this lifetime.

"You said you were a VP of engineering. What are you now?"

"Unemployed."

"Yeah, that's the advantage with my job. We don't get fired and we die with really good benefits. The clergy is probably out for you. What's next in your life?"

Thoughts of the events of the last few weeks race through my head, culminating in the botched suicide attempt. "Don't know."

"Got a family?"

"Wife and two kids."

"Get to spend more time with them while you search for your new occupation."

"If only it were that easy."

Without bothering to rise, the visitor scoots his chair closer to the bed. The feet of the chair drag, causing a high-pitched squeak to echo through the room. The perpetrator flashes an apologetic smirk while simultaneously raising his legs so his feet hover over the edge of my bed, "Mind if I do?"

Before I can respond, he brings his feet to rest on my bed and eases himself into a more relaxed, almost supine position in his chair. I give him a look that is meant to show him how strange I find this latest act.

He continues without a pause, "A man of your former position can't be accustomed to everything being easy."

"Not at all. Just used to having things planned out, not so abrupt."

My strange guest nods his head. The smirk on his face

fades into a full toothy smile. His teeth have an equine feel to their appearance. Too big for his mouth. I've never trusted people with big teeth.

"Probably annoys you when someone throws a wrench in your big plans. Us little folks are supposed to be just puppets on the stage of some big production you're in charge of."

A nerve in my upper leg starts firing as if it has a mind of its own. I jerk upright for a moment and adjust my position in the bed. In a few seconds my leg and buttocks begin to feel normal again. When I look up, the pastor is watching me.

"Never said I was mad at anyone."

"You find change exhilarating?"

"When it's planned."

"Ah. You're not *agitated* by this life altering decision, just...disturbed." The slouching man winks at me. "Because things are not going as planned. How long does it usually take for you to accept that things have changed outside of your control?"

"I'll let you know when it happens."

A nurse flits into the room on her appointed mission. She exchanges nods with my guest. No greeting for me. This one I've trained well. She examines the bag of medicine connected to my IV and jots down a few numbers from the equipment hooked to my body. Satisfied with her work, she leaves silently.

My guest eases his chair back from the bed and rises to his feet. He reaches for his blazer as I speak.

"Your work here is done?"

"Timing's not right. You still think you're the one calling the shots. You're not going anywhere soon. Maybe we'll talk again."

I hear myself saying, "Can't wait." It doesn't come out

with as much sarcasm as I hoped.

Chapter 40

Stacey is due here any moment. I love this woman and always will. There is much that lies between us, unspoken. Every relationship has these things, but ours feel suffocating. Her haphazard plan to right our family. My ultimate response, heroic or cowardly. How much credit should we give each other for good intentions? There is so little black and white to be found in our marriage. I need to place everything in its appropriate box before I can move on.

I decide to count the ceiling tiles one more time. Checking my math. There are ninety-nine in my room. Sixty rooms per floor in this four-story hospital. If I add another twenty percent to each floor for public restrooms and break rooms, then there are about 28,512 ceiling tiles in this building. I've asked every nurse I've seen this past week to wheel me around the building and assist me in verifying this theory. Some say no. Most look at me and walk away unspeaking. Mathematical cretins.

Used the phone yesterday to ring the hospital maintenance department. They hung up on me when I asked if they knew the exact number of ceiling tiles in this building. You'd think the group assigned to repair the tiles would know the number they are responsible for.

Focused on these relaxing thoughts, I miss Stacey entering the room. A perfunctory kiss is exchanged and she moves to lean against the far wall. She's wearing a pair of sun-faded blue jeans, worn spots in the knees, hand prints on both thighs where she has wiped them numerous times. Topping this is a tattered blue plaid shirt; the long sleeves have been cut off for functional reasons. She has removed the shirttails also, not bothering to hem them; there are threads unraveling in many places.

Her hair is tied back in that work-around-the-house-ponytail again. She's not wearing her Padres baseball cap which completes the outfit. Probably left it in the car. Leaning with only the back of her head touching the wall, her lower body is arched slightly forward to allow room for her hands to be clasped behind her back.

She makes the first overture. "You look better."

"Better than a man in a coma?"

"Good to have you back."

The sunlight peeking through the window obediently highlights the contours of her face. On her right cheek there is the faintest of streaks in her makeup. Most likely missed it when she was touching herself up in the car. I shift my focus to the happenings in the hallway. Can't allow such thoughts to occupy my mind.

"You've been working in the yard."

"Been pruning some of our neighbor's roses and hydrangeas. Good people, but they don't know anything about flowers."

"Last time you wore a uniform top for Mickey D's. Fast food and neighborhood gardening. Are you trying to piss off the illegal aliens by taking away their two best jobs?"

She snorts, the traditional Pederson female's response to humor when they can't help but laugh. Despite the trials we've faced in our lives, I've always been able to make her laugh. A lengthy pause ensues.

"What's next?" she asks.

"Doctor says I should start therapy next week. If that goes well I can make plans to break out of this place."

"Next for us?"

"I can't see that far."

"You can't or you don't want to?"

"I'm not ready."

"I needed to get your attention."

I cast a glance at my casts. "There were much less painful ways to accomplish that."

A nurse softly knocks at the door and begins to move toward the patient monitoring station, a Philips MX800. She's a little thing, probably not five feet tall and just doing her job, checking my stats periodically. It's not her lucky day.

"Find another room to haunt," I say.

She whips her head around, staring at me. I hear the sounds of disappointment murmuring from Stacey's side of the room but I go on undeterred. "Come back in an hour and you can get your numbers."

The nurse averts her eyes from mine and looks for support from Stacey. My wife just shrugs and mouths the word sorry as the petite nuisance flutters from the room. Run away Tinkerbell.

Stacey admonishes me as soon as she's out of earshot. "You can be such an ass."

"She needs to get used to grumpy patients."

"Can't you get over this?"

"Not as fast as you."

Stacey moves to the end of the bed and smooths out the blanket near my legs. She sits down gingerly on the edge of the bed. "I'm in this for the long run. I know I've hurt you deeply, in ways I can't understand, but I'm not going to throw in the towel."

She leans forward and places her hand on my cheek, turning my face so our eyes align.

"I know I'm fighting this battle alone for now. Soon enough you'll join me."

Her fingers are soft with an earthy smell. Comforting,

loving, even peaceful. I twist my head away to free myself from her hand.

"I'm not ready to forgive you."

"You're a bigger man than this."

"Don't be so sure."

"I have faith in you even if you don't."

"Damn you!"

I feel her weight rise from the bed as I examine the contents on the other side of the room. I pretend to be fascinated by the window blinds. Minutes pass with us sharing nothing but the same oxygen. Only one of us has the ability to leave. I wish she would.

She finally speaks, "What kept you so late that night of the accident? You were supposed to meet us at the restaurant and we couldn't reach you on your cell."

I keep my face averted from her as I respond.

"My hubcap fell off and I was retrieving it."

"On the highway? That's… dangerous."

"Do you know what a BMW hubcap goes for? Pretty pricey for a household being run by fast food and landscaping."

"More costly than this hospital stay?"

I turn my head to confront her but notice a nurse apprentice is at the door with my dinner tray. Stacey mumbles something about needing to use the restroom and heads down the hallway. The young lady places the tray on the table that swings over my bed. I leave the cover over the plate.

"I don't want any more visitors and you can take this food away too. I'm not hungry tonight."

I turn away again to face the portion the room inhabited by cards and balloons. The sounds of her picking up the tray, her footfalls retreating from my room echo too loudly. It's silence I crave. No more distractions to keep me from my resolve.

The motion of her body leaving the room creates a draft; the get-well balloons, some almost a week old and long past their peak of happiness, move slowly, silently. The sunlight shines off the twisting Mylar creating colored swaths on the wall, the table, and my bed. Our lives are just like these balloons, swaying in the ripple of air caused by some unseen force.

I love my wife and it hurts to be stuck in this state of limbo. I'm not sure what role is left for me. My life no longer makes sense. I should have died that night. I didn't develop a plan for where I'm at now. Everyone else seems to have the script for this play and I'm left adlibbing it.

Chapter 41

There exists an unseen and mysterious document for every patient. A protocol. Those in the medical field speak of it in hushed voices normally reserved for holy writings. As a patient I never get to see it. Supposed to be some kind of get-well plan for me, a program. It seems that behind the veil of confidentiality all manner of evil pleasures may be enjoyed.

A certain type is drawn to the nasty underbelly of the medical world. If you desperately enjoy being mean to others, consider physical therapy. Dennis, this hospital's resident schmuck, has just arrived for our fourth session. He claims his goal is to help me regain the strength, flexibility, and range of motion in my legs. Not so. Pain is his pleasure and he gets to inflict it on a daily basis.

I've been lying in this bed for four months. Nerve endings tingle at irregular times. Muscle cramps hide like thieves behind every rock, waiting to pounce on me unexpected. The added weight of the casts exacerbates the difficulty of physical activity. Nurses and doctors regularly ask me what my pain level is, on a scale from one to ten. Earlier this morning I was sitting at a two. I told Dennis I spiked to a four when he came in. He just smiled.

As instructed, I roll to my stomach to work on inverted leg lifts. Sweat begins to run from my forehead, dripping on my pillow. My instinct is to grab hold of the end of the bed for leverage, but this is not permitted. He claims that keeping my hands by my sides will strengthen my core. Sick bastard. Right leg. Hold it up for ten seconds. Eight...seven...six. I've never been one who follows orders blindly. Mitch Pederson will always question authority.

Switch to left leg. Nine...eight...seven.

These casts are due off tomorrow. Not sure exactly when. No planning in this environment. This is forced intervention for impatient, type A control freaks. Rebellion is futile. The options: submission or insanity. The doctor said that if my condition remains stable I can be freed. They're concerned about my mental facilities. I'm not. It's theirs I worry about. Back to my right leg. Ten...nine...eight.

Dennis is mumbling platitudes while he pushes on my leg to stretch the unused muscles. It hurts like hell, but I'll make it through this. He acts like we're a team, but we're not. I'll exceed all his trivial goals in spite of him. The next command comes. Roll over.

It's then I spy the hospital evangelist leaning against the wall, just inside my room. Not sure how long he's been there. Another pain-seeker, he's probably enjoying the show too. He nods. "Thought I'd stop by and talk with someone who isn't on death's doorstep. You up for that?"

The pain master instructs me on a new set of exercises. As I shift my body to begin, a cramp shoots down my right calf. I reach down hoping to punch my fist into the afflicting muscle, a technique I developed as a teenager when I was the victim of numerous nighttime leg cramps. I stop when I remember the cast on my leg.

"What makes you so sure I'm not about to die?" I nod my head in the direction of the physical therapist. "The angel of death is here amongst us."

Dennis doesn't react, staying focused on his job. Paul chortles. "I always pictured him as being bigger, more sinister."

Against my will, a small laugh escapes me, followed by the return of leg cramps, more intense then before. My body screams at me to stop for a moment, but I won't allow myself any sign of weakness.

My jolly visitor continues, "So what is it that you've got against God?"

Leg lifts, elevation of thirty degrees. Both legs simultaneously. Hold it for five seconds, rest for five. I wait for a rest period to respond, "Religion's for the weak."

"Weak? Help me with that one?"

"People who can't deal with reality."

Legs elevated again. My quadriceps start to tremble. Sweat drips in my left eye, blurring my vision. Rest period begins. I wipe my eyes and glance at the wall clock. Two minutes left in the session.

The pastor looks at me closely for a minute and then continues, "So you've got reality all figured out."

Dennis turns me sideways on the bed with my legs hanging over the edge. Done this exercise before. It's going to really hurt. I go through two reps and add an extra one. He chides me not to push it beyond his instructions. I point to my ass and pucker my lips.

Change my focus to the pastor. Amid deep recovery breaths I speak. "Ah, here we go. Been waiting for you to start your sales pitch."

"You're working hard here to fix the outside, but it looks like there's a big wound on the inside."

Dennis picks up a clipboard and begins to make notes. Says there'll be another visit after I get my casts off. Going to need to schedule outpatient treatment when I get home. Maybe, but not with you, prick.

Back to the pastor again. "Look, you're a passable break from the boring routine here, but I'm not even close to buying the placebo you're selling."

"There's no selling going on here. Consider me a rubber-necker who slows down on the freeway to take a close look at a gnarly wreck. Your life is flipped on its roof, the air bags have gone off and gas is streaming from the tank. And now God's got a semi barreling down on you. Going to be a fiery crash. I love this stuff."

Thoughts of my last highway experience play in my head. Walking the balance beam between a shitty life and death. It's strange that decisions that seemed so clear during one season in our lives are absolutely absurd in the next.

"You might be disappointed."

A look of what I assume is pain comes across the pastor's face. His eyes are locked on mine.

"At some point we all end up on our knees. It's only a question of how long you fight this."

A wave of nausea rises in my throat. I must have pushed it too hard on the last set with the physical therapist.

"With these legs it's going to be a while before I can hit my knees."

"Love and our desire for love can lead us to do amazing things," Paul says.

"Dedication and discipline can accomplish the same things."

"Some would have you believe that. I've never seen things done from personal ambition really last. Love conquers all they say."

My last disagreement with Stacey comes to my thoughts. Love doesn't seem to be winning that battle.

"My experience differs from yours," I say.

"Maybe enough time hasn't passed yet in your life? I liken love to a stream of flowing water. Given enough time it crumbles rocks, boulders, and eventually whole mountains."

A cramp erupts again in my right leg. I use my hands to help shake my leg, hoping this sudden movement will magically alleviate the pain. After a minute the intensity of the cramp subsides. I can't be sure if my efforts sped up this process.

The pastor continues watching me closely, making no effort to help me in my distress. You'd think he could show me a little compassion just now. Not that I want anything from this man, but hey?

"Have you ever heard of a fellow named Pascal?" the pastor asks.

"Blaise Pascal, seventeenth-century French mathematician and physicist? Nope, never heard of him."

"Then you've heard of his wager?"

I grab the remote on my bedside table and hit the nurse button. A voice quickly responds. I ask for an orderly to bring me more pillows.

Paul continues, "Pascal's Wager. Look it up some time when you're bored with just lying there in bed."

The orderly enters the room as the pastor exits. She goes about her duties as I stare at the ceiling tiles above my bed.

Chapter 42

Ninety-four minutes ago my legs were freed from the casts I've been wearing for almost five months. The resulting stench, akin to a bologna sandwich displaced under a teenager's bed for the entire summer vacation, still permeates the room. My neighbors must have enjoyed the sponge bath as much as I did.

Thoroughly washed, these two pale, scarred sticks aren't mine. I've always considered myself an athlete. These are not the legs of an athlete. Not one this side of seventy.

Today is my scheduled day of emancipation. In a matter of hours, I'll have beaten them. They wanted me to be grateful and humbly take their assistance. I am thankful for their help in my physical healing. The man I want to be, the one I hope to be again, doesn't do subservience. Real leaders stand tall no matter the obstacles. They can all kiss my flaccid, freshly wiped, bed sore-covered ass goodbye.

The elevator bell echoes down the hall. I steel myself for the things, physical and otherwise, I'm not sure I can handle. Stacey enters my room with a smile fastened determinedly to her face. She is wearing a red blouse with a collar that rides high on her neck. The blouse opening plunges deep. She has paired it with a tan skirt that screams look at my curves, look at my legs.

She moves quickly to present me with a hug and a kiss. I return them dutifully. Her smile seems to slip for a moment, but quickly regains its rigidity. She takes a seat in a chair near the end of the bed.

"Good enough to come home?"

"Physically."

A nurse appears at my doorway with a wheelchair. Stiff white face, stiff white uniform, stiff white hose all riding atop stiff white cankles. Gonna miss this place.

"Ready, Mr. Pederson?"

I launch myself into a vertical position. I have been upright only three times in the last month. Both women jump forward to steady me, but I brush away their assistance as I fight to maintain my balance. "I know your insurance says I have to ride that out of here, but I'm going to walk over to it and sit down like a man. On my own."

It takes me almost two minutes to make it the six steps to the wheelchair. The nurse slips on the chair's brake as I reach out for the arms to steady my descent. I almost fail in this regard and the chair rocks precariously as I drop myself into the seat. Without looking, I sense the women passing disapproving looks. Screw 'em both.

"You can push me now."

The trip down the hall, onto the elevator and eventually through the lobby is filled with conversation between the two women. I haven't the interest or remaining breath to participate. The mini-van is parked in front of the hospital, primed to convey me back into a life I know I'm not ready for. I allow the women to assist my efforts to get in the van. I'd like to go solo again, but I'm at my limit. My point made earlier in the room will have to do.

Her only willing conversationalist left behind, Stacey makes no attempt to speak with me during the drive home. Home. 1503 Simpson Place, a house that a few weeks ago I said good-bye to forever. Can a relationship be continued when one of the parties has chosen to exit with such finality? My house and my marriage are mere shells that this hermit crab once inhabited.

The mini-van swings into the driveway and my eyes

are drawn to the rose bushes in our front yard. The reds, yellows, even the whites are scene-stealing. Our bushes are thriving, having returned to health from the savage pruning they endured at this woman's hands just weeks earlier.

She must have caught my staring, "Look pretty good?"

A wave of disappointment comes over me as I contemplate the rest of the house. What else has she improved upon?

"You know your roses."

As I struggle to swing my legs out of the vehicle, Stacey scampers from around the back with a pair of crutches. She leans them against the van and walks toward the front door. By the time I have righted myself and begun to progress at a painful pace, I notice the front door has been left ajar. Stacey has gone inside.

The gauntlet has been tenderly thrown down. It's time for me to begin to move from helpless coma victim to captain of my life. I know she needs me to step up. Nothing will work in my relationship with this family until this is addressed. If only I could have the faith she has.

Between the healing bones and recuperating muscles, I am learning to walk anew. A stage in life I thought I'd never return to. Discomfort and shortness of breath cause me to pause twice along this journey. Mobility was always a given. Now my legs demand that I stop a third time, just four feet from my destination. I refuse to obey and push forward, my leg muscles shaking, twitching more as each moment passes.

A sweat drop is running down the bridge of my nose. There is no free hand to wipe away this nuisance. I shake my head violently, causing the perspiration to flee my face. The abruptness of this motion sets off a chain reaction. I struggle to right myself, but I haven't the motor-skills to accomplish this task.

I twist my upper body, aiming for a landing spot on the front lawn. The grass will be more forgiving than the cement walkway. This last contortion causes the process to accelerate and I'm forced to hurriedly cast the crutches away from my falling body. I land with a thud and a whoosh. My right elbow catches between my ribs and the ground. There is no additional pain, but I'm in that surreal state where all the oxygen has left my body.

Youth sports taught me that this will pass in a few minutes. I lie on the ground, focused on recapturing my ability to breathe regularly. The sounds of birds in trees and a lawn being mowed fill my ears. A neighbor's cat runs across the lawn between me and the house. It ignores the human lump on the grass. I notice the curtain in our living room window swaying gently. Maybe the air conditioning just kicked on.

Lying on the ground, waiting for my body to recover, I'm brought back to another painful time I found myself in a supine position. It was a late summer day just prior to my junior year in high school. Our football team was in the midst of two-a-days, four hours in the Southern California heat spent pushing yourself beyond what you thought you could endure. It was a grueling experience that brought out the true character of your team.

Our school's homecoming game and the accompanying dance were early in the season that year. Two days prior, the coach's daughter, an outspoken, not overtly feminine version of her dad, had proposed in front of my friends that I take her as my date to the big dance. The unexpected nature of this request and the audience of my peers had no doubt caused my response to be less kind than it should have been. The exact words I used escape me, but the picture of the wounded girl retreating in tears does not. I knew at some point I would pay for this indiscretion.

When things were going well for the team, the coaches would end our practices with a one-on-one drill. Our favorite involved having the entire team, about forty of us, stand in a large circle and face off. The defensive assistant coach would call out the name of one his charges and then the offensive assistant would reply quickly with one of his players. The two selected individuals would then charge forth screaming and meet with great force in the middle of the circle. The goal of each combatant was to knock the other man off his feet. The rest of the team would whoop and yell, girding on the combatants, celebrating the winners and chiding those beaten.

On this day, the skill-training portion of our practice ended about thirty minutes early. Following a water break the assistant coaches lined us up in the circle. This was the part of practice where we were allowed to be vocal, keenly aggressive. As the volume of noise began to pick up, I sensed a presence behind me. It was the head coach. He put his mouth to the ear-hole of my helmet and whispered slowly, in a calm, measured tone, that by the end of this practice I would beg him to quit his team.

Before I could process this message, the assistant coaches began to call out names. The defensive assistant called out a cornerback, small but fast. He had the chip on his shoulder necessary to play this position. The offensive assistant bellowed out "Pederson."

I was the back-up quarterback and because of our value to the team, the quarterbacks were seldom picked for these encounters. They couldn't afford for one of us to get hurt. I met my foe in the middle of the circle with a loud crash, helmets and shoulder pads colliding in a moment of violence. He stumbled and lost his balance while I stood over him and hands on my hips, staring down in contempt. For a defensive player to be knocked around by a quarterback was demeaning and his teammates let him have it.

Returning to our positions in the circle, we waited for the next names to be called. A defensive lineman, a stones-throw from 300 pounds. Again the name "Pederson." I attacked with the same desire, but the results were predictable. It was me who ended up on my back, vision out of lock momentarily. As I stumbled to my spot in the circle, the coach's words began to make sense.

Over the next ten minutes the remainder of the starting defense took its turn punishing me for my careless treatment of the coach's precious daughter. Nine more players. After the fourth time hearing my name called, much of the yelling stopped. The field was eerily quiet except for the calling of names and the crashing of bodies. The last name called was our team's middle linebacker. Vince Wilson was the most gifted athlete in our school and the only man on the field who struck fear in me. His collisions had a different sound to them. I had seen more than a few players shy away from taking this guy on.

By now my legs were masses of jelly, no spring left in them. I stumbled toward him and he caught me with his pads right under my chin. I was launched backwards, feet flying out from under me, hands flailing in the air, mouthpiece askew. As my eyes regained their focus, I saw Wilson's face inches from mine. He growled for me to stay down.

Blood was running from a cut on the bridge of my nose. It took me almost a minute to regain my feet and another to locate the head coach. He was hovering outside the circle, a sneer on his face. Without taking my eyes from him, I yelled for the defensive assistant to call out the next name. A look of satisfaction momentarily left the coach's face when I raised both hands and flipped him off.

Confidence and trust in yourself must precede leadership. A smile comes to my face now as I recall guiding that team to the playoffs the following year. My strength returning, I crawl to my crutches and use the exterior wall of the garage to help bring myself upright. The doorway is within arm's length. I complete this adventure.

On my own.

Chapter 43

Two days have passed since I returned to Simpson Place. I'm recovering, but not at the pace I desire. Walking down the twenty-six-and-a-half-foot hallway to my bedroom I'm forced to pause for a rest. This brings a pleasant encounter with that pictorial display of my family's history. Two rows of photographs, one for each child. Swatches of time, frozen in space, serenity for the asking.

The early shots of Alyssa, in her pre-school splendor, now produce a remorse for innocence lost. Jacob's images also cause mourning. Not for what he's already lost, but for what I know must be. Time is the most unrepentant of thieves.

In one photo I'm teaching Alyssa to ride her bike, *sans* training wheels. In another Stacey combs our son's hair on his first day of kindergarten. I look closely at our glowing parental faces. The children are not the only ones whom time has stripped of youthful enthusiasm.

Caught in this land of reverie a flash of light startles me. I look to my right and witness the action end of a Nikon D90. Two more photos are squeezed off and then the camera is lowered, revealing a large smile on the face of a captivating young female. She has blond hair with the slightest of brown highlights surrounding a face that has only a touch of makeup. The proof that there is injustice in this world is that the camera she holds is not pointing the other way. Cameras were invented to capture the hope and beauty that lie behind this face.

I hold out one hand and Alyssa comes to me for a hug. I point at the camera. A temporary frown shifts to a smile of understanding as she hands over the D90. I quickly click off four or five shots of my own. Peace envelops my soul. Camera in my hands, beautiful subject to shoot, loved one in my presence. Alyssa moves toward me again and brushes aside the camera to give me the hug she'd intended. At a loss to understand her need for physical affection, I hold on as long as this teenage daughter will allow. She eventually breaks free of my grasp.

I stare at her past the point of her comfort. So much has changed in the five months since my *accident*.

"You've let the beauty that was always in you come out."

Color rushes to her face as she focuses on putting a loose strand of hair in its proper place. Classic woman's move. She doesn't want me to stop admiring her. Just as well, I've no intention of doing so.

I should know better than to tinker with a good thing. Still, the engineer in me won't let this go uninvestigated. I must learn what has brought about this amazing transformation.

"You look so happy. How did it happen and what can I do to make it last?"

Alyssa points to the camera. "That."

My cheeks hurt as I realize that I've been holding a smile on my face for an extended time. Despite the pain, I can't stop. Don't want to. I nod my head as a signal for her to continue.

"You loaned me the camera and that book and…"

I wave my index finger in a corrective manner. "*The Art of Photography*. I gave it to you."

"Thanks. Anyways, I liked the pictures and what it said in the book so I decided to see what I could make with this thing. I took some shots. They weren't all that good and I began to mess with Photoshop. Love that program. So, I started looking at stuff on the computer in the photo lab because the monitor was bigger than my laptop. Hope that's okay?"

I feel the smile abandon my face as I remember the last time I saw this precious girl in my photo lab. I've never understood all that happened that day.

"You hurt yourself in that room. You were so angry."

Alyssa replies softly, "It was just a bad time…"

"Those things you said. My hurting your mom that way. I wouldn't do that."

"Mom said that too."

I look at her, waiting for my silence to draw her out.

"That day I didn't come home, I found out Dillon was sleeping with someone else."

My stomach drops. Playing back the sentence in my head. Did she say that they were also sleeping together? Stop it. Not the time for that.

"How did you… handle it?" I ask.

"I cried a little then told him to go shove his penis in the nearest garbage disposal!"

A small unfettered laugh escapes me. "Good job, baby."

"Why do men do that?"

"Real men don't. Just the weak ones. The ones who will never be of any consequence."

"I thought he was."

"They fool you sometimes, but you'll get better at picking up the signs."

"Why did you leave me the camera and the book?"

I look at the camera's settings. She has switched to manual focus and bumped up the shutter speed. Probably trying her hand at subjects in bright sunlight. Every junior photographer goes through this stage where they muck with the focus settings. Think they're smarter than the camera. Kind of like being a kid and questioning your parents. Eventually you realize it's better to just stick with the auto-focus and your parents' advice.

"Because I wanted you to love photography as much as me."

Alyssa removes a memory card from her pocket and replaces the one in the camera with this new one. She uses the buttons on the back to scroll through the photos until she arrives at the one she is looking for.

"After I read that book I wanted to learn more about photography. You were kind of dead." She smiles a nervous smile and I nod at her choice of words. "So I asked around at school. My history teacher has an after-school class he teaches. Bunch of nerds, but I went a few times anyways. He said I was a natural. A photo contest was coming up and he pushed me to enter."

She hands me the camera, softly adding, "I won."

Tears form in my eyes. That photography could free her from her troubles and bring us together is the kind of dream reserved for other, storybook fathers. As I look at the picture displayed on the camera monitor, I'm instantly reminded that in fact I'm not that kind of father after all.

The photo shows three people standing side-by-side, Jacob next to Alyssa and then their mother. It's late afternoon and the shot is on our front porch. Unkempt clothing, squinting eyes, despondent faces, disheveled hair, arms hanging limp by their sides, the shot has an air of one taken during the Great Depression. Next to Stacey is the ragged outline of another human. It's filled in with white and has the look of kindergarten art. The crude, rough work is intentional. Nice use of Photoshop.

The spot where the father, this father, should be

standing includes the words "Have you seen this man?"

In this moment I can fully see the wide chasm I have created. It forms the gap between the Pederson family and happiness. I've let them nibble on crumbs of joy, but never allowed them to fully sate themselves at the table of bliss. Is it any wonder that this wild hunger for something so basic drove them to such irrational acts? Despite this sudden clarity, I sense there is much more that I have done to hurt this family. Things I cannot yet see. My being gone from their world, for such a short time, brought them closer to where they always should have been.

I turn my head so my daughter doesn't have to witness her father crying.

Chapter 44

Many events around us don't break the pane of our consciousness. The elevator music of our lives. Not in this category are the sounds of domestic chores being done with excessive fervor. Pans clanking, cupboard doors shutting a bit too firmly, dining room chairs planted back into place, a vacuum jostling furniture and walls more frequently than needed. These are sounds not to be ignored.

Pete called earlier today and invited himself over. I've opted to meet him in the bedroom instead of the kitchen or family room. A mistake on my part. My general fatigue is not sufficient reason for such inconsiderate behavior. Message received. A price will be paid.

The sounds of shuffling footsteps in the hallway somehow make it over this din. They signal the arrival of my best friend. Can he still retain that title? There have been only a short phone call and a get-well card between us since the accident. Repairing our relationship is needed. A quick but unnecessary check of my emotional tool box shows no such skills. The bigger one of us will need to do the heavy lifting here.

The sight of Pete in the doorway pushes a smile through my lips to the forefront of my face. As I struggle to put words to a greeting, he asks, "Good to be home?"

"Better than the last place."

I consider rising from the bed to greet my friend, but before I can make such a move, Pete pulls up the only chair in the room. A hickory chair, spindles for legs, seat cushion covered with a pastel print. It's an antique from Stacey's grandmother which she uses exclusively with a matching vanity table. As he sits, the chair whines, announcing to all its peril. Pete leans forward so his head is less than a foot from mine and the chair groans louder. I make a mental note to add "respects personal space" to the requirements for my future best friends.

"How soon before you try to kill yourself again? It's not going to happen while I'm here?"

I quickly glance at the doorway, hoping no one is within earshot. My friend goes on, undeterred. "You came very close to getting your wish. Every day we waited for news. The doctors said the odds for your survival weren't good."

"I'm innocent. Do we have to replay it?"

"Yeah. You hurt yourself and all the people who are stupid enough to care about you, but it's not your fault."

"I …it didn't work. The plan failed."

"Obviously."

"I remember parking my car just off the I-5 and walking the shoulder hoping to get picked off by a negligent passerby. I couldn't follow through and flung the hubcap I was carrying in disgust."

"A hubcap?"

"Then I woke up in the hospital and weeks later my friend is grilling me about shit I still can't remember."

Pete uses the arms of the chair to lift himself. The chair trembles but survives. In the afterlife, Stacey's grandmother lets out a sigh of relief. Pete moves to the window. He crosses his arms and begins nodding his head, ever so slightly. His signature move when he's working something out. I whistle softly; my traditional countermove. His processing speed is not in my realm.

"Witnesses said you were standing in front of your car when another vehicle slammed into the rear of your BMW. You were sent flying into an open field. The cops don't know why you were standing on the freeway."

"I was looking at the front of my car where the hubcap hit it."

"You went there to kill yourself and you were worried about your car?"

"Not my best moment, okay?"

"So this was an accident? A coincidence?"

"Yes," I say drawing out the word.

"What's next?"

"Everyone keeps asking that."

"Because it's a damned good question. Answer it."

"I'm working on it!"

"You act like you expected no hiccups in your perfect life."

"Hiccup? This is a kick in the nuts."

"So is a shoe in the crotch worse than one in the ass? In front of your peers?"

An image of Jimmy Lee moaning and rolling on the lab floor flashes to the front of my memory.

"He didn't quit, you know? Came to work the next day. Walked with a limp for a good week."

I grunt in acknowledgment as I try to picture what that looked like. A frail, misunderstood man from another culture, clinging to his tattered dignity. Head held upright, black shock of hair bobbing with each painful step. Co-workers he annoyed in the past enjoying his pain in mocking silence. Company execs sitting in their offices, fearing he would bring a lawsuit that could bring to a stop the whole enterprise. Everyone from the janitor up just wishing he would go away. The injury forcing him to parade slowly through the hallways enduring more public scrutiny than anyone should be forced to bear.

"I bet his dreams of coming to America didn't include

being kicked in the ass by his boss. And yet he soldiers on. What about you?" Pete said.

"Not the same story."

"Right, your wife didn't actually kick you in the ass."

"What do you expect from me?" I snarl.

Pete's voice rises with mine, "You got hit by a car at high speed, shattered bones in both legs, suffered swelling around your brain, were put in a medically induced coma for almost four months, and come out of it with no permanent damage. It's a bloody miracle. How 'bout you stop feeling sorry for yourself and move on?"

"I spent hours lying in a hospital bed revisiting everything, looking for the answer. It's not there."

"There are other paths to the promised land."

"Teach me, Yoda."

"If being an asshole paid, you'd have no worries for employment."

"Your family wouldn't be going hungry either."

Pete moves his hand as if tipping an imaginary hat. He does it with the grandeur and enthusiasm of a starving actor trying to land a role in a third-rate off-Broadway play. I find myself laughing.

The big man smiles and pauses a moment before going on. I know he's enjoying that he was able to break down my defenses.

"What if you began again with a company that was just forming?"

"A start-up?"

"You could come on as an executive and not have to spend years climbing the ladder again. Maybe even as CEO."

"They're risky."

"You're in a position to take risks."

"I've got some baggage now."

"You know you like a challenge. Sell 'em. You've got no shortage of people who could vouch for you."

"Maybe."

"Huh?"

"Let me think this through," I mumble.

"You've gotta start somewhere."

"I said maybe. Don't push. That's all you're gonna get from me right now."

"What's there to think about? You gonna come up with another selfish scheme?"

"Selfish my ass! I was willing to give my life for my family."

"Oh you're no hero, buddy. Let me tell you. Could be someday. But for now, just another chicken shit!"

In lieu of delivering a fully justified, righteously angry response, I choose to re-position myself in bed. Through the break in our conversation, I notice that the noise of domestic chores has also ceased. My mind is suddenly focused on calculating how long the quiet outside the room has been present – how much of our conversation may have drifted to unwanted ears.

Pete glides to the edge of the bed in a way a large man shouldn't be able to pull off. He stoops until his face is inches from mine.

"What's holding you back?"

"I can't figure out why I'm still here, still alive."

"Is that really necessary? Just jump in the water and start swimming."

"How do I know if I'm swimming the right direction?"

Pete stands tall and backs away from the bed a few feet. He locks his hands behind his head, looking like he's about to lean against an imaginary wall.

"I don't think anyone knows that answer. We all kind of figure it out as we go."

From the hallway the sound of a toilet being flushed enters the room, soon followed by the creak of a door being opened. I listen for the sound of footsteps, advancing or retreating. My ears pick up on no useful clues. After a few moments I give up.

"I'm not wired that way. I have to have a plan."

"How has that I'm the man with a plan thing worked out for you?"

Pete playfully swats my leg as he heads toward the door. I know this is the hug he would give me if I weren't lying on this bed. What I have done to deserve such a friend is beyond my reasoning. I stare at him as he stops and turns before leaving.

"I suggest you get to swimming quickly before everyone you love has left you in their wakes."

Chapter 45

At CommGear I had a habit of checking the calendar and email on my phone several times an hour. I was always looking for clues as to how the rest of my day might turn out. Good, bad, or terrible. No surprises, I wanted to know in advance. Unemployed and barely mobile now, there is no longer a need to examine my barren to-do-list.

As if in answer to my boredom, the phone rings. Any relief I feel is instantly doused by caller ID. It's my attorney. He proceeds to offer greetings and concerns for my health.

"Where are we with my case?"

An audible sigh comes over the phone. He wants me to believe I've somehow hurt his feelings. Hah! Lawyers and human compassion. There's an oxymoron. All I need to know is what combination of prison, fines and probation I'm looking at. Making nice with this piranha doesn't even enter the equation.

"There are two phases of your defense against these assault charges, criminal and civil. Things have progressed nicely on the criminal front."

Nichols pauses. The silence approaches twenty seconds. I'm sure according to his script I should be reverently requesting his guidance. I grab my laptop from the bed stand and turn it on.

"Are you still there Mr. Pederson?"

I grunt while considering starting another game of computer solitaire. Nichols continues his diatribe.

"I spoke with the district attorney's office and they are willing to settle for misdemeanor assault. They took into consideration your lack of a criminal record, the fact that you didn't use a weapon and the minimal risk to repeat this offense."

I decide against the solitaire and opt instead to visit Wikipedia. I have nothing specific that I want to research, so I look around the room for a topic to explore. My eyes come to rest on the rack of ties hanging in my closet. I type necktie into the search box. One of the listed choices is something called the necktie paradox. Gotta be more interesting than lawyer drivel, so I select it.

"The next step would be for you to enter a guilty plea in front of a judge. With the prosecutor's recommendation, you'll probably be sentenced to four to six weeks of community service and some anger management therapy."

"This would go on my record. It'll show up every time someone runs a background check on me?"

"Yes. However, most employers and creditors only pay for searches for felony convictions. In two years after you have completed your sentence we could petition to have this offense expunged from your record."

The Internet article states that the necktie paradox is really just a variant of the two-envelope paradox, a classical study for applying statistics to decision making. I remember reading about the two-envelope case when I was interested in game theory. The twist with the necktie scenario is that it's based around a wager between two friends. I feel a prolonged silence pulling me back to the phone conversation.

"What's my other option?"

"You could plead not guilty and fight this as a result of extenuating circumstances. If we are successful in convincing a jury, you'd be declared innocent. Risks are higher here. The prosecutor would likely go for a felony conviction. Sentencing for felonies are much longer than misdemeanors. You lose and you'd be looking at some jail time. Less than three years."

"I could walk away free and clear."

"Yes it's possible."

"Extenuating circumstances?"

"We'd have to prove that your behavior was the result of some other person's actions. Something a normal person would have a hard time ignoring. Have to get the right jury, but it could be done."

There is really only one choice to be made here. Logically the risks are too great for me to fight this. Society will demand that someone pay for what was done to Jimmy Lee, and rightfully it should be, must be, me. The time to accept this fact is upon me. But not before I screw with this arrogant ambulance chaser a bit more. Even a prisoner with a death sentence gets to savor his last meal.

Looking back at my computer screen, I think about betting, wagers. A snippet of a conversation comes to my head and I type "Pascal's Wager" into the Wikipedia search box.

"The judge let us push this out during your coma. You're probably looking at a preliminary hearing in two weeks. I'll need time to build a defense. An answer today, now, would be best."

I start to scan the article on my screen. Memories of reading about Pascal, the mathematician, come back to me. I recall being impressed by the extremely logical, dispassionate way he broke down complex problems.

"Mr. Pederson…"

The Pascal article is worthy of my complete focus. Time to get rid of the audio annoyance. Before my bedroom can be filled with more lawyer droppings.

"Take the DA's offer," I say as I push the button to terminate the call.

***

The sun is only an hour away from calling an end to the day as I head out our front door. Stacey asked if I wanted company and I said no. I told her the walk was part of my physical therapy. It was a lie. That article on Pascal's Wager is not settling in my mind.

As I reach the sidewalk in front of our house, I have a choice to make. Left or right? I choose left, west. I walk toward the light.

My pace is slow, but it has improved over the last four weeks. I take a deep breath and settle into a comfortable shuffle. This will not be a quick walk; the conflict in my mind isn't a light one.

The rules of Pascal's wager: God exists or He doesn't. A game of chance is being played with all of humanity. There is no way to reason, scientifically, rationally, or philosophically, that either choice is correct. There is not enough information to make a good choice and yet the universe demands that we must.

I hear the patter of paws on cement behind me. It's a little dog who is moving fast to catch me. I don't look back, hoping he won't find me interesting enough to investigate. The mongrel begins to yip and yap. Hello Mitch, he barks, you will have no peace while I'm here.

I look down as the Chihuahua arrives. An oversized rodent. The dog moves to nip at my foot, but backs off quickly as I take a step. It barks again, in that annoying little dog manner, and moves in as my closest foot comes to a rest. A dance between us begins. The dog lunging forward first, then retreating, yapping out a canine salsa beat as it looks for an opportunity to sink its teeth into my person.

I decide to ignore my miniature deterrent. Pascal, a brilliant mathematician and physicist, argues that the only way to make a choice in this wager is to consider the results of each choice. If I continue on my path of denying God's existence and I'm correct, I have neither gained nor lost anything. If He does exist, I'm destined for an existence of eternal suffering. The equivalent of several hundred Chihuahuas attacking me simultaneously, never relenting?

The dog succeeds in getting his teeth around my shoelace. I swing my foot in an exaggerated arc hoping to loosen his grip. It doesn't work. I come to a stop as he tugs with all his might. I look around hoping that his owner will arrive to reclaim his vermin and rescue me. The street is empty of other humans. Looking down again, I kick hard in the dog's direction. This frees his toothy hold on my shoe and sends his body skidding several feet on the sidewalk. I scan the street again to make sure I have no witnesses.

The dog recovers his footing and I'm grateful. I wasn't hoping to hurt him. He shakes his head rapidly, resetting his vision and resumes his barking. My gratitude for his health diminishes quickly.

In the article there were those who found fault with Pascal's logic, claiming among other things that his wager didn't prove God's existence or that He may not be all that nice a supreme being. Flawed thinking on the part of his critics. Pascal wasn't trying to prove God was real, just that we'd better make a decision and do some real digging. Pascal was a Christian. In the interest of being complete, one should consider spiritualism, Buddhism, Confucianism, and all the other "-ism's". Not sure I'm going to give that much effort. I can't see myself getting in line with anything that doesn't make intellectual sense.

If I choose to believe in a supreme being and He does exist, I win a life of bliss, whatever that is, and an infinite future in heaven, wherever that may be. Although I cannot comprehend this, I'll give Pascal the benefit of the doubt here. This would be a great return on my wager.

Where I cannot agree with him is in the last outcome. Pascal says there is no cost beyond wasting one's time for believing in a God that does not exist. What about the intellectual humiliation? Other rational men of science would rightfully mock me. That is not to be ignored in my book.

The dog returns, ready for round two. My frustration with his interruption of my walk is tempered by a respect for his determination. I know despite his size he is a worthy opponent. He won't quit. His heart is bigger than his body suggests. There is no escaping his pint-sized fury.

I stand still now and let him have at my shoe. He growls and tugs, his little body shaking with the effort. For me the choice is an eternity in hell versus a lifetime of mockery by men I claim to respect. I know the derision I would face because I have participated in the ridicule myself. From the universe's perspective it would be poetic justice for me to switch sides and fill the role of a fool.

Inwardly I shudder. I just don't see that kind of emotional bravery in myself. I have always thought I didn't care about another man's opinion of me. Is this yet another thing I believed about myself that isn't ringing true?

With the little dog still attached, I turn about and begin the trek back to my house. I have not gone very far in my walk but distance was never the goal. This is a journey that will not be completed today. I'll leave my choice in this wager for another time. My little combatant friend remains locked on my shoe as I drag him toward my front door.

Chapter 46

A small yellow plane banks overhead, making a final turn to line up for its landing at a nearby airfield. The engine sputters as the pilot reduces his speed. It's lower than the normal approach, about 100 feet above the tree line. From my seat in our backyard, I can make out a passenger. The plane moves faster than I can easily track. I piece together visual snapshots my eyes manage to capture. An elderly female. She appears to be enjoying herself.

I've never liked to fly. Not sure why. The numbers show it's very safe. The engineer in me knows this. My discomfort is buried deep within that emotional part of my brain. Could do without that part.

Stacey is approaching with another lawn chair and a glass of iced tea. After several weeks we have arrived at a détente in our relationship. Real peace seems to be just out of our grasp. Neither of us is inclined to speak of our troubles; the status quo feels preferable to another round of going-nowhere talks.

She hands me the glass and arranges her chair to face mine. This upcoming scene is probably her attempt to urge along the healing process. Or she's about to insist we enlist a marriage counselor again. Either way I'd rather be on an airplane.

"Good workout?"

"The only thing good about this round of physical therapy is that it was my last one."

"You've hit all their goals?"

"All my goals."

"Is this about money? I could ask my uncle for a

loan."

I take a deep breath followed by a sip of the tea. No man worth a shit wants to borrow money from his in-laws. Some things women will never understand about us. I continue to nurse my tea for another minute, waiting until I can reply with no visible exasperation.

"We're going to be okay financially."

"How's that?"

That marriage counselor admonished me to never lie to Stacey. Now that's some make-believe bullshit. Is it really loving to share *everything* when you know it's only going to hurt her? I know the right path here.

"We could last several years, longer if we cut back on things."

"You sure?"

The woman's not going to make this easy. "Spoke with our insurance agent last week. HR at CommGear yesterday. We've got enough left in my 401K if things get real bad."

"What about health insurance?"

The sound of an airplane engine straining against the effects of gravity invades our conversation. I pause until it's out of earshot.

"CommGear has to let former employees stay on their policy for at least eighteen months. They could have denied us because of my actions but Frank stepped in and vouched for me. I wasn't guilty of gross misconduct. Premiums are higher now that I don't work there, but doable."

"No lapse in coverage?"

"My hospital bills will be covered by the other driver's insurance."

Stacey tilts her head slightly downward, maintaining eye contact. A librarian looking over the top of her eyeglasses. She doesn't wear glasses, but I recognize the move. There's more to what she's saying and I'm missing it.

I take a deep breath and let it out slowly as I slink down lower in my seat.

"Don't make me guess."

Her mouth opens and closes again without a word being uttered. Her eyes begin to glisten and she turns her head away. Shit. I toss the remaining tea from my glass as if it's the drink that's causing my stomach to turn over.

Why didn't she just tell me it was something serious?

I place the glass on the lawn and advance toward my wife. The gap between us is only four feet, but it seems to be growing as I struggle to bridge it. Damn these legs and damn the physical therapy that has left them even weaker!

I finally reach her, take her hands and ease her to her feet. We hug silently. I hold her as her breaths return to a normal pace. In my periphery I notice the yellow plane again lining up for its final approach. The first attempt must have gone awry.

I break the silence. "We'll deal with this."

Softly she speaks. "Our family is...growing."

Growing? She can't be pregnant. We haven't been together since my accident. Stacey wouldn't stray. This might be nothing after all. Probably that loser brother of hers got his girlfriend knocked up again and wants some help. Just till he can get on his feet. Not going to happen.

"Now's the time to focus on immediate family," I say.

I try to ease Stacey away so I can see her face. She buries her head in my chest. Her muffled voice reaches my ears.

"I need you to...help."

I shouldn't have told her we'd be okay money-wise. Now she's bent on giving it away. To a loser who fathers kids with no thought of their future. My wife will probably always let her emotions lead her actions with no thought to the consequences. It's her marital yin for my yang. I know I should be grateful for her balancing effect and maybe someday I'll learn to be. The best I can do now is to feign patience.

"Let's get our money situation straightened out here before we go reaching out to help your brother."

Stacey pulls her head away from me enough to shake it and then returns her body to its previous position, coupled closely to mine. Her arms squeeze me in a hug that seems to have the goal of combining us on a molecular level. My back and sides ache from her efforts. I sense that her pain in this moment is greater than mine. This will soon change. Our agony will even out. My shirt muffles her voice as she continues.

"No more trips to the highway."

My breathing sputters, not from Stacey's grip. This lady has always known me better than I know myself. It's good that I can't see her face now. There is nowhere to hide, no more lies left to tell.

I look for words to express the disappointment I feel in myself. To let her know that I realize I hurt her with my stupid act of cowardice. No matter what she did, nothing justifies my actions that day. In the end, I push my lips into her hair and whisper.

"I'm so very sorry. I never stopped loving you."

The words fall from my mouth and lie at our feet. We continue holding each other, staring at the words I have spoken. Slowly we sway to some unheard music. Healing is taking place and neither of us moves to interrupt the process. After a few minutes I feel the tension leave Stacey's body. She has picked up my words and brought them inside her. I can only hope they reach their intended target, her heart.

I take Stacey's arms and position her to face me fully. Gently I place my mouth to hers. We hold this kiss as tears fall from our eyes, mixing on our lips. How could I have wanted to cut short even one second from the time I've been given with this beautiful lady?

Our kiss ends and we separate slightly, smiling at each other. The emotion is too raw for me and I look away after a few moments. Stacey pulls a Kleenex from her pocket and dabs at her face. Her makeup has smeared and her efforts are futile. With no mirror she can't see this. She looks at me for confirmation that she is presentable. I lift her hand to my mouth and kiss her palm.

Both of her hands cradle my face, forcing me to look directly at her. I open my mouth to speak, not knowing what I will say. Her hands squeeze my cheeks, ever so slightly. I stop as an unspoken signal passes between us.

In the distance I hear wailing sirens. They could be coming from the airfield. Stacey doesn't seem to notice as she speaks.

"Alyssa's pregnant."

Chapter 47

We're seated in our normal spots around the Pederson table. Jacob is to my left, Alyssa to my right, Stacey straight on. Most evenings Jacob can be relied on to carry the bulk of the conversational load. I'm counting on his help tonight because I'm beyond reluctant to join in the suppertime bibble-babble. My mind is still churning from the natal bomb my wife dropped on me.

The oversized sunflower clock behind me ticks off each second like a cheesy gong in a Chinese restaurant. The clinking of silverware on plates adds to the melodic sounds of our dinner. Jacob had to pick this night to be stoic.

Stacey made corn on the cob for our meal. A noisy food that is almost impossible to eat with your head down. Looking up means that I might make eye contact with my fifteen-year-old ex-virgin daughter. A movie with my half-naked teenage girl starts to play in my mind and I shake my head violently to bring it to a stop. Butter flies from my lips as a result. Jacob laughs. I continue attacking the corn.

I rest my elbows on the table, creating a human shield between myself and the things I'd rather not encounter. This posture is not allowed at our family dining table and Jacob begins to protest. From the bowels of my stomach I pull forth the coldest look I own and toss it haphazardly in his direction. I'm not really angry with him, but he had the misfortune of walking through my crosshairs.

This loveless gaze does its job too well. Jacob's bottom lip starts to quiver. Stacey rises from her chair and moves to soothe our son. I'd like to apologize, explain that it's the circumstances of my life that are annoying me, but

I'm paralyzed. I remove my left hand from the cob and shift my body to protect myself from the motherly scorn that will soon be upon me. My defenses are in place too late; her disappointed glare is a spear stuck in my ribs.

I turn my focus on the mound of mashed potatoes on my plate. I caution myself to take small bites, chewing thoroughly. Too fast and I'll need to refill my plate. The bowl of potatoes is to my right, near Alyssa. I've got to draw this out. The order of meal conclusion is static in our house: Jacob, Alyssa, then Stacey and me. To finish early would break a routine that has long ago been adopted.

I wish I'd have thought to fake an upset stomach.

Stacey is self-conscious about her mashed potatoes, sure that they're never good. She's tried numerous recipes and alternative methods to prepare them. Success has always eluded her and not by a narrow margin. I've told her that her spuds are great for almost two decades and I'll keep right on lying until they bury me.

This brings forth another problem. It's better to eat her potatoes quickly. The faster the lumpy mass gets past your taste buds, the easier it is to hide any telling facial expressions. Pull the Band-Aid off fast and get the pain over with.

My toil continues until I scoop the remaining heap of potatoes on to my fork. It's too large for one bite. I realize my mistake instantly, but shaking some of the stubborn goo back onto my plate would necessitate a violent movement on my part. This would draw too much attention so I plunge forward recklessly.

The natural gag mechanism kicks in. I toss my fork to the table and grab my water glass. I take a large gulp but my throat is clogged and there is no place for the water to go. I breathe deeply through my nose as I wave away everyone's concerns. Any hope for flying under the radar is lost.

At last the water does its job and I'm able to swallow a clump of the vegetable. A loud wheeze comes from my throat as I greedily suck in air. My chest hurts and I lean back in my chair, enjoying the prospect of returning to normal breathing. I glance at Stacey and try to offer a pacifying look. A look of pain begins to creep over her face.

A voice comes from the one I wish to ignore.

"Good potatoes, huh?"

I give her the thumbs-up sign. Not sure my voice has returned and I don't trust what I might say.

Alyssa continues. "Want some more?"

I look at Alyssa, then Stacey and finally back to Alyssa. Left with no other choice, I nod my head dutifully.

Alyssa grabs the bowl and scoops out a large spoonful of spuds. She plops it on my plate and goes back for a second helping.

"Say when."

She is moving faster than I can respond. Before I can signal her to stop she has put three heaping mounds of the white clay in front of me. I'm looking at the mountaintop of potatoes cresting at almost four-and-a-half inches, wondering how I will force myself to get this down.

Alyssa grabs the gravy boat. "You're going to need some of this, too."

The brown substance plip-plops, chunk after chunk, until it annihilates the white mound. I never put Stacey's gravy on my potatoes. I'm not that good a husband.

Stacey tries to intervene. "Don't be wasteful."

"Don't worry Mama," Alyssa goes on, her voice almost breaking, "Daddy would much rather eat all these fine potatoes than talk to a daughter he's embarrassed of."

Stacey grabs her napkin from her lap and dabs at her

eyes. Her lips move as if to speak, but no sounds come out.

Alyssa grabs a spoon and slowly scrapes the last of the congealing mass of gravy onto my plate. Satisfied with her effort she puts the gravy boat down with a thud.

"Bon appetit."

I stare at my daughter's handiwork as I slip into reflection. Alyssa was ten days old before Stacey and I were allowed to hold her for the first time. A preemie, we could only touch her through a plastic shield. It was almost three weeks to the day when we were finally permitted to bring her home.

There are times I still feel cheated over those lost moments of holding her, smelling her newness. CommGear generously gave me extra time off to spend with our little girl. It wasn't enough. Never could be. I greedily lapped up every second I could spend with this tiny package.

Stacey and I would run in stocking feet down the hallway, out-of-control roller derby stars, jostling each other with love, laughing as we bounced against the walls, striving to win the chance to pick our baby up first after a nap. The victor received the right to inhale the sweetest of nectar, baby's breath. Our home has never been the same since Alyssa entered it.

I recall the prize-winning picture my daughter took and I know I'm being punished for not being the dad she needs. She gets pregnant and I'm expected to masterfully continue the fatherly dance, not missing a step. I should somehow be understanding, soothing? I'd like to be able to offer those things, but that cupboard is bare.

I stare at my hands as if in them lies the answer. All feeling has been removed from me, leaving a hollow void. I want to scream at my daughter that I do love her. I've never stopped. I long to be all that she needs, wants. My eyes begin to get moist, but I cough loudly, three times, creating a diversion while I rein in my emotions.

There is no alternative except to soldier on until my life clicks in gear. There have been dry gullies in the past, but never so long and so deep. I have no remedy for this situation but time. All things, good and bad, must eventually end.

I pick up my fork once again.

Chapter 48

I keep my head lowered and eyes averted from passersby as I pull Stacey's minivan into an open spot between a Mercedes and a Land Rover. This Starbuck's is in an upscale location which is frequented by execs. I would have rather parked some distance away, but running late, I had no choice. I try to calm myself by thinking that this would make a good Hollywood story. Arrested, fired from my job, almost killed, pregnant teenage daughter. Pull myself up by my bootstraps. Rise from the canvas. You can do this, Mitch. Just one thing, Mr. Director, please, no more potatoes.

"Mitch."

Frank is sitting at a table on the patio. Black V-neck sweater, dark slacks, casual shoes. There's no such thing as a power suit. If you need clothes to make you feel in control, you'll never have it. My old boss, the man who has been my mentor for most of my adult life, has never come up short in that area.

Frank taps the half-empty coffee cup in front of him. "You want something?"

"I'm amped enough without the caffeine."

"Feel like you're ready to get back in the game?"

I move to take the seat opposite him. Despite my continued exercises, it's a slower process than I like. I use the extra time to consider a response. This man spent years grooming me to take his place only to have all that washed away in one embarrassing moment. It seems that he should be looking for any way to distance himself from the mistake that I turned out to be. Finally seated, I look him in the eyes.

"I am."

"You might be looking at going the start-up route."

"Pete mentioned something similar."

"A friend of mine has a concept to provide a seamless link between social network sites and TV. Got some angel investors lined up, but he needs a face for the company. He's the kind who doesn't want to leave the lab. I could put a plug in for you."

"I'd be grateful."

"You made a mistake which shut the door for you here, but you'll learn from this and go on to be a better leader somewhere else. Life doesn't end outside the walls of CommGear."

A pigeon lands on the ground at the feet of a nearby table. He hops about poking at an empty muffin wrapper. Searching for his next meal. I kick my foot in the direction of the bird and he flies off.

"The court came back with sentencing for the Jimmy Lee incident. Forty hours of community service and a $750 fine. In four years it'll be wiped from my records. Need to get the forty hours done before I start my next position."

Frank takes a sip of his coffee and nods his head. "That'll solve the public restitution, what about the personal side?"

I stand up, jarring the table slightly in the process. Frank's cup doesn't topple.

"Think I could handle something to drink after all. Want a refill?"

Frank shakes his head. There is no line at the counter and the barista asks what I want. I search the menu board over her shoulder and choose raspberry passion tea lemonade. I feel my manhood ebbing from my body the instant I order it, but it's cheap and quick. I'm back at our table in less than three minutes.

Frank picks up our discussion. "I spoke with your sister-in-law before we let her go. Family is more important than work, but it's not the place to solve marital problems. How's that going?"

I take a sip of my tea and grimace. I think about adding something, but what do you add to sweet toilet water to make it taste good?

"We're hanging in there."

"There's still a loose end that needs your tending. It'll make it easier for me to attract backers for you."

I take another sip of the tea and let out a big sigh. When does this stuff begin to calm a person? Did they make it wrong?

"There are many execs with bad marriages," I say.

Frank half-rises and tosses his empty cup toward a nearby trash can. It hits the lip and teeters for a moment before falling in.

"True. Stacey's a good woman. I trust you'll fix that. I was thinking of something else that needs to be repaired."

I get up and toss my ill-conceived purchase in the trash. I've got no idea what loose end he's referring to. A sourness is growing in my stomach and it's not just the tea. I return to my seat.

"You're going to have to spell this one out for me."

"Jimmy Lee."

Frank is looking at me, unblinking. This is why he invited me here this morning. He could have helped me out without this get-together. This was always the main item on his agenda and now we've arrived.

"What are you looking for?"

"You need to apologize. In person. That's the kind of leader a company needs and the kind I will feel good about recommending."

Scenes flash through my head. A closed office door cutting an anti-social engineer off from society, black shock of hair continuously falling into that perpetually arrogant face, and finally his body curled in a fetal position. A pool existed in the shipping department to pick who would hit him first. Seems like he chose this path as much as I did. Life's not fair and maybe it's his turn to find out. No one's running up to apologize to me.

"Not sure about that. My lawyer probably doesn't want me talking to him until the matter is settled in court."

"Lawyers are there to advise, not direct. Leaders lead. You need to do this for yourself. Not out of concern for your career or fear of a lawsuit."

My last exit from CommGear was in handcuffs. I spent almost two decades with these people. Surely they know that wasn't the real Mitch Pederson.

"I'm gonna have to think this one through."

"Don't think too much."

Frank shakes my hand and apologizes as he leaves for some important meeting. There's not a damn thing pressing in my life, so I stay in my seat. Three pigeons begin to scavenge at the foot of Frank's chair. They're timid at first but begin to get bolder. I move my leg in their direction and they fly away only to swoop back in a matter of seconds. Each time I kick at them they return quicker. Tiny vultures not to be denied. Willing to put up with a slight nuisance to get what they need.

After a few minutes I get up and buy a banana nut muffin and return to my table. As I break off tiny morsels and toss them to my new friends, scavengers like myself, I realize that I have yet to hit bottom. When faced with a difficult situation in the past, I've always felt like I knew the right thing to do, the path of integrity.

This time the path is clear, but will I walk it?

Chapter 49

I turn my car toward a visitor space in the CommGear parking lot. A quick glance to my right evidences that the VP Engineering spot is vacant. I know that someday it will be filled, but I also know I'm not ready to see this just yet. I was the prince who all knew would someday become king. Today I'm a disgraced knight returning and no one gives a shit.

With the car parked and engine silenced, I rustle through papers sitting on the passenger seat. They have nothing to do with my visit here, but do offer me a pause to collect myself.

The theme of my entire life, as far back as I can remember, has been one of competition. To apologize to another man, if not defeat, is a sign of weakness. I know that I could forgo this next step, tell Frank thank you for all he's done for me, and move on. Deep inside of me, at the core of my being, I feel something gurgling that will not permit this. It's not about the prospects of a new job. I stole something from Jimmy Lee and I must return it. To do any less would be an act of cowardice.

I called ahead and spoke with Pete. Asked him to set up the meeting in the conference room just off the lobby. The receptionist isn't expecting a visit from this ex-executive, and looks away quickly. Just as well. As I'm about to poke my head in the conference room, I notice Pete entering the lobby.

"He won't come out to see you."

"You assured him it was okay?"

"He tells me it's not necessary."

"Take me to him."

The receptionist, no longer pretending I don't exist, says that she's not sure if she can let me go back there. A look passes between Pete and the receptionist. Pete uses his employee badge to open the electronic lobby doors and motions me in. I toss him a thank you and head toward my quest.

The door is closed, but the light leaking through the glazed window shows me he's in there. I knock and enter, not waiting for a reply. This needs to be done quickly, before security or other witnesses arrive. He raises his head from a lab notebook, his eyes quickly displaying recognition and then confusion. "Why are you here?"

"I want to tell you something and then I'll leave."

Jimmy Lee rolls his chair away from the desk and leans back. I expected fear to be present his eyes, his manner, but it's strangely absent. In all the years we have worked together, I have never seen him so relaxed. He doesn't speak but a nod of his head suggests that I have his permission to continue.

"I will stay over here, no closer."

I keep my back pressed to the closed door and lower myself into a sitting position, legs crossed, Indian style.

"I'm ashamed of what I did in the lab that day. No man deserves to be treated that way. I have struggled for the right words to tell you how sorry I am. I have humiliated myself and my family by my thoughtless actions. Whatever reasons I may have had are worthless as an excuse for such behavior."

I look at the man I have embarrassed, waiting for some sign. Passive aggressiveness, cool indifference, full frontal attack. I've imagined them all as responses to my apology. The slightest of smiles forming on his lips catches me off guard. Is he finding joy in the moment before he goes in for the kill?

"I have forgiven you."

My mouth kicks in before I can stop it. "How can you do that?"

He uses his right hand to move that ever-present shock of hair from his eyes. His gaze is locked on mine.

"I must."

Between this job and his time in college I know that Jimmy Lee has lived in the US for over a decade. Some pieces of our country and its laws must have still escaped him. He doesn't comprehend there is no danger left for him.

"No one will harm you," I explain.

Jimmy Lee shakes his head. I expect that for centuries his people have submitted in fear to their rulers, good and evil. No exceptions. How can I hope to overcome this culture? I know that I must try.

"There's no reason to be afraid. The laws," I wave my hands to encompass the whole building, "the management of this place are here to protect you."

He is shaking his head with even more passion. "I was adopted by an American family when I was eleven years old. They brought me to San Francisco when I spoke no English. My step-parents spoke no Korean. There was food and a warm bed. I was lucky. Such older boys in the orphanage often go unclaimed.

"Television was my teacher and for years my only friend. I worked hard in school. My mother treated me with love, but she was a busy woman. Helping at food shelters and halfway houses. My father pushed me. Always better. B's were not good enough. Must be A's. He said I had come to them later in life and there was much ground to make up.

"He whipped me with his belt. Leather end for getting only a B. Metal buckle for C's. Always on my back where it wouldn't show. In my ninth-grade physical education class I saw that other boys who were not good students had no bruises. I was confused. What had I done to deserve this?"

The muscles in my legs begin to cramp as nerve endings fire randomly up and down my left side. I'd like to stand and walk it off but I settle for uncrossing and stretching my screaming legs. I cough to cover any facial reactions. What is my temporary pain compared to what is being described to me?

Jimmy Lee continues, "I learned to forgive my father for what he did. It was not out of fear, but love. I've chosen to forgive you in the same way too."

Love? He loves me like his father? I lick my lips, but the dryness I feel is deeper, in my throat. I struggle to make my words audible.

"There may not be a way to make this right, but I'd like to. Is there anything I can do for you, your career, your family to make this good?"

"I forgive you; there is no more debt. Nothing you need repay."

How much more has this strange man had to forgive? From where does he get such wisdom? Such peace?

"Is this a Korean thing that you're talking about? This forgiveness."

Jimmy Lee emits a small chuckle. "Silly American. It's there for anyone."

Before I can slow myself a question leaps from my mouth. "Where?"

He is smiling now. A big toothy, broad one. Not pretty, but happy in a way that I never expected to see on this man. I try to look away but am compelled to keep his gaze. He does not speak, but slowly reaches into the top left-hand drawer of his desk.

From my lower vantage point I can't tell what he pulls from the drawer. His right arm goes back slightly and he flips it at me like a Frisbee. It appears to be a book, black, soft cover, maybe leather, obviously weathered.

The pages flap wildly as it tumbles toward me. I lurch forward to save it from any further damage. It comes to rest upside down in my hands. The back cover is blank. I feel the sound of my heart beating in my ears as I turn it over.

We had one of these in our house when I grew up. Not sure what became of it when my mom passed. It sat on a shelf, dust-covered and never opened. This is not to say it served no purpose.

My old man would pick the opportune moment to take it down from its resting place, blow off the dust, and make me swear on it. He thought it useful for determining guilt and extracting oaths. It might have worked had I believed in its contents. Maybe if he had shown me that he did.

Staring at the cover of The Bible for a few more seconds, I make no move to open it. The book feels cool to my touch. I think of the pastor's visit in the hospital and the article on Pascal's wager. A chill rises up from my stomach to my throat. I feel like I'm Custer in his last moments, utterly surrounded with no hope of escape.

I rise to my feet, legs arguing against the process the entire way. Jimmy Lee is watching me. I know this without looking. I place the book carefully, front cover down, on his desk and mumble, "Thank you for listening to me."

As I open his office door to leave, I notice two security guards standing outside. They appear at the ready to stop a skirmish. I've no idea how long they've been there or why they didn't announce themselves. Swiftly, for a man with lingering injuries, I step between them and move toward the lobby. I've accomplished what Frank asked of me. My words to Jimmy Lee were rehearsed but true. On the drive here I had played out this scene in my mind; always I had expected to feel relieved. My stomach is anything but peaceful in this moment.

Chapter 50

A noisy fight is mounting. Squeaking tennis shoes on a gym floor wage a battle against exuberant yelling. Each rises in frequency and volume, waves crashing on a cliff. A basketball game is going on, but it seems of little importance. Childhood-generated noise, unrestrained by adults, is the true measurable. I'm in a small room just off the court, where I'd like to shut the door. I can't because my visitor, my tutee, hasn't arrived yet. I need to make him feel welcome despite my distaste for what we must do here today.

The judge gave me forty hours helping seventh through twelfth-graders with math. Arithmetic was my first love. In my early teens when I found myself alone, I'd make up math problems and solve them. The kids I'm here to help were the type that thought me socially unfit back then. I felt the same about them. Decades later the battle continues.

The twenty-first century version of James Dean walks through the door. Mad at something, everything, and he doesn't know why. Long red hair brought into a ball on top of his head, Chinese warrior style. White tee shirt with an obscenity emblazoned across the front, baggy jeans riding below his hips, athletic shoes with no laces. Probably doesn't know how to tie them anyways.

"You Pederson?"

"Yeah. Can you grab the door?"

He kicks the door shut with excessive dramatics and plops into the chair across from me. A table and a mountain of differences lie between us. I notice that he has no books or other material. "What do you need help with?"

"Nothing. Just want my old man and the AP to get off

252

my ass."

"AP?"

"Assistant Principal." He stops to roll his eyes. "Said come down to the Y, do my time with some number-head and I can stay in school. It's all bullshit, but I'll play their game for a while."

"It's going to be hard to play the game if you didn't bring anything. What kind of math are you taking?"

He leans back in his chair and crosses his arms, holding them at chest level. His red ball of hair starts bobbing in time with some imaginary tune. "Algebra."

A loud thud reverberates through the room and I jump involuntarily. Something hit the door. Voices seep into our space, unintelligible yet excited. The game continues.

"So you don't want to work on any math?"

With excessive flair he uncrosses his arms and reaches into his right front jeans pocket. He swings his arm in a fully extended arc and slams a wad of bills, about four inches thick, on the table.

"The only math I need is to count my money."

The stack is askew and I can tell that the bills are twenties. A few thousand dollars. I stop myself from calculating an exact figure. He wants me to ask where he got that kind of money. I won't.

"We're both supposed to sign paperwork showing we worked on math for an hour. What say we both just do that now and you take your money somewhere else to count?"

I realize the judge would frown on the lie I've proposed, but my real debt to society was paid when I apologized to Jimmy Lee. Wasn't that the payment the world should have been looking for, the face-to-face admittance of wrongdoing? There is no greater cost to a man than to humble himself. The court system gave me the equivalent of forty hours of adult timeout. Which lesson is there left for me to learn here?

Fraudulent papers signed, I have thirty-five minutes to myself before the next tutee arrives. I pull a copy of Popular Photography from my briefcase and glance at a few articles. Nothing is grabbing me. The magazine that was once the sprinkled sugar on the dessert of my life is now without sweetness. No job equals no discretionary income for hobbies.

The inability to enjoy the magazine reminds me of the things that still need repair in my life. My career, my marriage and what in the hell am I going to do about my daughter. I'm not completely sold on going to work for a start-up, but it's the best path available at this time. Turning over a few rocks in that yard will probably yield an opportunity or two are worth pursuing. Anything I find is going to take a great deal of time to get going. Time away from my family. Stacey will need to understand this one last time.

No father enjoys the shame of a teenage daughter getting knocked up. I can only hope that my shame passes. As her father I'm obliged to guide her toward good choices. She doesn't need a baby at this young age.

Motion in the doorway breaks me from these thoughts. Teenage girl, long brown hair, skinny jeans and an oversized letterman's jacket. The owner of the jacket stands behind her, his arms around her waist. His hands start to slide where they shouldn't go in public and she swats them away with a giggle. Early in the romance stage when you can't keep your hands off each other.

The young man speaks. "One of us is here for math tutoring."

"Guessing that it's not you," I reply.

The young lady has her hands on her hips in a mock

annoyed posture. "Why would you think that?"

I counter with my own theatrical pose, that of a wizened teacher lecturing his freshmen class. "Females don't often appreciate the beauty of mathematics."

The boy nods his head as I motion his partner to have a seat.

"Name's Mitch."

"I'm Lisa and he's Tim."

Tim crosses his arms and smiles. It's a crooked smile, not the kind for a family portrait. "I could help her with this stuff but she can't keep her hands off me long enough to catch on."

He leans in to kiss her cheek but she turns her head away laughing. "Go play basketball with the other little boys."

The boy steals the kiss he was after and swiftly exits the room.

From her backpack she pulls a math book, pre-Algebra. Some cute girls have eyes that reflect light, twinkling. This one's eyes are that rare kind that seem to draw you in, a well with no bottom, a long fall to your death. Dangerous. A man would give his soul to be drawn into those eyes. I knew a girl like this once.

"Let's get going on this so you can get back to your boyfriend."

She smiles, not so innocently. "He'll be there when I'm ready."

I notice that the noise has stopped. Suddenly the silence is broken by an announcer identifying players for what must be an upcoming game. A smattering of applause follows each name.

As I begin to walk Lisa through the first problem, music infiltrates the room. Lost in the glow of mathematics, I hum along for a few moments. At last the lyrics of the song, the national anthem, rise to the forefront of my consciousness. Memories flood my thoughts and I feel my face breaking into an unbeckoned smile. I know I should snap out of this, but I've no desire to curtail this feeling of bliss. After another minute I push myself back from the table.

"I'm sorry but we're going to have to reschedule this. I just realized there's something priceless I need to go repair."

Chapter 51

My uncle Greg once said wives were like cars. When they're new you love looking at them in your driveway. Over time they develop signs of wear. Newer models have some appeal, but the wise man realizes they'll need maintenance someday too. Unless you're going to be trading her in every few years, it's better to just stay with what you know.

Won't see that in a Hallmark card.

I have too much respect for Stacey to think of her that way. Still, somewhere along the way our relationship shifted from happy to content. I can't pinpoint an exact time, not even a year. It's not something I sensed happening. I would've stopped it had I known.

I need to talk with my wife. The goal for the conversation is clear enough, but I don't know how to start. She'd accuse me of over-thinking this. Probably true. It's twenty minutes from the school to our house. Longer if you take the back streets. I choose the rural path; it's longer.

The objective is to return to a point where our marriage was good. For me goodness departed our relationship just after that photo showed up in my office. Clearly it was bad for Stacey for much longer. How long? One year, five years, just after our honeymoon? I replay random events, happy and sad, from our marital history. I've missed signs along the way. Some intentional? I shudder when I realize I've got no idea how long she has been unhappy. Maybe she doesn't know either.

Uncle Greg preceded his wife in death. During his last two weeks we spent more time talking than the previous two decades. He spent a good deal of his final moments reflecting on his life. Mostly his failings. He danced around his regrets with his children, but spoke frequently about how he'd let my aunt down. I remember asking him what he intended to say to her.

He told me he had tried but couldn't get it out. How do you apologize for treating someone like a possession for thirty-seven years? How could he say it on his death-bed without it coming across as being selfish? Would they think he was just trying to make amends so people would think well of him after he died?

Several times during those final meetings my uncle cried. He said he'd had the ability to have been so much more. Never lived up to his potential. A wasted life. Through his tears he made me promise not to follow his example. I said yes because he was dying. What choice did I have?

Auto horns snap at my ears like that neighborhood Chihuahua. The traffic light before me is green. I have no idea how long I've been waiting here. I wave my hand as a form of apology and move forward. Ten minutes of the commute are left and the answer is still cloudy. Pete would tell me to just jump in. Just trust that a solution will come to me. That's how he runs his life. It works for him because he's a good man who people want to root for. Not the same for me. I collect adversaries more easily than well-wishers.

I'm not sure I'll ever really understand what drove her to pursue that phony blackmail scheme. She could have left me, but instead she concocted a crazy plan. The thought of quitting was not in her. She loves me more than I deserve.

An apology is due. To do it right I need to take her back to the point where I first went off course, where the hurting began. I'll need her help locating that place. A lifetime of vegetation has overgrown that painful landmark.

A chill causes me to shiver momentarily. Without thinking I immediately reach for the car's climate control knobs. I stop myself when I realize the cold is coming from my inside.

Will it take me lying on my death bed to finally get this right? The desire is within me, but I don't feel I have the tools to repair the damage I have caused. Something gnaws at me. I need help but don't know what it is or where to find it.

Chapter 52

Pulling onto my street, I can see that Stacey's car is not in the driveway. For a moment I think of running to the store to get flowers. Pathetic. A better thought comes to mind. I last helped out with household chores the night I was prepared to sign off.

Once inside, I quickly attack some mid-level domestic chores. Vacuuming, dishes, picking up after the kids in the living room. No need to do the laundry or scrub the toilets. That's hardcore. I didn't have an affair for God's sake. She'll be pleased with my help. Mostly because she didn't have to ask.

I'm just putting away the last of the clean silverware when the front door opens. Stacey walks in, no kids. Great. I'm saved from devising a plan to get her alone. A smile quickly covers her face. I've done well.

"It's good to see you smile."

"Good to have a reason," Stacey says.

I motion her to take a seat at the kitchen table. "That's an area I should have addressed long ago."

The smile dissipates from her face, replaced by a look I know too well. She's confused by my actions. Waiting for the other shoe to drop. In this moment I get a glimpse of the naked root of our problems. A long-rehearsed game is about to begin. My next move has always been to calm her and then explain why the thing I'm about to force her to accept will be in her best interests. The utter selfishness of my actions stares at me now, unblinking. Well Mitch?

The marriage counselor tried to warn me about such ritualistic arguments. It only takes one to stop this train. This time it will be me.

"Much of what happened between us I still don't understand, but there's a long list of the things I must have done to hurt you. I've made you feel so hopeless that drastic measures were needed to save our marriage. It was selfish and I want to begin to apologize."

Her face is pointed down as she moves the chair back from the table. I stare at her, trying to glean what her response will be. When she finally sits and returns my gaze, her eyes are moist. Her mouth opens and after a few moments shuts. Seconds later she tries again.

"Begin to apologize?"

I take my seat opposite her. Her hands are below the table, probably folded in her lap. I stretch my arms across the divide between us. She reads my signal and places her hands in mine.

"This is going to take time to turn around. I'll need your help."

A tear escapes from one of her eyes. "What caused this?"

"I saw something just now. Something innocent, beautiful. It reminded me of what we had, what I've thrown away."

She smiles. Memories of our early romance must be playing in her mind's theater. I give her hands an extra squeeze and lift them to give each a gentle kiss. We look at each other, no words pass between us until she simply says, "Thank you."

I nod my head in agreement.

"I have failed you when I've tried to fly solo."

Stacey cocks her head to one side, waiting for my next move.

I pause as I run through my options. A bad choice here

could bring the whole effort to a fiery end. Finally I select what should be the safest path.

"Alyssa's making a mistake."

Stacey separates her hands from mine, using one to push her hair back from her face. Her hands don't return to mine. I've blown it.

"Making?" Stacey asks.

I search the extent of my being for a loving response, but only logic comes to my mouth. I will always be an engineer.

"What else would you call not terminating a high school pregnancy?"

Stacey leans back as she runs her fingers through her hair. Front of her head to the back. Slowly.

"Our daughter doesn't see it that way."

The temperature in the room seems to drop a few degrees. Just minutes earlier Stacey had been smiling. Bliss was within my grasp and now it's slipped through my fingers. I struggle to locate the words. The ones that will bring us back on course to harmony.

"We have to work together to help her through this."

Her hands continue to make passes through her hair before finally stopping, forming small fists, and pulling, not so gently.

"And what would you suggest?"

Her voice travels past me, bouncing from wall to wall. I stare at her words looking for clues. This isn't going to end well and I'm pretty sure there will be no points given for good intentions.

"She can't keep it," I say.

"*It?*"

I stand and walk to the fridge. Reach inside for a bottle of water. We always seem to end up as combatants on a marital battlefield. I think about asking if she wants a drink, too, and decide against it. Is that against the Geneva Convention?

"Why don't you tell me what you want?"

Stacey rises and slowly retrieves her own drink from the refrigerator, shutting the door a bit too forcefully for my liking.

"I'm not ready to sign off on killing our grandchild."

I return to my seat, hoping she will follow my lead back to the peace table. She does but without amicable intent. She grabs her chair and turns it away from the table. She sits with her chest pushing against the back of the chair. It's an awkward position that probably hurts to maintain. She's facing me, but I'm not sure that's a good thing.

She takes a long swig from her bottle and then thoroughly examines the remaining contents. Seemingly satisfied with her efforts, without standing she tosses the half-empty container into the sink. The cap isn't on the bottle and the end-over-end path causes water to splash haphazardly on the floor and countertop.

We both stare at the mess she has made. Neither of us makes a move to clean up. I've done enough domestic chores for the month. A sarcastic reply shoots through my thoughts, but I keep it inside. I choose instead to focus on removing the label from my own water bottle.

"This isn't going the way I imagined," I finally say.

"It's going as I expected."

"Why are you so pissed?"

"How can you still not understand?" Stacey says in a higher octave.

Extricating the label is a process that will take several minutes if I hope to do so in one piece. One of the corners begins to show signs of tearing. I take a deep breath and move to a new corner. Not bothering to look at my adversary, I speak.

"I'm sitting here putting up with this shit. Doesn't that count for something?" I ask.

"You've got a better place to be?"

I slam my open hand down on the table. The glasses in the cabinet behind her rattle for a moment.

"Damn it!"

After six minutes of silence, the label comes off. It's not perfect, but it's intact. I allow myself a small smirk.

"You know I love this family," I say.

"You hide it well," Stacey adds softly.

I sigh audibly. "Why can't you make it easy for me? Just this once?"

"Life's not that simple," she says as stands and exits the room.

Chapter 53

I read somewhere Colonel Sanders was sixty-five and penniless when he finally got his big break. I'm still a couple of decades ahead of his pace. Leaders often see things others can't or won't. I just need someone to open the door a crack and I'll go storming in. Waiting is no longer an option.

With my community service complete and the apology delivered to Jimmy Lee, I'm primed for the next chapter in the Mitch Pederson success story. I turn my car into the gated entrance for Frank's neighborhood. I'm still driving a rental because I'm hoping to purchase a car fitting for my new role. An older model BMW was fine for a VP, but it won't do for CEO. The security guard allows my mid-tier Chevy to pass, but not without a look of disapproval. My mode of transportation should cause me to feel unworthy, outclassed. Not so today. Around the first corner, I sound the horn unnecessarily. Hear me, see me. The next time I return it will be in a chariot more fitting of my standing.

Frank's wife answers the door and directs me to the study. My former boss is seated in an oversized chair, feet bared. His toes stretch out individually in a slow rhythm, like tiny, fat snakes trying to capture the warmth of the sunlight as it pours through an immense window. He places the book he's been reading on the table nearby. Jane Austen. Never cared for her work. Aren't there enough good writers in our own country, our own generation? Waving to a white leather couch to his right, my former boss invites me to sit.

I shake his hand and then comply. "You look relaxed."

"You should try it some time."

I'm on the edge of a cliff grabbing at the last root that stands a chance of saving me from a black abyss. With this man's help I could soon be leading a new venture, a role where men have invested millions in the belief that I can make them even more. It's a surprise I can even sit. This is as relaxed as I'm going to get.

"Maybe next decade," I say.

Frank smiles and positions himself more upright. He takes a sip from a nearby cup. Smells like tea. It's probably English like the book. He moves the cup in my direction.

"Want some?"

There's only one thing I want right now and the glacier pace of this conversation is about to bring on apoplexy.

"I completed my community service and apologized to Jimmy Lee."

"How was that?"

"Not so bad. I like math."

Frank takes another sip of tea before replying.

"The apology."

Snapshots of that time spent in Jimmy Lee's office flash through my head. An unexpected visitor, my moment of humility, a piece of his childhood shared, and that toothy smile when I asked him how he could forgive me. My placing the book, unopened, unwanted, back on his desk. The trip's objectives were accomplished, but something is still unsettled.

"I got through it."

"I spoke with him."

I stand and walk to the window, my back to him. Across the street an elderly woman is tossing bread crumbs on her front lawn. Bluebirds, wrens, crows, sparrows and a pigeon yell at each other in their own avian dialect. Fighting for the prime spot to secure the next morsel. The woman isn't smiling, but there's a calmness about her demeanor. I feel as if I could watch her for an hour as she performs this simple task.

"Did I do okay?"

"He said that he respected you for what you did. He knew that it took a lot for you to humble yourself in that way."

"It needed to be done."

"I'm glad you see it that way."

A larger bird from a species I don't instantly recognize glides to the forefront of the bird skirmish. Its size and sudden appearance seem to startle the kind lady as she pauses and retreats a step. Taking advantage of this lull, I turn my attention back toward Frank.

"When can I meet with the investors?"

Frank refills his cup from a tea pot resting on the table at his side. One and one-half spoons of honey added. Five swirls of the spoon to mix the ingredients. Never does he vary.

"The meeting is not the issue."

Sudden movement through the window and across the street pulls me back. Birds scream as they depart the feeding grounds. All but one. It lies beneath the paws of a cat. A tabby, the sort of benign variety you might see in one of those ubiquitous cat food commercials. The cat is tense, the majority of its weight bearing down on the bird. It's a wren. Brown stripes covering its tiny body. Writhing frantically. One of the cat's paws slips from the prey's breast. The bird begins to flex and flap its wings with renewed vigor. Freedom and continued life are only a moment away. Nonplussed, the feline assassin lowers its head between the wings and the pattern of movement changes. The bird's body is now swinging from side to side in rhythm with the cat's head. The cat lowers itself on its haunches, no longer needing to pin the bird down.

Without facing Frank, I address his last comment.

"I'm not following."

"I can get you the meeting, but the prospects aren't good."

Spinning around now, I cross my arms and lock my eyes on my former boss. A defiant pose, but I've lost any desire for restraint.

"I did my part."

"The economy isn't what it was a few years ago. Seems they're skittish to invest in all but sure things just now. Give them some time."

Time is the one thing that I don't have. Well, patience too, but he already knows that about me. It might be months before something promising comes up again. Everything is riding on this. My family's well-being. This ain't a damn chess game being played over brandies in an oak-encrusted study; it's my life.

"How much time do they need? Five years, a decade? Should I just go back home and wait till they grow a pair?"

"I'd front it myself if I had enough capital."

"That's so comforting. I'd keep feeding my family if I had enough capital."

Frank's jaw is set, but no words come from his mouth. I've hurt him but he chooses not to retaliate. We look at each other for a few strained seconds. There's nothing left to say between us. I'm screwed and he can't help me. I nod my head and leave, not bothering with goodbyes.

As I pull from Frank's driveway, I notice the elderly woman sitting in a chair on her patio. Her placid demeanor is now replaced by a smile as she pets the satiated cat sitting in her lap. The innocent routine of an old lady feeding birds was just an act. A life lesson. The world enjoys setting you up just to watch you fall on your face.

The tabby stretches out, relaxed on its partner's legs. I

slow my car in front of the reclining old lady and lower the window on the passenger side. The purring of the cat is loud enough for me to hear it almost twenty feet away.

The woman looks up, having taken notice of my slowed vehicle. The smile remains fastened on her face as I stop the car and walk around to face her fully. I increase my gait and rapidly close the gap between us, all the while flapping my arms in the manner of a crazed bird. She sits paralyzed. The cat stands at attention now, stiff, frozen between the choices of fleeing and defending itself. When I start to throw obscenities in their direction, they both scurry from the front lawn in a desperate retreat.

I spit in their direction, smiling as I return to my outclassed car. It's a four-minute drive to exit this community. I keep my hand on the horn the entire way.

Chapter 54

The car is heading north. Home is south, but peace is not to be found in that port. As long as I thought myself to be the captain of my destiny, there was an ever-present wind billowing my sails. My hands firmly grasp the tiller, but I'm not in control. My only hope is to run aground somewhere before my boat breaks to pieces from a rogue wave. At least my father had the courage to end the charade.

I need to keep moving. I look down and the car is reaching sixty-five. Something pushes me faster. The highway is best. I-5 north. I spot a freeway entrance sign and jerk the wheel to the right. The tires squeal but hold fast. A car behind me toots his horn like a squawking bird. I've got to get free before I hurt anyone else. Oceanside is twenty-two miles.

I thought I had everything in my grip. After thirty-eight years of sleep-walking through my life, I wake up to find I'm screwed. I thought I was winning this game. My boss, my best friend, my family. Spectators who have been waving their arms like mad men, trying to get me to slow down. They saw the cliff I was heading for. I can almost see my father calling me now to follow him.

The interstate is five lanes wide here. My automobile hits eighty as I veer left and then right. Rocketing past bogies. The car is chewing up pavement as my mind races toward nowhere.

Throughout the past decade when rough times hit, I've rested my head on the notion that if my career worked out everything else would fall into place. It's clear now that Stacey would've eventually left me if I had taken over CommGear. A man standing on a mountaintop with no one to cheer for him. I was playing a game with no way to win. Why did it take me so damned long to see this?

There must be a path to happiness. Others seem to get there. Frank, Pete, Jimmy Lee. My map is no damn good. The boat I'm on is caught somewhere deep in the Bermuda Triangle.

My car's engine hesitates, then sputters momentarily. I'm no mechanic. If the car dies I can only call for help. The temperature gauge is well above normal. Damned rental. They should make them tougher. I guide the car onto the shoulder and press the brake pedal to the floor. The car shudders as the anti-lock brakes take control. I come to a stop just inches from a signpost.

Zombie-like, I pop the hood and exit the car. I walk to the front of the vehicle as if I have the skill to solve this problem. That's what we're supposed to do, right? Smoke and gurgling sounds escape from inside the engine compartment. I raise the hood and stare at a broken machine I can't fix.

After a few minutes, I break free from my trance. I look around, not for help, because I know there's no one coming. To my right, I see a hill. It's familiar. Spinning back to my left I see the bridge. I laugh out loud as if there's someone here to witness the irony.

I walk into the field where I had once aimed a hubcap. God knows it's stupid to stand in front of a car on the side of the highway. After twenty feet I turn toward the freeway, clear a spot in the grass and sit. I may not be able to see the ocean but it's late afternoon and I've got no place to be. I will not be denied a chance to witness another sunset.

This is my life. It's the only one I'm going to get and I've blown it. Everything I've done up till now to fix it has only made it worse. I need help; I see that now.

My vision lands on the spot where the accident took

place. I stare at the patch of asphalt as if the answers I need will suddenly appear.

Why did you let me live that night?

Am I the example you'll use to keep everyone else in line? Pay attention people, you don't want to end up like that fool.

Mitch Pederson, a cosmic joke.

Where's the fun in that? You're toying with me because you can? How insufferable are you? I thought you were the essence of love. Why don't you play fair? Show me the rules for this game you're playing and I'll win. This much you should know about me, if you really did create me. Wanna bet on me?

I grab my cell phone and begin to Google a name, a place, and directions. If I'm right the car will make it.

***

Early evening on a weekday. Are these places even open at this time? I didn't call ahead. Not sure what I would have said. I pull into an empty slot, far from the entrance.

I reach for the key to turn off the car, but pull my hand back. I could leave now and no one would notice.

A real man of science, an educated person, mocks what's in the building in front of me. The man I thought I was does not belong here. Where did that get me? Who cares anymore if the world sees me as an idiot? They should have seen me as a fool all along. Some of them probably did.

I open the car door and exit quickly. If not, I'll lose my nerve. Whatever lies before me can't be worse than my current state. They might have that map I'm looking for here. I have no real idea where I will end up.

Please forgive me, Dad, for what I'm about to do. I'm not the man you hoped I'd become.

I walk in the front door and follow a sign to an office

manager. Didn't know they had these here too.

It's past six and there's someone at the desk. After all I've been through, should this surprise me? A middle-aged woman greets me with a smile and excessive warmth.

"Can I help you?"

Several answers run through my head. Probably not…God, I hope so…If you can't no one can.

Finally I just settle on, "Is Pastor Paul available?"

Epilogue

"Hush little baby, don't say a word. Momma's gonna buy you a..."

Alyssa walks in the room, hands extended, her presence interrupting my lullaby. The bottle of formula she went for is tucked under her arm. I sneak a little kiss to the boy as I hand him back to his mother. "Drink up big man."

My brain tries to regroup from the sweet diversion of holding my grandson. What was on my list before I was hijacked into grandpa duty? Proofs. I've got some I need to print if there's time. From the lobby Stacey pokes her head in to announce that Pete and his family have just arrived. Despite numerous attempts, I can't manage to get a handle on the schedule in my new life. The funny thing is I don't care. A smile seems permanently fixed on my face in spite of the calendar chaos.

As I walk through the lobby to greet my best friend, the phone rings. My wife/receptionist/office manager picks up the receiver.

"Touched Up Photo Studios. We preserve families through photography. What part of your family's life do you want us to capture?"

I escort Pete and his brood to the sitting room in the back of our shop. They're a lively bunch and it takes me almost fifteen minutes to get them set for their first pose. Not a problem, we assign each family a two-hour block. To rush them would take away from the experience.

Unable to resist the temptation, I pull the new Hasselblad from its case. I convinced Stacey that we needed this camera for the business. It isn't really meant for portrait work. I'm pretty sure Stacey knew I wasn't being honest when she agreed to the expense. Some parts of me will probably take longer to change. I'll find a way to make it up to her.

I decide to take a few freehand shots before I use the tripod-mounted Nikon. Suppose when we get busier I won't have the time to do this. I slide to my right and drop to a knee. As I move my eye closer to the viewfinder, I hear the sound of metal on plastic. My focus is distracted by the reflection of the studio lights coming from my chest. I smile again as I tuck the tiny cross hanging around my neck back inside my shirt.

ACKNOWLEDGMENTS

Thank you to my editor Jason Buchholz who pushed me to make this story better every time I foolishly thought it was good enough.

My eternal gratitude goes to my writer's group friends whose critiques helped me painfully produce the story God wanted: Dan Jeffries, Deborah Reed, Lisa Shapiro, Graeme Ing, Adrianna Lewis, Linda Mitchell, Lee Polevoi, Tim Kane, and Peggy Lang.

Chet Cunningham is the grandfather of writers in San Diego who through supreme fortitude has kept alive the longest running writers' group in San Diego. Despite being in his eighties, publishing over 300 books, and still writing daily, the first words out of his mouth for all of us are "How's your book coming along?" I will never forget the day you invited this naïve, wanna-be writer into your hallowed group.

Thank you Robyn Russell for inspiring me to continue. The changing dynamics of the publishing world didn't allow us to work together this time, but I hope we get to in the future.

The utmost thank you must go to my wife, Cindy. She put up with years of me talking about "the book". Never once did she complain and she always stood behind me in pursuit of my dream. She is the ultimate wife and friend.

ABOUT THE AUTHOR

The son of a career Air Force serviceman, Leo spent his childhood living the nomadic life of a military brat. Having survived the constant uprooting, Leo draws upon the time spent in the four corners of the US as well as Europe to develop his characters.

Leo has finally settled down in San Diego, California with his wife of over thirty years. Aside from writing, and engineering (the necessary day job), he enjoys time with his children/grandchildren, running distance races and all things baseball.

Leo Dufresne

Touched Up